Murder Once Removed

Murder Once Removed

Kathleen Kunz

Walker and Company
New York

First published in the United States of America in 1993
by Walker Publishing Company, Inc.

Published simultaneously in Canada by Thomas Allen & Son
Canada, Limited, Markham, Ontario

Library of Congress Cataloging-in-Publication Data
Kunz, Kathleen
Murder once removed / Kathleen Kunz.
p. cm.
ISBN 0-8027-3230-5
I. Title.
PS3561.U58M87 1993
813'.54—dc20 92-43527
CIP

Printed in the United States of America
2 4 6 8 10 9 7 5 3 1

Murder Once Removed

▽

Prologue

FROM THE OVERLOOK on top of the bluffs, Cecile Girard could see the slight chop in the Mississippi's current, stirred up by a breeze that made her shrug the deep blue cashmere cape closer to her neck. Once you pass seventy, she thought, the infamous damp cold here settles into every last arthritic joint and makes the ache all the worse. She flexed the fingers on her right hand and felt a twinge.

Not that bad, she told herself, coming to the defense of the city she loved. This would be a glorious October, much the best month of all in St. Louis, except for the one nagging problem. If only she could share the secret with Terry. Cecile sighed audibly. But a niece is not a mother to run to, and Terry would want to make it all public. Besides, Terry must be kept out of it, just in case . . .

No, the idea was unthinkable. She shook her head and that generated a shiver as the breeze cut through the sheer hose she kept for Sunday mass. The Ferragamo pumps, bought on sale ten years ago and usually so comfortable, had begun to pinch.

She shouldn't have agreed to meet this late in the day. Whatever needed saying could have been said at home after church or even in the office this afternoon. Since when was Mumpet too proud to come to either place? But at least this was on the way home, and Cecile really didn't want to put it off any longer. There could be no backing down; it was imperative that all plans be halted.

Cecile was rehearsing how to sound convincing when she

heard the gravel crunch behind her. Gasping, she felt the cool air strike her lungs as she spun around. "Mother of God, you scared me. Didn't you drive?"

"Of course, but I parked below and walked up for the exercise. Unlike you, I have to watch my weight."

"Nonsense. Your weight is fine, Mumpet." Cecile saw the wince when she used the old pet name. "It's your judgment you have to watch."

"You always did get right to the point, Cecile. What exactly do you want?"

It wasn't going to be easy, Cecile thought. "I told you this morning. You simply have to drop the whole thing. It would be positively immoral even to think of going on."

"Immoral?" The familiar eyes narrowed as they always did when anything desired was not immediately forthcoming. "Let's not throw around such scandalous terms—unless, of course, you can back them up. Do you have proof of what you're saying?"

"Of course I have proof. Good heavens, you don't think I'd poke my nose into your affairs unless I was sure, do you?"

"Cecile, you've poked that Gallic nose wherever you've pleased for so long, you don't even see the trouble you stir up with it. And to think we brought this on ourselves!"

Cecile saw the familiar anger building, felt her own impatience rising, and tried to erase the exasperation from her voice. "That's what I tried to make clear this morning on the phone. I didn't go hunting your family's scalps on my own, but once I saw—"

"Yes, yes, I know what horrors your conscience must be suffering. Let's just see what you have. It may be all a ridiculous mistake."

"I'm afraid I forgot and left it under my office blotter, dear. Besides, it didn't dawn on me that you would doubt my word." If she just spoke calmly and reasonably, Cecile thought, maybe the rightness of her position would come across. "The record was in his Bible, tucked behind an endpaper he'd obviously pried loose for the purpose. I copied it and tried to check it out downtown, but their files were damaged in one of the floods. Nevertheless, it's irrefutable."

Cecile watched a marshaling of physical parts—jaw muscles tensed, hands came out of coat pockets, feet sought a steady purchase on the grassy berm—that made her own heart thud against her chest. Surely no harm was intended? The blood was pounding in her ears now, and her heart seemed to skip a beat. Instinctively, she drew back from the guardrail and immediately felt her cheeks warming with embarrassment at such a silly idea.

"You mean there's nothing more than that one moldy sheet?" The tone was light, slightly mocking.

"That one moldy sheet is the truth. It's in the office, where we should have been in the first place. Come along and see for yourself."

"All right, but it's so unbelievable. Maybe you can make me a copy."

Cecile let out the breath she didn't even realize she'd been holding. "The copy shop is closed on Sundays, but you can have the copy I made. I just knew you'd do the right thing."

Relieved that Mumpet seemed to be persuaded, Cecile allowed herself one last look at "her" river, where orange from the setting sun edged the ripples. From the corner of her eye, she saw a blur of tan raincoat just before she felt the blow to her lower back. She drew breath in to scream but panic choked off all sound. Surely Mumpet didn't mean to hurt her!

But the pressure didn't stop. She realized her high heels—silly and now dangerous—were slipping on the loose gravel. She felt her knees against the lower rung of the guardrail, felt the unyielding metal edge on the upper rail dig into her hip bones, felt the unbearable pain in her chest as panic squeezed her heart. She tried to reach behind her for any handful of poplin she could grab but strong arms pinned hers to her sides. A knee was beneath her buttocks—how degrading!—boosting her forward and upward.

She willed her voice to work.

"Don't, Mumpet!" she screamed.

"I can't let you ruin me, Cecile."

The voice held no trace of human warmth and those hands were too powerful. Thank God she'd kept Terry out of it. Such *evil*—

Cecile pitched forward. Her body turned like a lever on a fulcrum as she was thrust over the railing. Terror filled her lungs, pushed out all the air through her half-opened mouth. The pounding in her head blotted out any sounds. Only her eyes still functioned, seeing the whirling bushes where sky should be, and finally the blackness.

The bluff was sixty feet above the riverbank but her body landed on the sloping grade only half that distance from the top and rolled a few yards to a stop in a patch of sturdy goldenrod.

Mumpet watched for any movement, took in the odd angle of the head on that slender neck, then checked both directions on the riverbank below. The meeting place had been chosen for its isolation; a few minutes observation before approaching had confirmed their privacy. No one was in sight, nothing moved nearer than the distant interstate, where cars carried picnickers home from leaf trips to Pere Marquette State Park. The World Series crowds, those who could afford it, were up in Minnesota; the rest were glued to their sets and would not storm Busch Stadium until Tuesday. Upstream, the top of the Gateway Arch was a shining apostrophe as it caught the sun's last rays.

With gloved hands, Mumpet opened the door of Cecile's Honda, parked by itself in the small paved area, and went through the worn Coach bag to find the spare ring of keys that matched the one dangling from the ignition. The search continued through the glove compartment, then the Sunday papers spread on the backseat. Impatient, Mumpet shook out the new umbrella on the floor.

The absence of any record wasn't surprising; Cecile didn't lie. That was the whole problem. She didn't understand that not everyone valued—could afford to value—such unrelenting honesty. She had brought it on herself.

The carefully cropped note was slipped under the black handbag and the door closed with a nudge on the window ledge. Then Mumpet—how detested that nickname was!—strolled down the path that led to the street below, moved along it to a paved lot adjoining a now-vacant auto parts store, unlocked the Mercury parked there, and headed for the offices of The Family Album.

▽

1

TERRY GIRARD MANEUVERED the dark green Mustang into its usual space in the parking garage between her office and the river, shut off the engine, and glanced at her watch. Just past seven-thirty, two and a quarter hours from Jeff City to the riverfront, including the Monday-morning commuter snarl on I-70. Not bad.

Next time, though, she would take the scenic route home along the Missouri as CeCe had suggested. Why had she felt so compelled to rush home this morning? Three days for research in the state archives wasn't long. Except she'd had only one, she reminded herself, and had to spend the weekend networking.

She opened the door and climbed out to stretch. The deep breath she took was laced with the smell of licorice from the Switzer plant. Maybe CeCe was right: in the year since she'd been back, Terry had rekindled her love for St. Louis in spite of its crime, blight, and—she smiled over her shoulder at Busch Stadium, crouching like a bullfrog at water's edge—lack of depth in the bullpen. The Cards had risen above adversity this year and so had she.

Be honest, Terry told herself as she hauled her briefcase from the backseat and locked the car. It isn't homesickness. You just can't wait to tell CeCe what a bore the professor was.

She strode up the steep brick sidewalk with its inlaid brass street names, rehearsing how she would convince CeCe, politely of course, to stop fixing her up with "suitable beaux," as CeCe called them. Terry wasn't interested in another relationship, suitable or otherwise. She hadn't finished grieving over Sean yet, hadn't even told CeCe much about him because he wasn't her aunt's idea of suitable. And it didn't matter now.

She was still arguing her points when she came to the corner building in Laclede's Landing that housed The Family Album. The lacquered brass lobby made her chestnut hair orangy, her charcoal knit separates a muddy brown, and her long legs into squiggly lines, but she only glanced at the distorted image to make sure her slip wasn't showing.

Satisfied, she raised her eyes to the directory and felt the old glow of homecoming. Beneath the listing of the firm was CeCe's name—and now hers. The warm feeling lasted until she climbed the unrenovated oak staircase and worked the key in the modern dead bolt between antique keyhole and frosted glass. Inside, the phone was ringing.

CeCe, she thought. Terry's briefcase landed on the barrel chair and she reached across the nearer of the two desks. Probably mislaid yet another set of keys this morning. I shouldn't have stayed over in Jeff City last night.

She picked up the phone. "The Family Album."

"Miss Girard?" A man's voice, businesslike, but not—the wall clock read 7:49—one of the helpful clerks at City Hall. They were never in early on Monday. "Therese Girard?"

"Yes, speaking." Terry moved around to the swivel chair behind her desk, careful not to snag her newest panty hose on the bottom drawer, which edged open. She sat and nudged it in two inches with the toe of her black leather pump. "Who's calling, please?"

"This is Officer John Freeman of the first district at police headquarters, ma'am. There's been an accident. Your aunt, Cecile Girard—"

Terry began to shake. "An accident? How bad? What hospital? Where—"

"I'm sorry, ma'am. She died last night. They found the body about an hour ago."

The room swayed dangerously. Terry pushed both feet

against the threadbare spot on the rug and held the desk with her free hand. She didn't dare close her eyes or she might fall. It was hard to get enough air.

The receiver squawked again. "Ma'am? I'm dispatching a squad car to your office. Will that be all right?"

"All right?" She groped for sense in the words. "CeCe's dead?" The motel's coffee was pushing up into her chest and she fought to contain it and the nausea. Of course it wasn't all right. Not CeCe, please God, not the only anchor Terry had, the only one left to love.

"Ma'am? I'll just tell them to come in for you."

Terry fought for control. She had to get rid of this man so she could be sick. What had he said? "Who's coming here?"

"The patrol car, ma'am. They'll bring you to the city morgue. We need you to identify the—"

"Cecile Girard. You're sure there's no mistake?"

"That's what the driver's license said, and the picture matches. I'm sorry, ma'am."

Terry hung up the phone. She ran to the office bathroom just in time and fell to her knees in front of the toilet. Her stomach heaved. No, no, no, she repeated to herself.

When the last of the bitter coffee was gone, she remained huddled weakly on the floor. There had to be some mistake. CeCe couldn't be hurt, much less dead, without her knowing.

Terry had just gone over to Jeff City for some census data and to sweet-talk a couple of researchers. CeCe had *made* her go, had said to stay over and not drive home Sunday in the dark. Had fixed her up with that damned history professor. *I'll be all right,* CeCe had said. And CeCe didn't lie. It was all a mistake.

But from that place deep inside her, where the wounds were not yet scarred over, the familiar feeling of powerlessness welled up. She hadn't been enough—smart enough, good enough—to save Daddy. She hadn't known Sean was dead either . . .

The patrolmen came, giving their names, but Terry couldn't sort them out and didn't try. They took her out to their car, handed her gently into the backseat, and laid her briefcase at her feet.

The ride took ten minutes in the Monday-morning rush hour but it seemed like seconds. Terry didn't want it to end. Fighting tears, she pressed her last tissue against her eyes. When the patrolman riding passenger silently handed her a packet from the glove compartment, she gave up all semblance of control and sobbed.

They reached the gray building on Clark and pulled into the driveway beside it. One on either side of her, the officers helped her from the car, walked her around to the front, up four steps under a fanlighted door, and into a lobby of cream-painted limestone walls and brassy brown carpet. Like a drowning man who clutches at every branch on the bank, she fastened her eyes on each detail. Nothing stopped her progress.

From an office ahead a voice was saying, "Cause of death was a gunshot wound, bullet entering . . ." She stumbled, and the patrolman on her right caught her. She stared up into his face, afraid it was like Sean again, afraid to ask.

He must have sensed her unspoken question. "No, ma'am. That's someone else," he said, shaking his head.

They went through a door on the right into what looked like a chapel or a courtroom. A lectern stood before rows of dark wood pews on blue carpet. Windows with clear panes, not stained glass, ran down the far length.

His firm hand still under her elbow, the patrolman held her back while the driver went through yet another doorway behind the lectern. "Do you want to sit down, ma'am?"

Terry looked at the pews and shuddered. The shudder turned into a violent shaking of her head. "No!" she said, too loudly for the quiet room. If she sat again, she might not get up.

The other uniform beckoned from the doorway. She followed him into a room empty except for two plastic chairs and some filing cabinets with bright blue fronts. At what must be a window on the far wall hung a sagging drapery.

Overhead the fluorescent lights glared on its abstract print of brown and blue and cream folds.

The driver peeked behind one end of the folds and nodded at someone or something. He turned. "Would you stand over here, Miss Girard?"

Terry's empty stomach lurched with every step forward, but she moved across to stand next to him. Was it colder over here or did it just seem so?

He pulled a cord at the side and the draperies jerked slowly apart from the middle to reveal a large window. Terry could see a man in a white coat standing behind a green-sheeted form atop a gurney. More green sheets were strung on rings like a shower curtain behind him, blocking out whatever else that room contained. The man in the window was looking at her, his head tilted as if asking permission. His hand hesitated on the sheet with its frayed corners that CeCe would never have permitted.

Terry gulped air. The smell of disinfectant filled her nostrils, stung her lungs. Faint, she nodded. The sheet was pulled away and Terry forced her eyes up to the head that was revealed, to a "Cecile Girard"—not CeCe anymore—whose face was bloodless.

The scratches on her cheeks were black under the light. Even the perennial red marks on either side of her nose where her glasses pressed were a dull blue-gray. Terry drew in another breath. The sticks of fluorescent light overhead began to rotate like overhead fans. Her legs no longer wanted to hold her up.

When Terry came to, she kept her eyes closed, clinging to the nightmare as she had in childhood. But the truth, looming infinitely larger than the nightmare, was there as always. The loss was real. She turned over on her side, retched again, opened her eyes just enough to see a plastic-lined wastebasket appear below her.

Nothing came. The heaving lessened and she felt a cold cloth pressed against her forehead.

Without raising her head, she could see a young woman in police uniform standing by the door. But it was the person attached to the cloth who finally spoke.

"Take it easy. You'll be all right. You just fainted." The voice was male, raspy, in command but a little awkward. "Thanks, Manning. I think we can handle it now."

The door opened and closed as Terry put her hand up to the dampness on her forehead and he released the cloth. She wiped her face and mouth. Embarrassed, she forced herself to sit up, fight the dizziness, swing her feet to the floor, and look up at him.

He was in civilian clothes, the knit tie under his corduroy suit knotted half an inch below the shirt collar. He was younger than his voice, though his black hair was already invaded by gray and lines webbed around the bluest eyes she had ever seen. A wariness in them contradicted his assurance to the matron. He probably thought Terry swooned regularly.

She scrubbed harder at her face to get the blood back. More than anything, she wanted to be out of this place, to be home in her room, but that would mean leaving CeCe here. She shivered. "I've never fainted before," she said.

"You had good reason." He moved to the desk, a matter of inches in the small office, and perched on one hip. The walls, cream again, seemed to bulge inward above tan files that were lined up against them. The nervous energy he projected crowded the room even more. "I'm Sergeant Dan Kevlehan. And I'm sorry about your aunt."

"Thank you," she said automatically.

"I was supposed to meet you, take you in there. I got tied up. Maybe I could have made it a little easier."

The image of CeCe lying there on that steel gurney came back, knotting her stomach again. "Nothing could make that easier." Slowly the ignominy of it all, the frayed muslin covers and the cold anonymity, seeped into her jumbled feelings. The anger it engendered warmed her more than the scrubbing. "And why was it necessary? How did it happen?"

"We haven't got all the details yet. She was found below the Riverside overlook. It's brush and weeds there, not visible from any street." He picked up a clipboard and bounced the edge on his knee. "Her car was parked there. She must have . . . fallen."

Terry felt the tears forcing their way out and down her cheeks. Tears of anger at a needless death. CeCe had laughed at Terry's suggestion of sensible oxfords. *I'm too vain for nun's shoes* was how she put it. And now CeCe, in those damned high heels, had fallen from one of her favorite spots for river viewing. Was gone, had left her. Terry fished blindly in her shoulder bag for tissues. The wet handkerchief could absorb no more.

Dan Kevlehan reached behind him with his free hand and brought a small box of them over to the couch.

"It's a bad time for this, but I'll need your signature on a couple of forms. First, to show that you did identify your aunt." He placed a multicopy form on the clipboard and handed it to her. A pen was attached to the clip with a beaded chain.

She signed at the *x*'d line and he retrieved the board, removed the first form, and clipped another to it. "This is a permission to perform an autopsy."

Nausea flooded her. The word transported her instantly to her father's wake: sitting on the footstool, smelling the spicy scent of mums—just after Thanksgiving it had been. Above her on a couch, CeCe had whispered the word tearfully to Nora. Terry had gone home and looked it up in her father's dictionary, desperate to make sense of what had happened to her seven-year-old world.

"Is that necessary? Hasn't she been through enough?"

"It's the law when anyone dies without the supervision of a doctor. I'm sorry," he said more gently.

"She'd hate it—she wasn't fond of doctors at all."

"They won't release the body without a lot of red tape. If you don't sign, they'll do one anyway but it might take a week or more."

A week! The idea of CeCe staying in this cold, awful place for a week made her shiver once more. Blinded by tears, Terry bent to sign the second sheet.

"I am bound to tell you, though, there is the suspicion of suicide," he said as he took the clipboard from her.

She felt her jaw drop in disbelief. It was bad enough, but this was too much. "That is . . . ri*dic*ulous! Give me back that form. I won't have you—"

He fended off her attempt to grab the clipboard, tossed it on the desk, and passed her a sheet of paper that lay next to it. "We found this tucked under her purse in the car."

Surrounded by the black of nothingness on the copy paper was a white rectangle filled with the boldly artistic script Terry knew so well.

This can't go on.
It's come down to
this and, believe
me, I'm sorry. I
couldn't live with
myself any longer

Words bubbled up in her throat, creating a logjam. There were so many names she wanted to call him but she needed fresh air, needed to be out from among four walls that were swiftly closing in on her. She would not faint again. She barely heard him order the patrolman outside the door to take her home.

▽

2

ONCE OUTSIDE, TERRY persuaded the patrolmen to take her back to the parking garage at Laclede's Landing. She would need her car.

But where should I go, she wondered as the patrol car picked its way through morning traffic downtown. She didn't think she could face going home. And she wasn't ready to talk to anyone yet. Telling people would be the final confirmation of a fact Terry wanted to deny. When they reached Commercial, she gathered her purse and her briefcase to her chest. "Right there by the ramp will be fine."

"You're sure you can make it home okay, ma'am?" the driver asked as the other one helped her from the backseat.

"I'll be fine. Thanks for the ride." She still didn't know their names.

She watched the driver lift a microphone to his mouth and report their whereabouts as they pulled away. She hoped it was Kevlehan they were talking to but it was probably a nameless dispatcher.

The Mustang was on the first level, facing the river. Its dark green paint was warm to the touch; the inside looked airless. Too confining. She opened the trunk and shoved her briefcase next to her garment bag, slammed the lid, and struck off down to the riverfront as though she were being chased. She breathed in deeply, as though CeCe's beloved river air could somehow heal. Through the high stone archway supporting Eads Bridge, she plodded along what was now Lenore K. Sullivan Drive but what CeCe still called

Wharf Street. When a woman tourist greeted her, Terry pretended not to hear. She couldn't respond to anyone just yet.

She turned right and climbed the steps leading up to the Arch area. Out of habit, she sidestepped the thin parade of tourists walking backward with their cameras, trying to catch the full scope of the landmark. Like a sleepwalker, she made her way slowly along the plaza under trees beginning to shed their first leaves. Most of the people were headed for the sloping walk that led to the underground museum but that, too, was confining. She reached the square in front of the Old Cathedral, but she would not join the stream of visitors filing inside. The glimpse of pews brought back the anteroom at the morgue. Besides, she was too furious to pray. Mad at God, mad at CeCe, mad at herself most of all. She should have come home last night, should never have left CeCe alone.

Should never have left him alone. That's what Sean's brother had told her at the funeral. She had confessed to arguing with Sean about his turning down a job offer, slamming out of the apartment, bunking with a friend. As usual, Sean hadn't gotten mad.

He'd gotten even. In spite of his promise, he'd gone down to his old haunts, trying to find Danny, who'd been his cocaine connection. But he'd found him at the wrong time, just when someone decided Danny had overstepped his bounds.

Sean had been caught in the crossfire of the drive-by shooting, the luck of the Irish deserting him as it always had. The sight of him at the wake, pushed to a dark corner of her subconscious for months this time, flashed on her mind's screen in tormenting detail. The same life-denying profile that she had seen in her father's coffin. The same etched lines as CeCe's face, the same blue shadows. That's what she got for caring, for letting someone get close. Her father, Sean, and now CeCe.

Stop it, she told herself, halting in her tracks to shake her head and breathe deeply, as though she could physically rid her brain of memory and her heart of grief.

Finally, she found herself in front of her office building. Braunigan's, the ersatz Irish pub on the ground floor, sent forth its noontime aromas: corned beef warring with pizza for recognition. Suddenly aware of the gnawing feeling in her stomach, she ducked inside and found a booth in the back. For now, the cool plastic and the dim lighting soothed skin and eyes and raging anger better than a hard wooden pew could.

"Corned beef on rye as usual?" Robin, the waitress, was smiling down at her.

"Please. And iced tea."

"Shall I get him to fix one to take upstairs for your aunt?"

Terry didn't trust herself to speak. She shook her head and slipped out of the booth. Clutching her shoulder bag to a cramping stomach, she hurried along the hall to the rest room and locked herself in one of the two stalls. Leaning over, she could produce nothing with her dry heaves.

She gave up, came out, and bent her face to the sink on the other wall. Cupped handsful of water cooled her cheeks. When she straightened, the face that looked back at her from the mirror was gray around the edges, as though some shadow was beginning to swallow her.

Who would want to comfort you? Terry asked the ashen face. Four years at Georgetown and the next five at the National Archives had distanced her from old school chums. In the past year she had discovered some old friends gone and others too changed.

Be honest, she told herself. You've pulled back. You don't want to get too close to anyone who might disappear from your life like Mom and Daddy and Sean.

And now CeCe.

In the hall outside, Terry looked at the phone on the wall and wondered if there was someone who would care, not about CeCe—there were scores of people in that category—but about her.

There was Kate, but Terry didn't want to get her out of class, and Bryn probably had a line of patients at the pediatric clinic. She transferred her own preference for privacy onto them and decided not to bother them. Their mother was a different story.

She fished a quarter out of her purse, slugged it into the slot, and dialed. The faint smell of disinfectant from the rest rooms brought back still more images of the morgue and Terry leaned against the hunting scene wallpaper, trying not to breathe. She wouldn't tell Nora over the phone; the shock might hurt her heart. But Nora was like a second mother—third, really—and would welcome her.

"Hello?"

"Nora, it's Terry. Are you going to be home for a while?"

"Sure, if you want to come by, but how come—?"

"Tell you when I get there. 'Bye." She didn't trust herself to say more.

Back at her booth she took two bites of the sandwich, washing them down with tea so cold it burned her throat. Then she gave herself a stern mental shake, paid the check, and marched downhill to her car. Nora would be waiting.

The traffic was mercifully light on Grand, and when she reached Carondolet Park only a car or two crept along the curving roadways. School wasn't out for the day; still, a few young teenagers huddled almost at the bottom of the incline to her left where the old MoPac railroad tracks cut through the park. Another memory, this time sweet, flooded back. She had played hooky from the eighth grade of her parochial school, joined several friends from the local public school, and dug a hole—they called it a cave—into the side of this same incline to use as a clubhouse.

Had these kids discovered and reclaimed it? Did they know what they were in for? Sister Mary Augustine had called CeCe, breathing fire, as CeCe put it. Terry had taken her lumps—detention for a month of beautiful spring afternoons—with CeCe neither punishing nor defending her. "We are all entitled to celebrate spring, but don't ever cut school again unless I know beforehand," was all she had to say.

Later, CeCe repeated Grandfather Girard's tales of finding limestone caves down by the river in his youth, of roasting potatoes over bonfires that threatened to swallow all available oxygen in the cramped space. He had taken CeCe and kid brother Paul down to the remains of one, tried to get a fire going, but the twigs sputtered and went out. Both children itched to be at the Saturday matinee, where they thought real adventure was, CeCe admitted.

Now, Terry slowed the car to a stop and watched the bucket of dirt being handed out and up by a loose chain of teenagers, to be sprinkled unobtrusively at the base of trees before being passed down again. Off to one side lay some squares of sod and what looked like half the staves of a barrel: camouflage and door for the opening. Now as then, secrecy was the most delicious aspect. She hoped for their sakes that they had parents as understanding as CeCe had been.

She gunned the engine harder than she should have. It had been to avoid these bittersweet, childish memories that Terry had not gone to Nora Carpenter's immediately. It would be a retreat to the helplessness of childhood.

CeCe's best friend even though ten years younger, confidante to the whispered "autopsy" conversation, Nora accepted Terry as another in her brood, accepted her defection to Washington, if not with the same generosity as CeCe, at least with no lasting resentment. Now, Nora was the logical person to help. And help, Terry finally admitted, was what she needed.

But Terry found herself on the giving end when she broke the news. The older woman swayed in the doorway.

"Mother of God, I can't believe it!"

Terry hugged her and when Nora broke down Terry let her own tears come. It felt right. Terry had spent after-school hours at Nora's while CeCe worked to supplement the income her father's estate generated for the two of them. Now, without CeCe in the offing, the parlor seemed empty despite its battered upright and scarred library table, chesterfield sofa, and silent television set.

"I can't believe she's gone either, Nora. It just hasn't sunk in yet and I don't want it to."

Nora led her out to the kitchen, where they fixed cocoa and sandwiches of chicken left over from Sunday dinner.

"You need something in your stomach to keep your strength up, love." Nora had faced down most of life's emergencies with a spoon and a teakettle. In spite of a stomach full of knots, Terry sat and ate at the round maple table while she told Nora what little she knew.

"But I don't see how she could have fallen off the bluff. Just like a mountain goat, she was, and always so careful when we'd stop there," Nora said when Terry told her where it had happened.

Should she tell Nora all of it? She remembered how horrified Nora had been at her father's suicide. But Terry needed someone on her side. Besides, she didn't believe Kevlehan's assurance that no one need know. It would be common knowledge inside of a week. She polished off her sandwich and launched in.

"I'll tell you what the police told me. But I don't for a minute believe it, Nora, and you won't either. The sergeant said they think CeCe might have jumped instead of fallen."

The older woman went white. She was leaning on folded arms at the table, which rattled under her. "Suicide? They think CeCe committed suicide? Oh, but they're wrong. They're *wrong,* Terry." Her jowls and the graying topknot quivered as she shook her head.

"You don't have to convince me, Nora. But they have what they seem to think is some proof."

"No. Not after Paul. You don't know what CeCe went through."

Don't I? The old loneliness was back. There had been such a concerted—if futile—effort to spare Terry that everyone seemed to think it hadn't touched her. She had finally stopped trying to talk about it with anyone, even CeCe and Nora. *Especially* CeCe and Nora, as Terry remembered.

"CeCe had dinner with you Saturday, didn't she?"

"Yes, and if I had ever thought . . . ever known . . ."

"We aren't meant to know. That's supposed to be the beauty of it, Nora. It feels more like one of God's bad jokes."

"Don't start in." Nora's mouth was a firm line, but her disapproval of Terry's ideas on theology was overwhelmed by her own grief and the line quivered until it was a grimace of pain.

Terry went around the table and held the woman's head against her waist. It felt funny, somehow, comforting Nora instead of being on the receiving end.

"Was she herself or did she seem worried about anything?"

"Nothing she'd kill herself over, young lady."

"I know, Nora. I said I don't believe it. I'm trying to make sense out of it. Was she ill? Having dizzy spells?"

"Don't be silly. CeCe's never sick. But . . ."

"But what?"

"Well, I will say I've never seen her so . . . skittish. It was like she was here and then she wasn't. Her mind was a million miles away."

Terry's stomach turned over and the fear grabbed her chest again. Still, Nora would be on her side. Terry had to ask. "Do you know what she was worried about?"

"Worried? Nothing. Oh, I don't know." Nora brushed at the crumbs on the table as though they were the enemy. "She'd been to lunch with Micheline Barron. She said something about 'setting her nibs straight.' You know how pushy that woman can get. She was tired from fighting the traffic on the highway. Just *little* things."

Little things didn't bother CeCe as much as they do me, Terry thought. She dug in her purse for pen and notebook. "I'll see that Sergeant Kevlehan has all the proof he needs that it was an accident if you'll take care of calling people. I don't think I can stand to answer all their questions right now."

Nora's mouth thinned out to a tight line again, anticipating how people could be. "Of course, love. Do you have any idea when the wake will be? They'll want to know."

"Not a clue—tell them to check the paper. Maybe we

ought to spell out just how it happened in the *Post* and save ourselves all the trouble!" Terry felt her anger rising at the thought of facing even sympathetic friends. She would prefer to grieve in private. CeCe would want everyone invited. And CeCe knew *everyone*.

She forced the angry thoughts out and concentrated on writing down a few names on a list. After the first half dozen, though, she gave up, tore the sheet out, and pushed it across to Nora.

Nora fingered the paper, smoothing it to the maple surface. "It's just that everyone loved CeCe so, and they'll expect a funeral mass, and if Father Morgan refuses . . . Oh, Terry!" Nora's head fell on her arms and she gave way to moans interspersed with deep ragged breaths as though nothing could ever stop them.

Terry seethed. Her jaws were clamped tight against what she wanted to say but dared not. That's what Nora had worried most about when Daddy died, she thought. Not why he did it or how they would deal with it but fear that he would be denied Christian burial. It was Nora who had urged CeCe not to fight the doctor's finding of mental impairment. Terry waited until the pulse in her temple faded before she answered.

"They just don't do that anymore, Nora. Even when Daddy died, you got all worked up for nothing. The Church has changed, or rather some of those who run it have gotten some sense." Terry couldn't keep all the bitterness out of her voice. "If the Church did that, then it wouldn't be the one I want to bury CeCe."

Nora raised her head and met Terry's eyes with a determined look. "It's the Church that CeCe wants, Terry. We don't change easily."

God's truth, thought Terry, wearily. CeCe's generation pretended that Vatican II was an old man's folly. It was an ancient argument she thought she had left behind when she went to Georgetown—only to find vestiges of it there, too.

"All right, Nora, don't worry. I'll take care of Father Morgan."

"If only Bryn and Kate were back from that marriage encounter convention, they could help with all this."

Terry's heart sank. "I forgot this was the week they were going."

"You know how involved they are, but it wasn't the most convenient, coming right in the middle of a semester."

Bryn was an associate professor in pediatrics at the med school up on Grand, and Kate, Terry's oldest friend, taught at the academy both had attended.

"We'll manage, Nora. And they'll be here before the funeral."

But Nora's apprehension was still there when, having agreed on the names of people needing to be called, she gave Terry a final reassuring hug. "Let me know when you hear anything, love. And don't forget to eat some dinner."

At home, Terry checked the answering machine on the front hall table. She kept trying to save enough money for her own line but a new computer at the office had taken priority; meanwhile, Terry had settled for sharing CeCe's number, and letting CeCe share her machine. Two messages, the first from the policeman who had reached her at the office, the other from her dentist's office. The calls would start soon, though.

She pushed the knob to mute so she wouldn't hear the inevitable condolence calls, then climbed the stairs to the self-contained apartment she had made out of the second floor of the house her grandfather had built.

She debated whether to put a TV dinner in the microwave, settled for soup, and curled up on the window seat to try to make sense of it. And mourn. For herself, for CeCe, and for the loss of the family they had made, the two of them, out of tragedy.

Suicide, indeed!

Through the years, CeCe had drilled three truths home to Terry: her father had loved her; her father had been ill; but suicide was not an answer.

Not for the first time, Terry wondered whether CeCe was

frightened that an impressionable girl might feel some irrational guilt of her own and try to imitate her father. God knows, the guilt was there, and hard to consider irrational in the darkest part of night. Just so, CeCe would never desert her by suicide when Terry was out of town and liable to feel responsible. Never, she shook her head.

She blew her nose and discarded the latest tissue casualty. Staring at the pile, she was reminded of the one offered by that detestably sneaky Kevlehan. To think that he had tricked her into giving permission for an autopsy before he told her about the note! She muttered something she had learned at Georgetown and for which Sister Mary Augustine would have given her another month's detention.

Of course, Kevlehan hadn't known CeCe and that was some excuse. But she'd be damned if she'd excuse him. CeCe, of all people. After all the pain they had both been through, CeCe would never renege, even in the face of a terminal illness.

Had CeCe been sick? Had she not wanted to worry Terry? But the picture of CeCe striding down long blocks, cheeks tanned or chapped rosy according to the season—"none of your creams, Terry, I rather like these wrinkles"—made a joke of that idea. CeCe hadn't been to a doctor in the year Terry had been back in St. Louis. Was this reason enough to demand an autopsy?

Any accident called for one, he'd said. So how had she fallen? That would be the question everyone asked Nora, who could put them off, honestly, with ignorance. They would ask again at the wake, whenever that would be. What could she tell them?

And what about that note? It was, as she had said, ridiculous to see it as a suicide note. But where had it come from? And what did it mean? She was sorry she hadn't gotten more out of Kevlehan, but she told herself he wouldn't have helped anyway. Evidently they taught trickery instead of tact at the police academy, or wherever he had gone to school.

She could assume that CeCe had suffered a sudden dizzy

spell or even a stroke. Those things happened, even to fiercely loved aunts. But that wouldn't do. CeCe had taught her to make sure of her facts, never to assume; their reputation depended on accuracy. A researcher couldn't assume the immigration official had misspelled a name or that a hungover stonemason had carved a different date on a tombstone. If the names or the dates didn't agree, look further.

CeCe was healthy but she had fallen off the bluff. She would never commit suicide and yet had left a note that gave that impression. Terry had to find some answers. Much as she hated to, she would have to call Kevlehan in the morning and ask him for whatever information they had.

Mumpet stared at the ceiling above the bed, thinking of what had been done and what still needed doing. The office had been given as thorough a going-over as possible in the time that could be spared. The copy had been readily at hand—Cecile had left it under her blotter—but the original wasn't there, too, as she'd said. My God, the woman was absent-minded—always had been. The file where it should have been was bulging with photostats and Xerox copies of news items, pictures, even book excerpts, everything but that moldy piece of paper. The Bible that had hidden it was propping up another set of files; its pages had yielded nothing but a pressed rose, a snippet of hair, and a collection of funeral-home holy cards.

The house would have to be searched. The problem was finding a time when Therese was away and no nearby homeowners were on the lookout. Daylight would be better and safer, what with people coming by with food, as long as Therese was out. Cecile was too secretive to leave it out in the open—but where could she have hidden it? Had Therese come across it accidentally? Would she recognize its connection to her aunt's death? No on both counts, Mumpet decided; Therese would have filed it or turned it over to the police.

There was still a little time to get it back. In any case, it was safer to try than to risk something so overt as an accident, especially so soon. But there was a family pattern established now. First Paul, now CeCe. If necessary, Therese would follow it. Things shouldn't come to such a pass, but CeCe was behind it all. She had to stick her nose in where it didn't belong. She had threatened ruin at the worst possible time.

▽

3

TERRY SLEPT ONLY in snatches. A jumble of wild dreams woke her repeatedly, beginning with Sean and CeCe arguing, then her father and Kevlehan, talking over her head as though she weren't standing between them. Finally, Nora and Sean's brother were shaking fingers at her, but when she reached to bite the nearest blaming digit, she woke for the last time.

At six she abandoned the bed, threw on a robe, and collected the *Post* off the porch. Her answering machine was flashing to signal all the messages that had come in last night, but she wasn't quite ready to listen. She compromised by turning the bell up and the sound on in case Nora tried her this morning; she would move it upstairs tomorrow. She stood in the hall to leaf through the paper and felt relief flood through her: no mention of CeCe's death, thank God. Then the guilt was back because she was glad to avoid facing reality and the people who would bring it down on her forcefully.

In the shower, Terry let the hot water run an extra minute on her shoulders, hoping to loosen her tense muscles. When she finally pulled back the shower curtain to reach for her towel, her reflection in the door's full-length mirror caught her attention.

She had come to terms at last with her height—five-foot-eight wasn't that tall except that she had reached it in seventh grade looking and feeling gigantic next to CeCe's five-two-and-a-hundred-and-two. But CeCe had taught her to stand tall and she did so now, her breasts rising and her stomach flat. The gangly, thirteen-year-old form was gone, along with the adolescent modesty that was built more on fear of ridicule than on virtue.

She had driven CeCe to hysterical laughter on one occasion with a demonstration of how she and fellow convent school classmates, under Sister's watchful eye, managed to change from uniform to gym clothes without so much as an inch of strategic skin displayed.

She still didn't spend much time in front of mirrors; she was content to know that her figure looked good in clothes and out of them. A warm glow spread through her at the memory of Sean's admiration.

She wrapped her shoulder-length chestnut hair in one towel, wrapped another around her torso, and peered at her face in the mirror. Automatically she smoothed out the frown lines between thick brows—another of CeCe's dictums that covered diet, posture, and personal grooming—and saw her face as a seismograph, recording all the worry and stress of the last twenty-four hours. Dark patches circled her wide-spaced eyes, making their light brown even lighter, and her cheekbones seemed more prominent because of the shadow of hollows below them.

Nothing to be done about that now. She shook her head impatiently and rubbed the towel vigorously over her creamy, untanned skin—avoiding the sun was her own, not CeCe's, idea, to keep those insidious freckles at bay.

After dressing, her hair hanging damp on her back, she made coffee and rehearsed what she would say to Kevlehan. She watched the clock by the bed until she figured he was on duty and punched in the number the patrolman had insisted on giving her. She had practiced a calm, low-pitched introduction, but still the choking anger made her voice squeak as she asked for Sergeant Kevlehan and was put on hold.

"Kevlehan here."

How could so much impatience be packed into two words?

"Sergeant, this is Therese Girard. I'm calling to see what

you've found out about my aunt's death, if anything. There seems to be a monstrous misunderstanding if you think there is even a chance that she committed suicide. It is simply not in her nature . . . she never . . ." Things were not going as planned. She was babbling. She took a deep breath to continue but he had grabbed the ball.

"On the contrary, Miss Girard, there's more than an outside chance of suicide, given the evidence. And I need to drop by to ask you some more questions if you'll be home for the next hour or so. By the way, did your aunt have an insurance policy?"

She gasped. The gall! He was going to call the company and warn them before he even talked to her! She wouldn't let him set one foot in CeCe's house. What's more, she would round up evidence beforehand to prove him wrong.

"I'll be in my office at ten, Sergeant. Once we hear each other out, I'll furnish you whatever information is necessary." Her voice cracked on the last word but she hoped the iciness had gotten through. She hung up before he could reply.

Terry was just rinsing out her cup when the door chimes sounded. She punched both arms through the sleeves of her London Fog, grabbed up her purse and briefcase, still untouched since her trip, and ran downstairs to the front hall. She hoped whoever it was would see she was on her way out and take the hint. At least it can't be Kevlehan, she thought.

But when Terry looked through the sidelight next to the door, she saw that it was just about as bad. The man on the porch stood erect; his eyes, watering like an abused basset's, were fixed on the bell. His three-piece suit was a darker gray than his hair but no less somber than his face, where the straight line of mouth below the slightly aquiline nose gave no quarter, no sympathy. Hugh Barron, CeCe's lawyer—and perforce Terry's—was an imperious but infrequent presence in the courtroom, doing most of his work in estate law. Terry wouldn't have picked him as a legal counselor but the ties that bind old family friends together make some choices inescapable.

Reluctantly, Terry opened the door. "Mr. Barron—Hugh." He'd been Uncle Hugh until she left for college but since her return it sounded too familiar, as did plain Hugh. "How thoughtful of you to come." A shade late, she stood aside and motioned him in. Instead, he embraced her awkwardly but briefly.

"Yes, my dear, please call me Hugh. I'm so sorry to hear the news. Tragic, that's what it is."

"Yes—" She wasn't adept at fielding sympathy; her hands remained at her sides.

"Ah, but I've caught you at a bad time."

"No, I still have a few minutes," Terry said, glancing at her watch even though she knew exactly what time it was.

"Well, I won't keep you because I have to be in court in an hour, but I wanted to extend my deepest sympathies," he said, sweeping past her into the parlor and hitching up sharply creased trousers to sit on the largest of the Victorian side chairs.

"Cecile was my godmother, you know. A pillar of the community, salt of the earth." His long pale fingers held the brim of a black homburg on his lap.

Did he always have to talk in clichés? She usually tried to tune him out until he ran down, which often took half an hour. This time was different. She had barely perched on the settee when he got to the point.

"I just wondered if I could be of any help. I have a copy of the will, of course, and your partnership agreement. Do you know the whereabouts of the deed to the plot?"

"I think the Fourcaults probably have it." She named the funeral directors who'd buried generations of Girards. "I'll ask when I see them today."

"Oh, I assumed you had gone there yesterday." He reached into his breast pocket for a handkerchief and sneezed into it. "Excuse me, dear. Hay fever season is lasting too long this year. Anyway, it was such a shock when Nora called. I'd just sent Cecile an invitation to the dedication."

Damn. The album she and CeCe were working on for the

Barrons was due as part of the celebration that day. Now it was all up to her.

"On the twenty-ninth. Now CeCe won't be there. We'll all miss her—Mother is devastated. Mother was going to run by this morning but I'll call her before court and tell her not to bother."

"If you wouldn't mind." Terry knew that was the last thing she needed right now. Micheline Barron would take over CeCe's funeral and orchestrate it like a charity ball if the mood struck her. "I was going to call her myself but it's all been such a shock. She had lunch with CeCe on Saturday?"

"So I heard. Cecile was one of her oldest friends. I believe she's already left a message on that machine." He indicated the answering machine on the hall table next to the phone.

Terry felt the old pull of guilt he always engendered. She had left St. Louis, left CeCe for a distant college, not come back until she herself needed emotional support. He had been cool to the partnership idea. "I haven't played them all back yet. I'll call her today."

"Well, I'll let you go. I just wanted to tell you that we are here for you. You know the terms of the will, I suppose. Everything is yours now, but we can go into the details later." He paused and his large wet eyes studied her like a lab specimen. "Do you need any funds to tide you over?"

Why did he always make her feel like a poor relation? "No, I'll be fine, really."

"Will there be visitation hours this evening?"

Terry felt the blush rising up her neck. She couldn't go into it all, not with Hugh Barron, but they might call him for something as the lawyer of record. She struggled to sound matter-of-fact. "No. It's a bit up in the air. Since she died in an accident they have to do an autopsy." She swallowed the lump in her throat and stood up.

"Autopsy? Oh, my dear child, how dreadful! Just like Paul." He looked genuinely distressed and his hat went rolling off his knee onto the floor. "Do you want me to intercede? I'm sure we could get a waiver on the—"

"It's too late. I signed the paper yesterday."

"You should have called me before signing anything." He had retrieved his hat and was fanning himself. "Well, water under the bridge. I must be off or I'll be late."

"Thank you again for coming. I'll call Aunt Micheline today." She ushered him out the door and out of her mind with a sigh of relief and dashed for the back door and her Mustang. She could dial up her messages after Kevlehan left.

When she reached the brass lobby half an hour later, the memory of yesterday, of coming back from Jeff City when she thought her world was still in one piece, made a heavy knot in her chest. She had been mad at CeCe. One of the researchers CeCe had steered her to had been an old college friend of Terry's father, and happened to have a son. An unmarried son. Urbane, well-mannered, a tenured professor of economics at Mizzou, not bad looking. And incredibly boring. He'd kept her from doing the last few bits of checking she had been assigned. She had seen CeCe's Machiavellian hand and was ready to call her on it.

Now she wouldn't get the chance. Now she was free. She bit her lower lip between trembling teeth, blinked back tears as she climbed the stairs and moved down the hall. Only as she neared the Family Album door did she look up to see Barry Malone—Uncle Barry—his hand on the brass knob, his lined face ashy except for the large red nose. The only suitor CeCe had been unable to discourage permanently, he had become a fixture at holiday meals and a reliable escort whenever needed. Now he stood looking like he'd slept in his suit, not the dapper Irishman she knew. His hand moved from the doorknob to brush hair back from a far-receding hairline.

"Terry, thank God you've come."

"Uncle Barry! Did Nora call you?"

"Of course. That's why I've been trying to reach you. I tried and tried the house but all I got was that damn fool machine."

Another rebuke from her elders, Terry thought. What did they want from her?

"I'm sorry, I just couldn't talk last night. Come on in." She pushed the door back and stood aside for Barry to precede her.

He crossed the floor and stopped in front of CeCe's desk, looking down at the jumble of papers and folders as he spoke.

"I'm sorry, too—didn't mean to be—it's just that I can't take it in yet."

"Here, sit down." She led him by the arm to one of the barrel chairs, turned it to face away from the desk, and almost pulled him down on it. "I'll put some water on."

"No, no tea, I can't stay. Just light a minute, will you?"

She chose the mate to his chair, scooted it closer to him, and sat on the edge. "I know the two of you were awfully close. "I appreciate your coming by. I miss her so much already and I know you do, too."

He looked at her as though he couldn't quite make out the meaning of the words. "Miss her. Yes, we will."

The silence lasted while he loosened an already drooping tie knot and rubbed both hands on the knees of his trousers. When he finally spoke again, he still wasn't looking at her.

"Is there a safe here?"

Had she heard right? "A safe?"

"That's where she would keep it. In her private papers."

"Uncle Barry, I don't know what you're talking about." Terry sat even closer, as though space was the barrier to understanding.

He leaned forward, too, finally meeting her eyes.

"God, I'm sorry she's dead, but since she is, I want—I need it back."

Terry felt the goosebumps on her arms. Was it a ring, some keepsake he'd given CeCe? And to demand its return before she was even buried . . .

"Terry, I'm not making much sense. Did CeCe ever tell you about some information concerning . . . me?"

"No, she didn't. If it was something told in confidence, you know CeCe wouldn't share that."

"Of course not. I thought perhaps she had left instructions to destroy certain papers or return them. If you've seen something with my name, some papers . . . ?" He motioned over his shoulder at the piles on CeCe's desk.

"I only got back yesterday morning, Uncle Barry. I haven't gone through her things. If I find anything—"

"I understand. I'd appreciate it. I'm sorry I involved her in the first place." His voice broke on the last words and he pushed himself up with both hands, an obvious effort.

Terry was torn between pity and irritation. Something was weighing on him, even more than CeCe's death, but my God, couldn't it wait until after the funeral? Pity and ingrained respect for her elders won out.

"If I find anything that looks like it concerns you, I'll call right away. Of course I won't open it."

"I knew I didn't have to ask that. You're too much like her." He bent to kiss her cheek and pat her arm. "Thank you, my dear."

He was gone without a question about CeCe's death or funeral particulars. This was an Uncle Barry Terry had never seen before. Everything had changed. The last of her family was gone, along with the life she had carved for herself, using CeCe as an armature but herself as clay. She felt it all melting away. The office was suddenly stifling and she marched to the window, raised the stubborn sash, and inhaled the riverfront air like a drowning woman. Today, the licorice scent was more like the undernote of a wine.

CeCe had taken the office in Laclede's Landing, not because it was trendy and "well-placed for the society you appeal to," as the real estate agent had said, but because it was handy to the Old Cathedral's records in the rectory basement and to the Old Courthouse and its files, which overflowed into nearby warehouses, awaiting the National Park Service's microfilm process. And Terry suspected that CeCe had chosen it partly because it had a view of the river closer than, but almost identical to, the one Terry's grandfather had had from his Wainwright Building office sixty years ago.

She leaned her forehead on the warm glass and looked for

barges moving on the slice of water she could see. The cobblestones leading down to the breakwater glistened with a sheen of moisture, as though the river had mysteriously developed a tide and washed over its banks in the night, but Terry knew it was merely the street cleaners tidying up for the tourists.

The latter had bothered CeCe, who pretended quite often that she was living back in the times she was researching so she could "get a better picture." This had disconcerted Terry at first, but in the last year she had grown used to looking at the area and seeing, not the glitzy fern bars and souvenir boutiques, but the original warehouses stinking with their "fur rows" destined for the backs of plump dowagers in New York and Paris.

Their own building hadn't changed all that much. Though the staid lawyers of her grandfather's generation had moved closer to the newer court building and would not have tolerated Braunigan's downstairs, such taverns had been commonplace earlier. Her grandfather's grandfather had run one nearby, tossing the too-boisterous drinkers into the muddy river to cool off, according to CeCe, who had made it all come alive for her.

Now Terry felt the beginnings of panic. Those comforting pictures of a past to belong to, would they fade as the color had faded from CeCe's face?

She must get busy. There were things to round up for The Diplomat Kevlehan. Proof to convince even his hard-boiled senses that CeCe had meant to stick around this place.

She sat down at CeCe's desk. Centered at the top of her blotter was a page-a-day calendar whose twin stacks of sheets had been left, for some reason only CeCe would know—if even she would—at the weekend sheets of Saturday and Sunday, the twenty-ninth and thirtieth, almost two weeks away. Penciled in on the left was the Sullivan–Gaines wedding at ten and the Barron Park dedication at two. On the opposite sheet the word *crystal* was crossed out and *Wedgwood* written below it, with a question mark under that—CeCe debating what to get the couple.

Terry riffled backward past pages noting other engagements, business and social, to last Friday. "T–JC 8am" was written on the left sheet: Terry *had* left at eight for Jeff City. Below it and on the adjoining sheet, in CeCe's arcane shorthand, were more reminders: "ck VPB fils–px–souv," "Cntrr–CD," "ck F lgt fils," "p/u cleng," all of which Terry interpreted quickly: check Veiled Prophet Ball files for picture of souvenir—CeCe wanted to use one in a montage for the Barron book; get over to Centerre Bank to reinvest a CD that was maturing; check the French land grant files; and pick up cleaning. Hardly the agenda of a woman contemplating suicide. She would stuff that in Kevlehan's pipe and let him smoke it.

She thumbed the page over. Saturday held four notations: "MM," "MB–lnc DM," "p/u Tbdp–Aub," and "N–dnr." The first was easy—CeCe paid monthly visits to her old friend and former teacher, Sister Mary Michael, at Gethsemane, the home for retired sisters. The second was lunch with Micheline Barron at the DeMenil House and the last meant dinner with Nora, of course. But the third entry puzzled her until, with a tightness in her chest, she remembered.

She would be twenty-nine next week; CeCe had planned ahead for once, and had picked up Terry's birthday present from Aubergine's.

Terry retreated to the coat-closet-sized bathroom, where she grabbed a paper towel, wet it, and held it to her stinging eyes. She wasn't ashamed of crying—CeCe had given her sound advice when Sean died: grieve without apology. But it made her look vulnerable and Kevlehan might not take her as seriously as she wanted him to.

It was as though he were reading her mind. She had her head immersed in the sink when she heard a rap on the glass and his deep voice: "Anybody home?"

Dabbing fiercely with the towel, Terry edged the door closed with her foot. He had to be early!

"Hello? Anybody home?" The office door creaked open.

"I'll be right out." Her reflection stared back at her: puffy eyes, a patrician nose that was now Rudolph-red, and chestnut hair that had pulled from a French knot and lay curled damply along her temples and jawline. She smoothed the hair back, stabbing viciously with the antique tortoise combs that had been CeCe's birthday present to her last year. Never mind her eyes. She would convince him with logic.

"Am I too early? I finished up sooner than I thought."

Yes, dammit, you are. But that's how you planned it. She pulled that imaginary string on the top of her head that straightened her spine, lifted her chin, and defined her breasts under the hunter green jersey dress. Then she took a cleansing breath, let it out, and opened the bathroom door.

▽

4

HE STOOD IN the middle of the worn kilim rug with his hands jammed in the pockets of a raincoat that was cleaner than, but just as rumpled as, Columbo's. His eyes seemed to rake the surroundings, missing nothing, and his chin jutted out to give stubbornness a whole new meaning. Again, she was struck by that barely contained energy—like a locomotive with a head of steam up and the brakes on. The eyes stopped at her face. "Are you sure it's not too early?"

A trickle of fear tried to crawl out of her—going up against such a force called for strength she wasn't sure she had right now—but she wouldn't let it show. "No, please sit down. The sooner this is over with the better."

She sank into the chair behind CeCe's desk, feeling out of place, a usurper, but at least her back would be to the light streaming across the blotter.

He swiveled the barrel chair Barry had just vacated, sat down, and leaned forward out of the direct sun, elbows on knees. "I'm really sorry about your aunt. I didn't handle it well yesterday. I should have realized how upset you were."

Terry was surprised at the unexpected apology. "Yes, it was an awful shock. She was my only family. But to have you accuse her of committing suicide is such utter nonsense . . . that's what really upset me."

"We have to go on the evidence we find—"

"And that's what I've started collecting for you." She leaned forward to turn the calendar so that he could read it. "You can see what she had planned for Friday and Saturday.

She led a very busy life." Terry translated the abbreviated notes for him. "Does this sound like a woman so despondent that she's ready to throw herself off a cliff?"

He examined the pages, including the blank Sunday sheet, before looking up. "We've learned from long experience that a facade of busyness often covers up certain depressions, and that—"

"Oh, come off it!" Long experience! He was hardly that much older than she was. "I've known this woman all my life. She doesn't—didn't—believe in suicide. It was against her religion, for one thing."

"Catholics aren't immune to suicide, Miss Girard." His eyes under those heavy frowning brows drilled into her.

This time the old fear came out, crept up her spine, and made her hair tingle. She hadn't wanted to bring up the other reason why CeCe had been so against it: she had seen the pain it caused those left behind. Did he know about her father?

"Are you talking about specific cases?"

He didn't answer immediately but shrugged out of his coat and settled one leg over the other as though prepared to make a day of it.

"Your father's religion didn't stop him. Sometimes people are too sick to see beyond what they think is an insurmountable problem."

She breathed in, filling her lungs for battle. In a strange way she felt better once the words were out. The fear had always been in the waiting, not in the actual question. The eyebrows raised in silence had been the hardest of all, for there was no fighting them. This time she could fight.

"Sergeant Kevlehan, let me tell you how it happened. My mother died in childbirth when I was five."

"From what?"

"Cardiac arrest, not that it makes a difference. She'd had rheumatic fever as a child and her heart was weak."

"Had she been warned about another pregnancy?"

"CeCe told me they knew the risk but Mother wanted at least one more child. CeCe came to live with us after that and went with me to the hospital five months later when I had pneumonia. While I was there, my baby brother died of sudden infant death syndrome."

"While your father was taking care of him?"

"Yes, he woke up and the baby was dead—that's usually how it happens. CeCe tried with all her might to convince my father that he wasn't to blame for either death, that there was still reason for living." With her mind's eye, Terry saw her aunt again, pointing to her over the dinner table, night after night. *There's your reason. She needs a father.*

"Did she get him to see a doctor? A psychiatrist?"

"Our family doctor sent him to one but Daddy wouldn't go after the first visit. CeCe kept after him for a year but when we lost him, she made no concession to the doctor's diagnosis of severe depression."

"Why not? He felt guilty for both deaths and it caused depression—sounds logical."

"That's what I'm trying to tell you if you'll just listen. CeCe just couldn't see suicide as a response to any problem. Knowing the pain it caused us, do you think she would make me go through it again?"

He massaged a jaw that probably never looked freshly shaved; his blue eyes looked through her for any hint of untruth. "No, she doesn't sound like the kind to do that, but she may have felt equally guilty about not preventing his death or about something more recent. It's possible she had—or thought she had—a terminal disease and didn't want to be a burden. Lots of reasons. Maybe we'll never know, but I've got a job to do, Miss Girard."

"And I'm trying to help you do it, Sergeant."

"*Was* there some trouble that she was worried about?"

"None."

It hadn't come out the way she wanted it: forceful, decisive, unarguable. The image of CeCe on Friday morning came unbidden and out of nowhere. Sitting in this very chair, watching Terry pack her briefcase. Frowning—and she never frowned, preferring to tilt her head back and look down her nose when displeased—quieter than usual, worried. Damn him! Why did he keep at it?

"You're sure?" He drummed large fingers softly on the chair arm but his eyes didn't leave her face.

"Yes, I'm sure." Better this time, but she still couldn't quite look him in the eye.

"The note indicates otherwise." He spread the copy on the desk like an exclamation point to his argument. Terry pushed back her chair, stood and turned to the window. The breeze cooled her face, if not her temper, as she tried to take in enough oxygen to break the vise around her ribs.

Turning back, she saw the paper fluttering as though it had a life of its own and slammed it down with both palms. "This is not a suicide note!"

"Calm down, Miss Girard. Is that your aunt's handwriting?"

"Yes, it's hers. But there's no signature, no reason. It doesn't sound like her. There's something wrong with it."

"Hold it." Kevlehan held a palm up to stop the flow. "I'm not calling it a suicide note as such. It may just be that she was practicing an explanation of how troubled she was. It may be she was seeing how far she could go to the edge before she pulled herself back and she misjudged. It may—"

"It may be bull feathers!"

He was unmoved by her sarcasm. Like a juggernaut, he plowed on, his voice calm and quiet. "If it was depression . . ." He left the sentence unfinished, hanging there between them like a pall over the desk.

"Sergeant, you may not have had time to study much clinical psychology on your way to your present position. Let me enlighten you. The tendency toward clinical depression may run in families. It is characterized by feelings of worthlessness, hopelessness, and worry that have no basis in reality."

"And your father, what did his death certificate say?"

"My father's depression had a sound basis. The parents of SIDS babies suffer such feelings—it's normal guilt, unreasonable but not necessarily clinical depression."

"Isn't it true that doctors can't really draw a firm line between the two?"

"Yes, but my aunt told me they put that on the death certificate just to get him buried by the church—and even that was needless." The old bitterness welled up in her at the memory, giving her final words an edge that was sharp enough to cut a lesser man off.

"Your father did commit suicide?" He wouldn't let her eyes leave his.

"Yes, he killed himself. But it is not *catching*." Her knees felt weak suddenly and she sat down abruptly.

He sat there looking at her with those damnably blue eyes and, without a word, he began applauding softly.

Terry felt the blush rushing up her neck, burning her cheeks. The gall of the man! "And what's that supposed to mean?"

"I'm sorry," he said, although his eyes showed suppressed amusement, and something else she couldn't put a finger on. "How many times have you had to give that speech?"

She poured a glass of water from the carafe on the desk to give herself time to calm down. They were getting off the track. How could you get through to a man like this?

"Enough. Why?"

"It's just that it sounds a lot like the speech I used to give years ago. It was in defense of a retarded older cousin, and I used the same last line—it isn't catching."

"Then you ought to believe it."

"I do believe it. But I've already talked to Mrs. Carpenter, and she told me something *was* worrying your aunt Saturday evening. 'She just wasn't her old self,' was how she put it." He read the last from a small brown leather notebook he had pulled from another coat pocket.

Why had Nora told him that? Didn't she realize how damning that sounded?

"I think you saw it, too. Then I add the note and the fact that she picked a spot that was both sentimental and isolated enough so she wouldn't be interrupted. I come up with a total of possible suicide. I won't say positive."

She felt the tears coming again and shielded her eyes with a hand, blinking rapidly. It was hopeless. Like beating against a brick wall. But she knew CeCe had not been a quitter and neither was she. And something was niggling at the back of her mind. "You're wrong, you know. And I'll prove it, somehow."

"You don't have to. Unless there's insurance involved there's no need to publish the autopsy findings. No one will know."

Her bitter laugh hiccupped out. "Oh, people won't *know*. They'll just whisper behind their politely cupped hands and I'll keep giving my speech. No, Sergeant. I don't intend to spend the rest of my life explaining another death."

"I know how you feel."

Her anger finally exploded, surprising her as much as him. She slammed both fists down on the blotter so hard that the calendar jumped. "The hell you do!"

He stared at her, not looking surprised as much as amused. "Listen, I don't want to fight you. But I have to know if there was insurance."

Like a safety valve on a boiler, the last outburst had taken off pressure. "No," Terry said through stiff lips. "She kept a savings account for emergencies—in case she was hit by a bus, she always said. We have partnership insurance for the business. I don't think it has a clause about . . . suicide." She could barely get the word out.

"What sort of business is The Family Album, anyway?"

"It's a professional genealogy service, mainly. We research family trees, but beyond the standard forms we create an album filled with marriage certificate copies, wedding pictures, death notices, newspaper clippings about notable achievements or good works, debuts, anything having to do with any of the ancestors in the direct line—or however many the client is willing to pay for."

"You know a lot about old St. Louis families?"

"My aunt did. I went to D.C. for college and worked at

the National Archives until last year. I'm still learning about locals."

He stared at her, his hand moving from jaw to ankle for massaging. "Is that so?" Another silence, then, "Can you put your hands on that policy?"

Terry moved to the file cabinet next to the window behind her and found it under "I" almost immediately; she had filed it there just six months ago. She passed it to him without a word, watching him scan the few pages.

The phone rang, making her heart jump. She shrugged off the dread as she lifted the receiver. "The Family Album," she said. Silence. "Hello?" But there was only a click. The line went dead until the dial tone buzzed in her ear and she replaced the receiver.

"Wrong number?" he asked, passing the document across to her. "No problem with this. We can go with accidental death if there are no surprises from the coroner."

"But you really don't believe it, do you?"

"Does it matter whether I do?"

"It matters to *me*! I want you to be convinced with logic and proof that she did not kill herself. If I can't persuade a disinterested bystander, then I won't have much luck with all the whisperers. It won't be a secret, not after the delay for an autopsy."

"Miss Girard, even if she'd suffered a stroke and died in the emergency room, they'd do an autopsy. She wasn't under a doctor's care."

"I'll use that in my repertoire of excuses," she said. Would he never finish?

"I'm really sorry. And her belongings still hadn't been released when I left. Dr. Wickers said he's running behind. But he'll call your mortuary as soon as he's finished and they can handle it."

Terry shivered at the thought of CeCe being laid out but she hid her feelings in what she hoped was brisk efficiency. "Tell him it's Fourcault's. And if you're finished, I'll get on with making the arrangements."

"Thanks for your time." He held out his hand.

Startled, she put her hand in his bearlike grip.

"Will you have wake services?" He seemed reluctant to let go of her hand.

"Of course. You ought to know that if you're Catholic. Why?"

He had relinquished her hand and moved to the door. "I wish I'd known her. I'd like to come pay my respects, if you don't mind."

She warmed to this in spite of herself. "If you'll keep your questions to yourself."

"Scout's honor. Just introduce me as a friend if you have to—I wouldn't want to embarrass you." He waved good-bye and was gone.

Rubbing her right hand with her left, Terry stared at the door. He did have some sense of decency after all, but now that he was gone, she felt drained. Emotional battles took so much more energy than physical labor. And—she had to be honest with herself—some of the emotional drain came from fighting feelings that she would rather deny. She had heard of men whose magnetism drew people to them but had never met such a perfect example as Dan Kevlehan. Did she want to get drawn into something she wasn't sure she could handle?

Her relationships, even with Sean, were always based on an emotional arm's length. She had always felt in charge of herself, hadn't "fallen" in love as much as nurtured a growing warmth that was trying to turn into love just as Sean died. No, she couldn't honestly say she'd ever felt like this with Sean.

The butterflies she felt now could not be charged to grief. In spite of his stubborn refusal to be swayed and his dogged attention to duty, he was so damned attractive that she was sorry he was gone.

Irrational. She was just lonesome for CeCe. And she still couldn't count him on her side. She would have to do it alone.

But though it was barely eleven, Terry was ravenously

hungry. Nora was right: she would keep her strength up by running downstairs to the pub for a corned beef on rye. With something in her stomach she could face the people at Fourcault's Funeral Home and, finally, Micheline. What's more, she would take camouflage to make that visit easier.

She looked around at the worktable and CeCe's desk and decided on the huge manila accordion file of pictures CeCe had collected for the Barron album. As far as Terry knew, CeCe hadn't finalized the selection with Micheline before she left. It would provide a good opening for questions about what was worrying CeCe. She hoisted it under one arm and headed off, still not feeling invincible.

▽

5

MUMPET STOOD ON the Girard front porch, clipboard in hand, and rang the bell. The belted raincoat and matching hat conveyed anonymity: this caller could be a politician seeking votes or a salesperson distributing brochures.

Calls to the machine inside and to The Family Album office had provided the reassuring knowledge that there would be no answer to the bell, but a short wait seemed appropriate. No one was out and about, not in the park or on the lawns of the nearby houses. The porch, even in morning light, was shadowy and not visible from neighbors' windows. Still, there was no time for hanging about. No telling how long Therese would be gone.

The key fit easily into the lock; in seconds, Mumpet was inside with the door locked behind.

The sudden ringing of the phone on the hall table shattered the stillness and Mumpet's nerves. The answering machine kicked in after the first ring and Therese's voice sounded loud in the hall, every word audible. After the beep, Nora's flat, no-nonsense tones rattled off the names of those she had gotten in touch with since her last call, ending with a plaintive "for the love of God, answer your phone."

When breath came normally again, the search began. The layout was straightforward: a formal parlor to the left of the front hall, a dining room beyond that, and a morning or family room—converted to Cecile's bedroom when Therese had returned—at the back. To the right of the hall was the small library in the turret. Old man Girard had had this lined with curved, glass-fronted bookshelves, which were now stuffed with most of the classics. Down the hall beneath the stairs was a maid's room and bath with a pantry connecting it with the kitchen on the back.

Disregarding the formal rooms, Mumpet headed directly for this servant's area, which had been converted into a cozy office. This was the most logical starting point. As at The Family Album, every surface was obliterated by photostats, genealogy sheets with their lines and forked branches, contact sheets with photos of oil portraits, most of it fodder for albums. Gloved hands shuffled through these, through each drawer.

In one of the small drawers of the apothecary chest that hung above the desk was something that seemed to burn the fingers when retrieved. Mumpet stood contemplating the situation. Not the document but—was it possible? If it were, then getting the paper back would be extremely risky but absolutely essential.

The thought was banished for the time being and the search moved through the sitting room and the parlor, furnished with reproductions and the few antiques Cecile had managed to avoid selling. Under, in, behind, atop—no cushion, decorative box, or picture left askew, the search progressed.

On to the bedroom, where drawer contents were lifted out carefully and just as carefully returned in spite of mounting anxiety and frustration. It was slow and tedious. And ultimately fruitless. Mumpet sighed loudly, hands shaking as the last drawer was closed.

Unless Cecile had hidden the document in some book—the several walls lined with crammed bookcases would take a year to go through adequately—it was not on this floor. But Cecile often acknowledged how disorganized she was and it was unlikely she would have trusted herself to remember which book among hundreds she'd chosen. And would she have gone upstairs to Therese's domain to hide something she hadn't seen fit to tell her niece about?

Mumpet debated for several seconds but the phone's bell stymied thought once again. This time the beep was followed by a tentative voice identifying herself as Nadine.

"I don't know whether you want company or not, but if you're not home, I'll just leave this pie on the porch."

All the hatred and frustration built up through searching in vain and feeling victimized by Cecile made Mumpet's head throb. Was there to be a parade of do-gooders this morning, traipsing up the front steps or wandering around to stow their goodies in the safer confines of the back porch?

Mumpet felt trapped. Therese herself might return for any number of reasons. But panic would only complicate matters. Think. Cecile hadn't taken it upstairs, that was almost a certainty. Had she cached it in some quaintly secret spot? Perhaps one of those antiques had a hidden compartment. And one of these days, Therese would happen on it and ruin would rain down. She was just too much like Cecile not to act on it, another do-gooder.

Stop torturing yourself. With Therese out of the way, the chances of it being discovered could be controlled—not perfectly, perhaps, but at least to a tolerable degree.

Mumpet was just passing through the dining room when the door chimes sounded ten feet away in the hall. Crouched beyond the breakfront, Mumpet froze. A mirror halfway along the outer wall reflected a shadowy form through the sidelights. Could anyone see through the curtains into the same mirror? Air refused to stay in its prison of lungs any longer and came hissing out. The room filled with dancing black spots and Mumpet leaned against the wall until dizziness passed.

When at last footsteps faded and an engine roared, Mumpet crept across to peer between the blue moire draperies at the front window. No one was in the neighboring yards and only one elderly man waited patiently for a slow basset hound at the edge of the park.

The shiny oak floors surrounding islands of worn Oriental rugs squeaked underfoot as Mumpet moved swiftly to the front door. This house, at least sixty years old, had undergone almost no restoration, despite the shift to two separate quarters. How old was the heating plant? Mumpet wondered, a hand on the doorknob. The seed of an idea germinated, its eventual bloom promising survival: a way to take care of Therese and the missing document at the same time, if it were, indeed, somewhere in here. With a little help, this place would go up like a tinderbox. First, the other possibility had to be attempted, risky though it was. Then, if that proved a dead end . . . Time to worry about that later.

Mumpet pulled open the door slightly as the phone rang again and was about to ignore yet another sympathy caller when, following Therese's greeting, a voice crackling with age identified herself as Sister Mary Michael. "Call me as soon as you can. I must see you," was all she said before the connection was broken.

Frowning, Mumpet crossed the threshold and pulled the door shut until the lock snapped into place. Was there yet another voice that had to be silenced?

The question hung on the brisk fall air as a raincoated figure crossed the street and walked into the park, someone in no hurry but with a purpose.

The people at Fourcault's were eager to help Terry. They had been burying Girards and other, more prosperous descendants of the "First Thirty" for generations, along with the later-arriving German bourgeoisie. No eyebrow was raised when Terry told them to expect a call from the coroner's office.

Still, Terry's stomach grew queasy as she confronted the ghosts each parlor and alcove produced. Visions of her father's wake haunted her: a series of painfully constrained introductions to distant relatives and teary-eyed friends of the family.

Though Nora would gladly have helped, Terry wanted to choose everything herself. The guilt still gripped her: she should have been home, should have somehow protected

CeCe. She had failed before; she would do everything to make certain these last rituals would be just the way her aunt would have wanted them. Once met, these challenges might somehow prepare her for the greater challenge of disproving CeCe's suicide.

First, a casket that, though reasonable, would have fit in nicely with CeCe's cherished parlor. Next, her favorite soft blue chiffon to dress her in, along with Grandma Girard's rosary. She had remembered this at the last moment. The seemingly endless choices were paraded for her decision: which holy card pictures, what prayer on the back, acknowledgment cards, pall bearers, the design of the funeral mass leaflets.

Finally, calling him from old Jean Fourcault's desk, Terry arranged for Father Morgan to say the requiem mass.

With the torment of deciding for CeCe behind her, Terry faced the next chore: Micheline Barron. CeCe had set her straight, according to Nora. About what? Had it to do with a problem that could mean the loss of that contract? Even if Aunt Mich had simply been put in her place when she got too pushy, she was still one of the last people to spend any time with CeCe. Terry had to know what they talked about.

She fluttered an apologetic hand at Mr. Fourcault, held up a finger to indicate one more call, and dialed the Barron house. When Emma, the maid, told her that Mrs. Barron was home to receive her, Terry was both relieved and anxious.

The anxiety was like a poison inside and her stomach knotted in defense as she left the mortuary. Ordinarily, her stomach was the uncomplaining recipient of late-night pizza, street-vendor hot dogs, and coffee from machines, not that she didn't at least try to eat healthy. But now, everything seemed to cause a rebellion in her innards.

Then Terry remembered the soothing chill of porcelain on her seven-year-old cheek as she laid her head on the washbowl between fits of vomiting. Every night for a month after her father's death, her stomach had rejected dinner despite CeCe's comfort-food menus.

Finally, CeCe began reading to her at the table and, caught up in *Alice's Adventures in Wonderland,* she forgot to be sick. And when Sean was killed, she suddenly realized, the vomiting had returned until she immersed herself in the details of moving back to St. Louis.

Nothing could take her mind off CeCe's death, but she would feel better if she could find out what had happened. She slid into the driver's seat of the Mustang and let the warmth stored in the tan leather seep through her raincoat, a welcome feeling after Fourcault's offices, still air-conditioned this late in the season. When she was finally warmed through, she cranked down the window to let the winy October air flood the inside. It was a day CeCe would have loved.

Let's get it over with, she thought. She started the car and headed for the Barron house on Lindell.

Dan Kevlehan rocked far back at his desk in the detective squad room at headquarters, but the squeal of the springs was almost lost in the din of typewriters, phone conversations, and a suspect's loud denials down the hall. Both hands cradled the back of his head as he stared at the fluorescent fixture above him. He searched for a way to tell Lieutenant Carney, who straddled the corner of his desk, waiting for a reason why the Girard case couldn't be closed.

"It doesn't feel right."

"Well, we don't always have time for feelings, Dan. Besides, you don't often play hunches."

"I just don't like it." Dan swung forward, torturing the springs, and shaped a square with his hands on the blotter. "Nothing fits into the suicide pattern."

"Except a note, distracted behavior, and witnesses who say she was worried. What more do you want?"

"A lot more. The note, especially, I don't like. Neither does the niece. It looks cropped—even the lab says the top is off a hair from being square, like it went through a paper cutter. Her niece said she was always disorganized and the worry could have been fear for her life. No, I've got a hunch we may be looking at a homicide, Lieutenant."

"Proof. We need some, Dan, maybe with a dollop of motive. And a suspect is always nice—the niece, maybe?" Carney was smiling but the needling came through.

Dan breathed a little quicker, remembering the way that soft green material had skimmed over sensational hips as Therese Girard bent to the filing cabinet. He was glad she was off the hook. "She's alibied up to her eyeballs. Spent the evening in Jeff City with a professor from Mizzou. He confirms."

"You've already been checking alibis?" Carney's eyebrows shot up. "Maybe she has friends. Any other relatives that inherit or otherwise benefit?"

"None so far. And I don't think there's all that much to inherit." The threadbare rug and spartan furnishings in her office had only served to make Therese Girard look that much better in contrast.

"I'll give you another day or so, Dan, but we're really backed up. We'll be shorthanded trying to deal with the sellout crowds every night at the stadium, not to mention Thursday's problem if we don't get him before that."

There had been a letter made of cutout words from the *Post*, warning that, if the Series lasted until Thursday—now a certainty since the Cards had split the first two with the Twins—a bomb would be detonated in Busch Stadium.

"I don't know what kind of mind can get its kicks out of maiming a bunch of bleacherites."

"Beats the hell out of me." Dan cursed the timing silently. It was Tuesday, which left forty-eight hours. He needed breathing room to develop any sort of case, and he didn't want to let the details leak beforehand if there was a good suspect. "I'd like to keep the coroner's finding off the front page at least for now. Can I get him to release the body without the paperwork?"

"If you think there's anything to this, I'd rather he keep the vic *and* the report on ice. But remember, Thursday afternoon you and Lucas get yourselves over to Wilson; he'll need all the extra hands he can find. And don't be surprised if you get switched before that. You can't ever tell about these crazies." Lieutenant Carney eased off the desk and wandered over to his next target for an update.

Dan liked the way Carney went around to his men instead of calling them into his office. It seemed to knock down the bullshit on both sides. And Carney cut a little slack when he thought you might be onto something.

All I need is a little time, Dan pleaded to Carney's back, but when he thought of how Terry Girard would react to their keeping her aunt's body, he groaned inwardly. Damn the timing. Damn the unknown bomber, if he really existed. Why Thursday, he wondered? Couldn't the guy get tickets for an earlier game? That narrowed it down to 50,000, though.

Bert Lucas eased into the chair opposite him, grinned across the width of the two desks between them, and stretched his feet out in the aisle. Dan's partner was tall, thin, black, and so laid-back that certain people missed the workings of his analytic mind until it was too late. Most of these people were now behind bars. "I thought I'd make myself scarce until the man had thoroughly digested you."

"Wilson's breathing down his neck and the bomber's making everybody goosy. But he listens, give him that. I get to persuade the coroner to sit on the report as long as he keeps the corpse, too. And how do you feel about a little honest work now that you've stuffed your face with lunch?"

"Do I have a choice?"

"No, but it's in a good cause. I haven't told the Girard niece what I think of this case. It stinks like a murder."

"I thought she was alibied. Make up your mind—you want a tail on her?"

"Hell, no. I'm worried she might be next."

▽

6

TERRY TRIED TO sort out her feelings about Micheline Barron as she left the southside mortuary. She headed west to Kingshighway Boulevard and worked her way north in the stop-and-start traffic until she reached the northern edge of Forest Park.

The newlywed Barrons, Louis and Micheline, had followed the path she traced now, deserting the bluffs of South St. Louis's riverfront during the Depression, when many fortunes were changing hands. Louis, craving a higher step on the social ladder than his Carondolet setting could furnish, had taken advantage of a broker's window leap to pick up a bargain in one of the stately homes overlooking the north side of the park. As a young bride, Micheline had set out at once to live up to the new address.

As a widow, she had made offers several times for a house in either Westmoreland or Portland Place, the two private places north of—and several notches of exclusivity above—Lindell, but each time the deal had fallen through. Not accidentally, Terry thought. Still, Micheline resisted the idea of moving farther out to whatever western suburb was currently "in," even though Terry had heard her daughters suggest it often.

Terry veered into the left-turn lane at Lindell with a flick of her signal and a baleful glance to the west. The doyenne of the Barron clan was not one of Terry's favorites. It wasn't just that Micheline had never done anything useful—Terry discounted the chairing of balls, where the work was artfully delegated while Micheline ended up on the society page.

Even the mothering of four children, once the sympathy-producing birth was accomplished, had been delegated to nannies and assorted boarding schools. Hugh and Evelyn, Frances and Claude, none of them had turned out to be people Terry could admire, but Micheline couldn't be blamed for that necessarily. No, it was more that Micheline equated wealth and position with personal goodness, or at least the results of goodness, worthy of adulation. Lack of money, therefore, became some sort of character flaw, the inevitable result of laziness and bad habits.

CeCe had chastised a teenaged Terry more than once for smartmouthing, as CeCe called it, in the presence of the older woman. "She's more to be pitied than condemned," CeCe would say once they got home. But Terry had disagreed silently: *She is a self-centered old bitch and I won't kowtow to her.*

Yet Terry had found herself doing just that when Micheline Dechant Barron had come to them several months ago as a client. Approaching her seventy-fifth birthday, Micheline had asked CeCe to assemble a thorough reprise of the Barron–Dechant families. It was the largest commission the new partnership had received and, though the lineage was already researched, both CeCe and Terry had kept busy tracking down proofs of authenticity and memorabilia.

Terry told herself it was in the name of business but resented Micheline's less-than-subtle steering. The finished product was due to be displayed—and a limited number of copies distributed—at a black-tie dinner celebrating the dedication of Barron Park in eleven days. The deadline would be met, if only to preserve CeCe's reputation.

Terry pulled into the curving drive that carved out a half circle of lawn, centered with one ancient blazing oak. Two Beamers were already parked by the door and she left the Mustang thirty yards from the nearest one. The rusty rose limestone towered three and a half stories, its copper mansard roof green from long exposure to the damp city air. Like its neighbors on Lindell, it commanded a lovely view of the park, enjoyed only from behind curtains: no resident would venture to relax on a front porch where he could be observed by drivers on the now-busy boulevard. One glance at the imposing front door and the familiar queasy feeling in the pit of her stomach was back. It was worse now, because CeCe would not be there to run interference for her.

Telling herself that honey would get more answers than vinegar, Terry nevertheless dragged her feet along the walk past a six-foot-high privet hedge. As she neared the steps to the wide porch Frances Devereaux's unmistakable trill of laughter coming from behind the hedge caught her attention. Evidently they had heard her also because Evelyn Devereaux, firmly girdled into a Carolina Herrera jumpsuit, came to the opening carved in the greenery and hailed her.

"*Dear* Terry. We heard from Mother about Cecile. Come sit a spell. We're both just horrified. She was such a dear woman." The staccato speech pattern made Evelyn sound like an irritating telegram.

Reluctantly, Terry followed the platinum-haired figure onto the side patio. Listening to these two was a steep price for delaying her confrontation with Micheline.

Plump-cushioned iron chairs and chaises surrounded a central marble fountain on the old brick patio, and were in turn flanked by spectacular beds of fall flowers. The smell of mums assaulted her; she must remember to warn the Fourcaults not to put them near CeCe's casket.

Frances lay stretched out on one chaise, her upper body in the shade of an umbrella table and her legs, where they extended into the sunlight, covered by a pale green angora throw. No sun, not even the watery October kind, for Frances. She fluttered her mascaraed eyelashes at Terry.

"Was it really an accident, darlin'? I can't imagine Aunt Cecile losing her balance." Frances's Virginia finishing school accent made it come out "Ohnt Cecile."

"The doctors aren't sure what made her fall," Terry said. She perched on the concrete edge of the fountain's pool with the bulky file balanced next to her.

"Well, she never got dizzy when she was younger. She used to swing us around until we were *senseless*," Evelyn said. "She played make-believe, let me be Joan of Arc. Frances was Scarlett. Fran was wild for *Gone With the Wind* back then. Wonderful lady. Fed our imaginations."

"The boys were her favorites, though. Her little one, Hugh," Frances said, with a slight edge in her voice, "and Claude, the Fat Cat."

"Yes, I remember," Evelyn said. "He's still roly-poly—and late with the drinks." She looked past Terry toward the French doors.

"She had pet names for everyone, even for Mama, but not to her face." Even Frances's laugh was tinged with a cultivated Southern accent.

Terry wondered what CeCe had called Micheline behind her back but wouldn't give this ersatz Southern belle the satisfaction of asking. The corners of Frances's mouth hung down in disappointment.

"Some tea, Terry? A drink?"

"No, but thanks anyway. I really came to see your mother."

Frances took off her broad-brimmed straw hat and fanned herself with it, probably for the languid effect, because a cool breeze already stirred her artfully lightened hair. "About that lovely old book y'all are fixing for the dedication?"

"That and some other things."

"Would those be the pictures?" Evelyn motioned to the envelope, and at Terry's nod she laid a perfectly manicured hand on Terry's shoulder and launched a verbal attack. "Just remember, Trep and Leslie are awfully sensitive. They should have only the most flattering pictures. And I won't have that hideous picture of me on the arm of Stuart Lenbeck at the ball. You use the one of me alone, curtsying."

Good God, the woman was insufferable. "I'll be sure to suggest that to your mother."

"Of course, Mama will use what she da-yum well pleases, Evelyn."

"And she'll certainly be pleased to choose the one of you up there on the dais with his veiled highness. Stuart was good enough for the ugly duckling who never even made the court of honor." Envy, so old it had long teeth, bit into every word.

"Well, *one* of us had to get that far or Daddy would have had a stroke a lot sooner. Besides, it was one evening. You didn't end up having to marry him, Evelyn."

"Oh, no. I must be forever grateful to you for throwing your future brother-in-law my way."

"Ah, but he's given you two lovely children, which is two more than I have, darlin'."

That quieted Evelyn momentarily, Terry thought. Frances's only child, an eight-year-old daughter, had drowned in the pool at Micheline's Pompano Beach condo. Evelyn had become obsessively protective of her children after that.

"Of course you'd bring up my only advantage in life. You could have had another child but your debutante figure might have suffered."

Frances turned even whiter. "I won't warn you again, Evelyn."

Terry could hardly believe her ears. Here CeCe was lying on a cold slab downtown and they were arguing about children and some Veiled Prophet Balls twenty-five years ago. She would have to sidetrack them or scream.

"I have some nice wedding pictures of both of you. Did your mother give you any idea of which she wants?"

"Mother's playing her cards close to the chest," Evelyn offered. "I wanted a full page of Trep in his honors gown at graduation. She made it clear that she was paying for the album. I tried to tell her Friday—"

"You just never learn, Evelyn." Frances had recovered her role. "You don't tell Mama what she should do. You—cajole!" She gave her hat a final flourish and plopped it back on her head.

Evelyn rolled her eyes at Terry. "I hope you'll excuse our little tiffs. It's not like we don't feel awful about Cecile. If there's anything either of us can do, just say the word."

"Thanks, I'll do that." When pigs can fly, she thought, backing slowly toward the gap in the hedge. "Now I'd better get inside before your mother wonders if I changed my mind. I'll tell Claude you're waiting if I see him."

Airheads, both of them, and without an ounce of loyalty to their siblings or mother. She fled along the walk to the porch, crossed the herringbone brick surface, and rang the bell. Opaque curtains prevented seeing beyond the door's oval beveled glass, etched with an Old English *B*. According to CeCe, it was the first renovation Louis Barron had ordered. She had joked about it standing for "bargain" and scolded Terry for saying it stood for "bitch." Now Terry stared at it, wishing that CeCe had been right.

▽

7

"LORDY, MISS TERRY! Come right in." The elderly black woman's smile was both sad and welcoming.

"Hello, Emma. You said Mrs. Barron would see me?"

"Sure, you come along with me, child." Her crisp black uniform and starched white apron rustled as she closed the door behind them. "I was awful sorry to hear about Miss Cele. She was one sweet lady."

"Thanks, Emma, that she was. No, don't bother," Terry said as the maid began to help her off with her raincoat. "I won't be staying long."

Terry followed Emma across the circular entry hall with its harlequin pattern of tiles and curving stairwell and down two steps to a room dominated by furniture stiff and unforgiving, its wine, cream, and navy striped upholstery barely softening the black oak frames. Beyond, a huge bay window spanned the back wall. The Barron and Dechant mansions built on the Carondolet bluffs, CeCe had told her, faced downstream, overlooking the river and Arsenal Island; the view here was tamer.

Terry could see more gardens and a gazebo, along with the now-covered pool. She had been allowed to swim there as a teenager, conscious of Claude's lascivious stares. The memory chilled her in spite of the gas logs turned on low in the fireplace.

Out from behind the bar in the corner, with three drinks on a tray, Claude Barron emerged as if sprung from her thoughts. His graying hair was worn long, the curly ends covering the collar of a cashmere polo shirt that was pulled taut across his paunch. He evidently hadn't heard her because he jumped, almost spilling the glasses. "Ther*ese*, what a surprise. And how is your dear aunt?"

"Didn't Hugh tell you? Or the girls? I was just talking to the two of them and they knew. She died Sunday." It sounded blunt to Terry's ears but she would have to get used to it.

"Oh, how perfectly dreadful of me. No, no, I hadn't heard. I just now got here and the girls sent me in to play bartender. And Hugh and I aren't speaking again this week. But this is simply awful. Was it sudden? Well, of course it was," he said, answering his own question. "Mother just had lunch with her Saturday."

A slight creak on the stairway made him shy like a crowded racehorse. "My heartfelt sympathy, dear," he said, running the words together. With a meaningful look over his shoulder, he whispered, "We'll talk later." He scurried through a side door to the sunroom and out the French doors that gave on the patio.

Terry turned to watch Micheline come sweeping down the stairs as though she were Mrs. Astor greeting the Four Hundred. Still vigorous, and with a flowing rose silk to soften her large frame, she strode up to Terry and embraced her gingerly, keeping her immaculately coiffed platinum hair a careful inch from Terry's cheek.

"My dear girl, I was shocked to hear about Cecile. Why, I took to my bed for the entire day!" Her own condition described, she held Terry at arm's length and scrutinized her. "And how are you bearing up under this tragedy?"

"I'll be all right, Aunt Micheline. But I'll feel better if I can find out how CeCe came to fall off that bluff. You had lunch with her Saturday?"

"Yes, I took her to the DeMenil House. Such a nice ambience and the salads—oh, gracious, here I am going on about food, and poor Cecile—do come over here and sit down." Micheline led the way to a straight-backed settee that was as uncomfortable as it looked. Her chin was tilted so that those icy gray eyes sighted down the length of her nose at Terry. "Now what was it you could possibly want to know about our lunch?"

Terry plowed on, ignoring the coolness. "CeCe was worried about something and I'm rather sure it had to do with work. Since you're our most valued client, I wondered if there was some trouble with the album. Did you have a complaint?"

"A complaint? Of course not." Micheline's eyebrows raised a quarter inch, not enough to furrow the well-creamed forehead. "I was simply getting a report on her progress so far. We went over quite a few details and I was satisfied that everything was on schedule."

Micheline's strong hands were folded motionless in her lap. Sitting bolt upright, she seemed to force a composure that she didn't feel.

"She didn't mention any snag that could jeopardize the project?"

"Heavens, no. Is there one I should know about?" For the first time, Micheline's wide eyes left hers to stare out toward the side patio and her offspring.

"Not to my knowledge. But when I left for Jefferson City Friday morning she seemed . . . upset. Did she act like she was worrying about anything or had another problem on her mind?" Terry watched the older woman's knuckles whiten in her lap, but Micheline turned again to face her.

"You may rest assured she was business as usual. Of course she did misplace her glasses and had to hunt them down in the rest room. But then that was business as usual for Cecile."

Terry didn't believe her. Of course the part about CeCe losing her glasses was true—God knew how many times Terry had found them this past year—but that was just diversion. CeCe's emotions were an open book, though, especially to those who had known her for so long. If she was worried, it showed; if she was mad at you, you knew it.

"She told me you were extremely organized, always on top

of things, not a bit like her." Micheline reached out and patted Terry's hand.

Terry felt the warmth of a blush on her cheeks. If she could have had more of CeCe's concern, she might have persuaded her aunt to share whatever was worrying her. "I wish I were half the woman she was," she said.

Micheline ignored the demurral. "So since you are that well organized, my dear, do you think—I hate to speak of my own needs at a time like this—but will you be able to gather things together before the dedication?"

The anger in her made Terry's blush deepen, warming her until the room's air felt oppressively hot. "I'll have it ready as soon as possible after the funeral."

"I don't mean to press, but our agreement had a deadline and if it isn't met—" The threat of nonpayment was politely unspoken but definitely present.

"You'll have it."

She was hurt, not for herself but for CeCe, who had been ten times the woman this one was. She stood up abruptly. "Had you and CeCe decided definitely on which pictures in our files are to be used?"

Micheline flinched. Had no one wrested control of a conversation from her in years? Or had Terry hit on the source of a disagreement at that luncheon? But Micheline's face smoothed over as she flicked her hand at the file. "I had her bring me the lot on Saturday. All the older pictures go in—they're marked on the back. There are so few from those generations and each adds its own character."

"There are quite a few of you and Mr. Barron and all the children and grandchildren. Do you—?"

"We discussed the later ones and I told her I'd think about it." Micheline cut her off without a glance. "It's a shame there wasn't a better selection for some of them."

That's it, blame the messenger—or the photographer. More and more, Terry was convinced CeCe and Micheline had at least disagreed over the pictures even if CeCe hadn't argued the point that strongly. She was determined to stay until she had some idea of what CeCe had objected to.

"I brought all of them with me so there wouldn't be any mistakes. If you have a few minutes, and you've made up your mind, maybe we can mark the rest now."

"Oh, has Evelyn been at you about that Lenbeck person?"

"I haven't shown the pictures to anyone." Terry evaded the question. "But I'll need a decision soon. Even though this will be camera-ready copy, the printer wants five working days to run a preliminary copy in the gold binder you chose."

"Well, let's just walk out by way of the patio and see who's depleting the bar supply today. Maybe they can help me make up my mind."

As if Micheline had ever needed any help in that regard, Terry thought. Why was she willing to involve them now?

Terry had her elbow gripped firmly and was led past the bar and through the doorway to the sunroom. It was too late now to tell Micheline that she'd already talked with everyone else, and an instinctive caution made her hope it wouldn't come out.

"Would you care for a glass of sherry?" Micheline asked with one hand on the handle of the French door.

Terry almost laughed at the typically lame offer, extended so late. "I don't drink when I'm driving, thank you."

"No vices at all? My, how—content you must be." She pulled hard on the door so that it banged against a verdigris frog doorstop.

"Look, everyone, Therese is here. I'm sure you've all heard about poor CeCe, so give this child some sympathy."

Terry winced inwardly. She hadn't come here for sympathy, she wasn't a child, and over Micheline's shoulder she could see that the three siblings didn't appreciate the interruption. The women sat sipping their drinks and Claude stood in the left corner of the patio plucking dead mums for a pile on the brick retaining wall. He turned a pouty-lipped face to his mother.

Don't blame me, Terry thought, *this isn't my idea.*

After a few seconds they all murmured condolences as though she had just arrived, but none came any closer.

"Well, I suppose you've already talked to her," Micheline tweaked them, "so you know Therese has all the pictures of the last three generations with her. She wants a decision on which to use." She picked up a glass from the nearest umbrella table as though it were filled with Socrates' hemlock. "Make some room for us to spread these out, and you may all have a vote—subject to veto, of course."

Of course. Terry watched Evelyn scurry forward to take the glass and a tray of crumpled cocktail napkins and set them on the table next to Frances, giving her a victorious look. Then she hurried back to claim a chair next to Micheline where the action was.

Frances roused herself languidly, as though she had no interest whatsoever, and sank down in the fourth chair. Claude dragged a fifth one over but instead of sitting down he continued to neaten the bushes.

"Let's start with the youngest generation, Therese. Perhaps Frances has a favorite of Pamela."

Micheline looked to Terry, who was obliged to rifle through the last section of the file and hand over a manila envelope.

Micheline in turn spread them out in front of Frances. There were two studio portraits, one of Robert standing behind Frances, who held a year-old Pamela somewhat gingerly, and one of Pamela at about four, in a long dress, holding a basket of roses.

Without a moment's hesitation, Frances picked up the one of Pamela by herself and handed it to Terry.

"A wise choice, dear," Micheline said quietly. "And we'll use the ballet shot, shall we?"

The one of a tutued Pamela, arms and feet in first position, lay next to several of Pamela in various bathing suits, posed on diving boards or the edge of a pool. Frances nodded silently.

Was there a hidden agenda of cruelty here? Terry remembered CeCe talking about the drowning, saying mother and grandmother blamed each other for not watching the child. Micheline had complained to CeCe that Frances didn't warm up to her daughter; afterward, Frances's lack of maternal feeling was never mentioned. Like mother, like daughter, CeCe had said.

"Now for Leslie and Richard the third," Micheline commanded.

"Trep, Mother. I know he's twenty-three, and he says that's too old for nicknames, but I still think of him that way."

Micheline stiffened beside Terry and dumped the pictures out in a heap on the table. Unaware of the effect her correction had on Micheline, Evelyn could hardly contain her eagerness.

"Ooh, aren't they adorable? I'd forgotten how cute Leslie was in her band uniform—and those two at her debut—definitely that one, right, Mother?"

"Oh, I think the other one shows off her beautiful figure, dear."

"But that's just it, she looks slimmer in this one."

"She has your genes, Evelyn—but if you insist." Micheline marked Evelyn's choice with an *x* on the back.

Belatedly, Evelyn must have realized she'd antagonized her mother, and now she chose a baby picture and the band pose—not really cute at all, Terry thought; those uniforms don't flatter anyone. Leslie, a senior at Wellesley, would scream if she were here.

Micheline handed the lot to Terry with a nod and spread her grandson's pictures out on the table. Terry could see the doting adoration on Evelyn's face. Trep had inherited his father's good looks and his political savvy. Just finishing law school at Emory, he had compiled a résumé of class presidencies and prestigious internships, and had even been an alternate delegate to the state convention last year. Evelyn cooed over each picture from kindergarten to mortarboard.

"For God's sake, don't drool on them, Evelyn," Frances told her. "Can we get on with it?"

Evelyn gave her a long look, then turned to Micheline. "They're all good. Trep never took a bad picture. Use whichever you think—I love them all."

Terry watched her caress one picture after another. It was almost scary.

Micheline deftly lifted several from the table, with Evelyn nodding again, loath to let them out of her hands. Micheline marked and handed them to Terry. "Now the fun begins. Claude? Chien Gras? That's what Cecile called him," Micheline told Terry.

Claude had moved over to the front opening in the hedge and was looking down toward Kingshighway. Now he crossed with slow, small steps, dropped one last mum on the tray, and sat down next to Terry at the table.

"Shouldn't we wait for Marie? I don't know whether—"

"Nonsense. Even at your most prosaic, you have more artistic sense than Marie."

This time Terry spread out the "Claude" envelope in front of him, then leaned back so he and Micheline could fight it out.

"I'd like the one that ran in the *Post* with the feature on *Beaux Arts*." He fished through the pile and held up a glossy that showed him with Marie at a pasteup table, putting together the newsletter they published.

"But Claude, that's so pedestrian. Marie doesn't even have her hair combed."

"*Beaux Arts* means more than anything to us—to me. It *is* me, Mother. *Nothing* can describe my life better."

"We'll run a blowup of the banner." Micheline turned to Terry. "Be sure you put in some glowing words about their little paper. That should get you a few more subscriptions, Claude. Then we'll use the shot of you and Marie at the governor's inaugural, all right?" She reached across Terry to lift a view of Claude and Marie in tux and black crepe, wine glasses in hand, in front of an ice sculpture of a giant fish, its open mouth threatening to consume Marie.

Terry looked to her right, where Claude's jaws worked and

his lower lip jutted forward. "Have it your way, Mother, as long as the banner shot is a decent size."

"As big as money can buy," Micheline said, pointedly. "We'll have a page of wedding poses, too, so choose one of you and Marie." She turned away with an air of dismissal.

"Well, we're down to you girls and all the fine offerings CeCe has gathered." Without looking at Terry, she held out her hand for the women's envelopes. "I'll bet you two have some strong opinions, don't you?"

"Haven't they always?" Hugh came through the archway in the hedge, crossed the flagstones, stopping to sneeze into a handkerchief, then stooped to bestow a kiss near his mother's head. "I hope you're not still arguing about escorts and offspring in front of Therese."

"We've just reached their pages. Therese, would you get Hugh's share of pictures out? He can choose his own."

"But mother—" Evelyn started, then subsided.

Terry passed the last envelope to Micheline, who dropped it on the flagstones. Hugh retrieved it.

"This won't take long," he said, riffling through the contents and extracting one of himself in judge's robes and another that showed him with a plaque from the city beautification committee.

"None of you and Schindler in there? That would make a good one," Claude said.

After a week of silence, Terry thought, this didn't sound like a peace offering. One glance at Hugh told her he was livid. Who, she wondered, was Schindler?

Micheline fanned herself with Evelyn's envelope. "It's so warm for October, I don't see how you younger people stand it out here. Hugh, would you get me a glass of water while you fix yourself something?" She brushed him toward the French doors.

Keeping warring siblings separated, Terry decided as she filed Hugh's choices away.

"Evelyn, I suppose you want the curtsying pose? Fine. Which of the others?"

Evelyn looked nonplussed. Her hand hovered over the batch as though this was a high-stakes card trick and her fortune depended on choosing the right one.

"Oh, come on, Evelyn. There aren't that many good ones," Micheline prompted.

"I'd rather have one with the children, but . . . I suppose the one on the podium with Richard when he won his seat. What do you think, Mother?" Evelyn was cowed now.

"Perfect. And one of your wedding, please. Now, Frances. Are we agreed on the one of you in the court of honor? I thought so. And those?" She collected a wedding shot and one of Frances at a political convention, holding the sign of a successful candidate who was now pushing Robert for governor. "Still toadying to Drake, I see."

"Drake is our ticket to the White House, Mother, after our purgatorial stay in Jeff City."

Micheline turned, her eyes boring into Terry's. "You didn't hear that, my dear. I don't expect it to go further."

"Of course not." Terry returned Micheline's look. "I don't dish gossip."

"No, that's right, you have no vices. Well, you have all the pictures now. Call me when you have it set for the printer and I'll give it a final proofing." Micheline was standing, an obvious signal that Terry's mission was over.

Talk about a bum's rush. "I'll have it done as soon after the funeral as possible."

"Oh, here's a copy of the newsletter so you can get a good repro of the banner." Claude pulled it out of a back pocket and proffered it.

Hugh came out of the house with a glass in each hand.

"If you need pallbearers, keep me in mind, my dear." Obviously, he wasn't including his brother.

"Of course, whenever the wake, whenever the funeral, we'll be there," Micheline chimed in. "Cecile was one of my dearest childhood friends. I wouldn't dream of missing it."

"I'll keep you posted, and thank you for all your help." Terry said the last with a straight face, sure that the sarcasm would go right over Micheline's head. With an all-encompassing wave, she backed toward the opening in the hedge. Above the spicy tang of mums, she could smell what must be cider in their glasses and, suddenly thirsty, wished she had asked for a glass of water, too.

On the driveway, Terry made sure the selected pictures were segregated in the file and wondered if Micheline was getting senile. The woman had seemed to relish pitting her will against her daughters, hiding behind her money and power to take potshots. And then to capitulate, give in to them on the pictures—it just wasn't like Micheline. Deep down, Terry felt that she had witnessed a fine performance in the living room, but Micheline might just be losing touch instead of lying. And what had Terry learned about the problem that CeCe was so upset about?

"Terry Girard, isn't it?"

Terry, deep in her own thoughts, hadn't seen anyone coming. Surprising, because the vicuna cape that enveloped all but the face and feet was bright gold, striped with the red, yellow, and violet of a Santa Fe sunset. Mahogany hair piled in several layers balanced a face with as many layers of chin below. The scarlet lips didn't know whether to smile or not but the eyes, squeezing out of their fat, didn't try.

"I'm sorry to hear about your aunt. I just heard from Nora Carpenter." Then, when Terry didn't seem to recognize her, "Marie Barron, Claude's wife?"

"Of course, I'm sorry." Terry tried to keep eye contact and avoid staring. The onetime artist's model had put on another thirty pounds since Terry had seen her last. "I was thinking about something."

"About Mother Barron giving you a hard time? If I were you I'd take her precious book and use it to line the zoo's bird cage."

"My aunt contracted to produce it. I'll deliver."

"Is it true that you've collected candid shots of us?"

"Yes, candid and formal. We've just been finalizing the selections."

"Using just what she picked?"

"It was more or less a joint effort." Terry didn't want to start a connubial conflict.

But Marie persisted, the layers of hair tilting toward the house. "Which ones of Claude and me *are* included? If you don't mind my asking."

Terry saw no reason not to tell her; she would find out from Claude shortly anyway. "The two of you by the ice sculpture and a wedding portrait. And Micheline agreed to run a shot of the newsletter banner. Nothing unflattering."

Marie slung the strap of a leather hobo bag over her shoulder and turned to climb the steps. "Don't bet the rent on it," the woman said without looking at her.

Terry watched from the driveway while Marie Barron punched the doorbell as though she hoped it would detonate a bomb inside. Terry could have called out to her that they were all on the patio; instead she climbed into her car, smiling. Nora put Claude a day down the list from Micheline; evidently CeCe had told her what she thought of his ogling Terry.

Terry ran the shift through four gears before she took a deep breath and leaned her head against the backrest. She could feel the tenseness of her neck muscles and Marie's heavy perfume still tickled her nose.

Had CeCe argued with Micheline about the choice of pictures? But that sort of thing was routine; now that she was away from those strange people, she couldn't see it causing the worry Terry remembered with increasing clarity. It had to be more serious, bad enough to cause a heart attack or perhaps a sudden stroke. God, if the results of the autopsy would only show that, at least it would simplify things.

The dashboard clock read a quarter to four when she pulled into the first level of the garage and headed for the office and her telephone. She would call Sister Mary Michael. Of all people, CeCe would have felt most comfortable confiding in her. Terry scolded herself for not trying to reach the nun this morning. *What's the matter with me? I can't even think straight.*

Terry felt calmer once she reached the office. CeCe was closest here, the rest of the world far away. And it was just possible that she would find more proof to show Kevlehan. She flipped idly through the calendar once more and stopped at an entry that startled her: penciled in on Tuesday at four-forty-five was a meeting with the Sullivans, parents of the bride-to-be noted in the calendar and old friends whom CeCe had taken on as clients. That's today, she thought, checking her watch. In less than an hour. Too late to reach them. "Dammit," was all she could say.

From memory, Terry dialed Gethsemane, only to get a busy signal. Letting the phone drop into its cradle, she went into the bathroom, took a long drink of water with two aspirin to dispel a nagging headache, and put the kettle on for tea. She dialed the Gethsemane number again: still busy.

She got out the file on the Sullivans and started to page through it, but the copy of the note Kevlehan had left fluttered in the draft from the window, drawing her eyes to it. What had prompted CeCe to write those words? Where had she been when she did? The paper was not from the loose-leaf notebook she carried in her purse. Not the bright yellow pad in the front hall at home. Not from the lined pads they used in the office. It looked more like her formal notes except that the name and address were not on top. The sheet was smaller, as though the heading had been trimmed.

Trimmed.

The lead ball that had been tossed down in her stomach when she first heard about CeCe dropped again with nauseating suddenness. Her head felt curiously detached from the rest of her. CeCe had written a letter to someone and this portion of it had been neatly cropped. And left in her car. Which meant that it had not been an accident or a stroke or a dizzy spell. Or a suicide as it was meant to appear.

CeCe had been murdered.

Terry screamed. It came out soft, hoarse, with little air behind it, and she covered her face with both hands, rocking back and forth in CeCe's chair.

* * *

Terry had forced near-scalding tea down her throat to calm herself. Her second cup was cold, and still she shrank from touching the paper, even though it was just a copy. A cold-blooded killer had handled the original. Now Terry knew what had been tickling the back of her mind. The note hadn't sounded like CeCe because of its grammar. There was no period at the end of the sentence for the simple reason that it wasn't ended.

Was it possible? Who would ever want to hurt such a harmless soul? CeCe was not perfect. She had been maddeningly absent-minded, losing keys, umbrellas, pens, and eyeglasses. Her work area always looked as though the '29 tornado had just passed through. But, to Terry's consternation, CeCe could generally put her finger on the paper she needed.

She loved her friends and Terry, but felt free to tell them how best to live their lives: according to her moral standards, which were high, if quirky in a few areas. What had she been, or said, or done that someone would hate enough to end her life?

But someone had. Terry was sure of it.

Should she tell Kevlehan? "Ha!" she said out loud. If she couldn't persuade him away from a suicide, she certainly wouldn't convince him it was murder. Not without proof.

Standing by the chair Kevlehan had filled this morning, she stared at CeCe's empty swivel chair and tried to play back the events of Friday morning. Had her aunt said anything that she, in her rush to be off, hadn't listened to?

Nothing. CeCe had been unusually quiet. Terry realized, ashamed, that she herself had done most of the talking, had not noticed at the time. And CeCe had spared her, one last time.

She retreated to her own desk and, hands trembling, punched in Nora's number. With her new realization, it mattered less that Nora had told Kevlehan about CeCe's preoccupation of Saturday night. Terry was determined to find any shred of information that would point to the source of that worry.

"Hello?" Nora's voice was hesitant.

"Nora, it's Terry. I'm—"

"Oh, thank God," Nora sighed. "I thought it was another one wanting to know *just how it happened*." Her voice sank to a dramatically conspiratorial whisper for these last four words. "You know how people can be."

"Yes, and the hell with them. Listen, I want you to try to remember everything CeCe said to you Saturday night."

"What? Are you serious?"

"I've never been more serious in my life."

"Everything?"

"Everything that wasn't your standard chitchat. Did she have any bits of gossip that surprised you?"

"Well . . . we talked about Sister Mary Michael. CeCe had just come from there. Sister's heartbeat has been erratic and her blood pressure was up even more but that's not really news. She brought me some windfall apples Sister had given her from the orchard. Then she told me she hadn't gotten by Aubergine's after lunch."

Terry's throat ached and she swallowed hard, trying to control her voice. "Did she say what Micheline and she had talked about at lunch?"

"I already told you about her saying she 'got the old biddy straightened out'—that's the way she put it."

"I've just come from there and Aunt Mich was not forthcoming at all. Can you remember her exact words?"

"Just what I said. Mich was one of your customers and you know CeCe never gossiped about the business. Maybe Mich was trying to talk down the price, knowing the Barrons."

"Come on, Nora, what did she say or do that made you think she wasn't herself?" Terry wasn't going to mention Kevlehan's previous call if she could help it.

"There was one question, now that I think about it. She asked me if I thought you were serious about making a career out of the business—if it were to go bust would you be heartbroken."

"But the business is doing better than ever!"

"Well, that's what I mean about her not sounding like herself. Then she said that some things had to be done even if innocent people got hurt."

"And?"

"And that's all she said. She clammed up and finished off her pie. Didn't even stay for 'Masterpiece Theatre.' "

"Strange, all right."

"What's strange is that your sergeant asked me the same questions you just did."

Terry didn't know whether to be frightened or comforted. She felt off-balance, the way she did when she reached for the doorjamb in the dark and it wasn't where she expected. If he were so dead set on a finding of suicide, why probe further?

"He wanted to know what all she said—not just how she acted?"

"Yes, but I just told him she wasn't her old self. It was the truth but beyond that I wasn't sure what you wanted me to tell him. Can you explain what's going on, Terry?"

"I'm not sure, Nora. But he did say they'd be finished in time for CeCe to be laid out tomorrow. I wish we could have put the funeral on Thursday." Her father's had been on Friday.

"But there are too many people coming. We have to make it two nights. CeCe has so many friends and they'll all want to come and—"

"I already told Fourcault's two nights, Nora. I know they'll come, even though the Cards play on both nights. But she'd understand if some of them go to the game one night."

"This isn't the time for humor, young lady. The phone hasn't cooled off since you left yesterday. I called a few people and told them to pass the word, but everyone called me back when they couldn't reach you. Don't get mad, but lots of old people don't like those answering machines."

Terry was ready to scream. Here was Nora worried about machines with CeCe's murderer at large! She tried to keep the panic out of her voice. "Nora, I'll call you later. I'm not home to answer the phone—I met Kevlehan here at the office before I went to Fourcault's and then I went out to the Barron house. Now I'm stuck back here at the office—the Sullivans are due any minute."

"You're working today? Merciful God, can't you give it a rest?"

"I'm trying to find out . . . why CeCe died. And I have to keep the business running. That's important."

"I'm sorry, honey. You do what you think's best. Be sure to stop for something to eat."

Terry hung up and tried to stretch the tenseness from her muscles. Her foot nudged the bottom drawer and she remembered closing it yesterday. She never left her drawers open. Her work area was as neat as CeCe's was a jumble.

Almost afraid to look, Terry nudged open the drawer and peered in. Three steno notebooks and a spare roll of tape, just what she expected. She lifted the top one by its spiral and flipped through it. Blank pages. But when she went to put it back, she realized she had turned it around automatically. Everything in her drawers was put in facing her—a compulsion as chronic as CeCe's habit of losing things. Terry hadn't put these notebooks in like that. Had CeCe? Or had someone else? Maybe Cece had simply needed a fresh steno pad.

But nothing was missing. Just . . . rearranged.

Her whole body was shivering as she slammed the drawer shut. Her eyes darted around the room for any other sign of a stranger's presence. The pictures on the walls were straight; nothing appeared changed on her desk. Yet everything suddenly seemed contaminated, just as the note had. She hugged her arms to her sides to control the shaking. Her heart sank as she approached CeCe's desk. Who could say if anything had been disturbed there?

She got out her keys and unlocked the lowest file drawer.

Clippings that were far from flattering to The Family Album's clients were usually destroyed, but sometimes a client would ask to have material saved for younger generations, letting them judge whether to be embarrassed or forgiving or merely amused. None of these files seemed disturbed but she couldn't tell if any were missing. It was impossible.

She retreated to the bathroom, scrubbed her hands with the thoroughness of Lady Macbeth, then warmed up her cup with more boiling water. The tea sloshed over her trembling hand as she tried to drink. When she heard the knock on the door the mug seemed to fly from her hands, shattering in the sink.

▽

8

TERRY LOOKED AT the shards of pottery. How would she face these people, knowing what she did? She would have to act a part, not reveal the awful truth. Everyone was a suspect and if she said the right things someone would have to betray their guilt.

"Hello?" Frank Sullivan was already peering around the frame with a puzzled expression.

"Mr. Sullivan. I just now noticed your appointment on the calendar. Nora didn't call you last night or today?"

"Nora? Nora Carpenter? Why should she? Besides we've been gone a lot."

"I'm sorry. Come in, both of you."

Frank Sullivan held the door while his wife Maura came to stand in front of CeCe's desk where Terry sat. Her lips were drawn in to a thin line, bordered top and bottom by short vertical creases, and her eyes sparked with anger. Frank, on the other hand, wore a salesman's overconfident smile.

"CeCe died in an accident Sunday night. We aren't open for business, but maybe I can help."

"My God—that's awful! We just saw her after church for a minute Sunday. She said we had a problem to deal with today. I just can't believe—I'm really sorry."

This was the closest link she had gotten to CeCe's last hours—she must have been here Sunday afternoon to have written down this appointment. And the problem CeCe had mentioned to them might be what she was so worried about.

"Sit down, please. Let me just run through your file. Would you like a cup of tea?"

"No," they said, almost in unison. "Thanks anyway," Frank Sullivan added.

"I didn't have time to go through your file before you came. I did collect some of the material, though, the passenger lists when your people immigrated and that sort of thing. But I haven't put it all together." Terry was winging it, like a schoolgirl called upon to play Ophelia on Broadway without rehearsals.

"Well, it's probably just a minor item to you. Just a mistake on somebody's part. But it has Maura really upset and she thinks we can come to some agreement on it."

Looking at the pedigree charts, filled in with CeCe's handwriting, Terry recognized in an instant what the hitch was. "I see what CeCe meant," she said as she checked the photostat of a marriage certificate from Arkansas.

"It's enough to make me cancel the whole thing." Maura Sullivan had finally found her voice. "Here we pay Cecile to put together this wonderful heritage book for the children's wedding and she wants to sabotage it."

Terry felt her hackles rising on the back of her neck. "You've only paid the twenty dollar contract fee so far. And my aunt doesn't—didn't—create facts, Mrs. Sullivan. We just collect and present them."

"Well, you can forget about presenting anything to our future son-in-law. It's like blackmail!"

"Now, wait a minute, Maura, honey. Let Terry have a say. What about it, Terry? Can we just leave that branch of the family out?"

"I'm not sure I have the whole story, Mr. Sullivan."

"Call me Frank. We're all friends here."

A cold chill sent the hair on her neck up even further. "According to these documents Maura's grandparents were first cousins to each other. Is that the problem you're referring to?"

"Yes. I had no idea until Cecile found the dispensation. They were married down in Arkansas where it's legal. But they had to file for a dispensation up here to be married in the eyes of the church."

"That's unusual but it's all legal. We come across that sort of thing now and then. It's ancient history. Surely you can't imagine that your future son-in-law will cancel the wedding if he finds out?"

Maura Sullivan's eyes filled with tears and her mouth worked for several seconds before she could get anything out. "Damn you, yes."

There was hatred on her face and Terry wondered if she could have wanted the relationship hushed up badly enough to kill. But it was so senseless.

"You're telling me that Jim Gaines would think this was scandalous enough to make him give up Kim? That's insane." As she said it, she realized that obsession over suppressing it might be insane, too.

"Let's say we have our reasons for not wanting it known, Terry, and leave it at that," Frank Sullivan smoothed over. "Now, what do you say? Can we agree on a little name change for Grandma Lynch?"

"We can agree on dropping the whole project, Mr. Sullivan." She didn't want to be on a first name basis with such a man. CeCe must have had great tolerance when it came to friends, but she wouldn't have buckled under.

"But that's impossible now." Maura Sullivan was almost whining. "We've already told both of them all about it. They expect to get an album full of details about Kim's ancestors—both sides. We can just say there wasn't enough information about that particular branch if you'll back us up."

"What you do with the album is your business, Mrs. Sullivan. But we stand by the facts we present and any changes or omissions constitute fraud on our part. We can't do your fibbing for you."

"But we can't let Jim Gaines see that. We'd look like hillbillies!" Maura Sullivan's voice was low but the final sibilant whistled through her clenched teeth.

"Then I suggest we drop the whole thing and we'll call it

even. You can tell the newlyweds whatever you want."

"What happens to the material then?" Frank Sullivan wanted to know.

"I'll destroy it, of course."

"How can we be sure?" Maura Sullivan's eyes squinted at Terry over a hanky held to her mouth.

Terry sighed in exasperation. Taking the first few pages out of the folder, she began tearing them into small pieces. When the pile was a few inches high on her blotter, she swept it into the plastic bag that lined the wastebasket next to her desk. Then she dumped the remains of her tea on top. Anger had dulled her sense of danger. Even if they had killed CeCe, they would not impugn her name by crying foul.

"Will that do?" she asked.

Frank Sullivan stood up with a curt nod, but Maura still wasn't satisfied.

"You'll always know about it."

"I can't undo that, but I would no more divulge your family's circumstances than I would change them to suit you." Terry stood up on legs that no longer trembled. "Now, if you'll excuse me, I have a lot to do before the wake."

When they had filed out without a good-bye, Terry collapsed in her own desk chair. The throbbing in her head had dulled but a desolate feeling of emptiness filled her chest. She could not imagine taking over for CeCe as the head of The Family Album. And with her anger spent, she realized how scared she was: those people might be murderers.

And if not, which one of the many she would greet tomorrow at Fourcault's? Once more, she thought of Dan Kevlehan and wished he were on her side. "Don't be a fool," she told herself aloud. It was up to her. She could have missed the Sullivans' motive. Was there someone else who would approach her, to find out how much she knew, to "work out a deal," as Frank Sullivan said?

She dialed home and let the machine play back her messages. Maybe one of these would be another offer to dicker with her.

As Hugh Barron had said, Micheline's message with her condolences was one of the first on the machine. Hers was followed by a dozen others, mixed in with updates from Nora that grew increasingly weary when Terry hadn't called back. Nothing suggestive. She was becoming used to the variations on the sympathy theme when a familiar, scratchy voice came through the earpiece.

"Terry, this is Sister Mary Michael. Call me as soon as you can. I must see you."

No comforting words, no preamble. Surely Nora had reached her, but as Nora said, many old people became nervous at the beep and froze. And Sister's hearing had been failing these last months. But this was not nerves or compensation for deafness; this was an urgent command.

Again Terry dialed Gethsemane, this time getting through. She identified herself, and asked for Sister Mary Michael. After a pause, a polite voice told her that Sister wasn't answering in her room, that she usually took a walk after lunch and frequently stayed out until afternoon prayer at four-thirty.

"We don't interrupt that for phone calls. In any case, Sister doesn't hear well over the phone. But she left an explicit message that if you called, to please come down at your earliest convenience. 'Urgent,' it says, but of course she doesn't mean it's a matter of life and death, my dear."

Fear overtook the muscles of her hand again, in spite of the reassuring words. *That's exactly what it is, my dear,* Terry thought. If CeCe had confided in Sister Mary Michael, it was possible that the nun's life was also in danger. Terry couldn't protect everyone. She would have to call Kevlehan and convince him to go down and hear what Sister had to say before someone else got hurt.

▽

9

ALMOST FIVE O'CLOCK. Dan checked his watch, aware that another of the forty-eight hours allotted him was gone. With both index fingers he pressed upward on his temples and stared out at the French Renaissance Revival backside of City Hall. Ornate window caps waited for a merciful rain to lessen, if only minutely, the accumulated grime.

The day, sunny and warm up until minutes ago, had turned cloudy and now rain was a distinct possibility. He wondered if a deluge would postpone the Series and give him a day's breathing room. Would that mean the bomber wouldn't strike until Friday or was there something magical about Thursday? *God, I hope he warns us either way*. But nuts weren't always that predictable. Life seldom dealt you the hand you wanted. That yanked his mind back to Terry Girard and her aunt, whose body still lay next door at the medical examiner's.

Bert had gone out to talk with Girard's neighbors and see if Nora Carpenter could fill in the spaces the deceased's calendar hadn't covered and approximate Cecile Girard's activities on the last three days of her life. Dan had gone to deal with the coroner. Now Bert sank into the facing chair, his coat covering a shirt that clung damply to his chest.

"So what did our grisly Dr. Wickers have to say?"

"The good news is that he'll release the body sometime tonight but, through a strange accident, he lost the findings under his blotter for now. I convinced Carney it might be more of a tip-off if we held onto the body."

"And the bad news?"

"He isn't sure enough to make it murder, but he's willing to look further if I can come up with something. Death from unknown cause is as far as he'll go for now."

"But you know better."

"Take a look." Dan spread the contents of a folder out on both desks: pictures, X-rays, written transcripts of Dr. Wickers's monotone as he described what he found.

"See these legs?" He pulled two photos out of the batch. "The bruising in parallel lines down the thigh and then the abrasions on the knee? They're deep, deeper than if she just bumped against the rail as she fell. She was fighting and she was pushed hard against it. There's some slight—too slight for Wickers—bruising on her upper arms, too. I say the clothing, especially the thick cashmere cloak, would have absorbed a lot of the pressure of hands clamped around them."

"You're sure these abrasions were from before she went over and not as she landed or rolled?"

"Wickers is, and that's good enough for me. He says she evidently went over it headfirst, rotated almost a full turn, and landed mostly on her back but enough to break her neck. The rolling was enough to bring up a few surface abrasions but nothing like these."

"That's it? Those cuts on the knee?"

Dan gathered up the coroner's file and put it in the interdepartmental envelope. "What more do you want? It's hard to distinguish a fall from being pushed when the trip down is forty feet."

"You're right, it does get some messy. The D.A. will want a stronger basis for murder, though. Time of death?"

"Five—give or take. No dinner in her stomach. Listen, that's not all we have, besides the doctored note, that is. Check out these scene-of-crime pictures. See how the rail isn't at the very edge of the dropoff? I mean, if someone was going to commit suicide, there would be room to climb over the rail and stand on that foot or so of ground. Look at the picture and go through it yourself."

Bert gave an exaggerated shiver. "That's not my style, babe. I'd do a nice dreamy OD if I had to."

"Dammit, try it."

Bert looked at the blowups of the overlook and the close-ups of the rail and grass where Cecile had stood. He said nothing at first. Then, "I see what you mean. She'd climb over and hold on. When she was ready, all she'd have to do is let go—nothing in her way to stop her then."

"Exactly! When those Black Friday stockbrokers took a dive out their skyscraper windows, they didn't lean over the sill. They got up on it or stood on a ledge outside and then let go."

"And Wickers is sure she didn't get dizzy and fall hard against that railing?"

"For the love of Mike, Bert, whose side are you on?"

"Devil's advocate, Dan. Good guy/bad guy. I's jes tryin' to he'p, massah."

"Don't give me that bullshit. What kind of a line did you get on her last couple of days?"

"Mrs. Carpenter says Girard did go down to Gethsemane—that's the retirement home for the sisters in South County—in the morning. She confirmed that lunch with Micheline Barron—Girard told her about it. Also told her she'd missed Aubergine's because she forgot they closed at noon on Saturday. Said she was going to do it Monday."

Both men were silent a few seconds. Close as they were to sudden death, the riskiness of "tomorrow" was an uncomfortable familiarity.

"What else?" Dan broke the silence first, with a glance at his watch. He knew he probably worked better when he was under the gun like this, but, damn, how he hated it.

"She went home early, earlier than usual anyway. Said she was going straight to bed."

"But Mrs. Carpenter can't vouch for the fact." It was a statement.

"Where does a seventy-year-old woman go on Saturday night, Dan? Pubbing in the Central West End?"

"God, but you're getting sassy now that you're thirty!"

"It saves the department my tuition for assertiveness training. Let's see now . . ." Bert flipped a small leather notebook open. "Mrs. Carpenter says Girard *always* went to ten o'clock mass. She saw her afterward talking to several people. Among them, Frank and Maura Sullivan—Mrs. C. thinks they're recent clients. Barry Malone, an old suitor, I gather, and Nance Phelps and his daughter Victoria. Mrs. C. says when she left the parking lot, Girard's car was still there. Doesn't know what she did the rest of the day. End of report." Bert flipped the book across to him.

Dan added the names to a growing list in his own notebook. Some he had gotten from a notebook in Cecile Girard's purse and some from her address book.

"Will you try to get hold of those five and ask them if she said what her plans were? See if you can find out what sort of cars they drive, and whether they're pillars of the community."

"Hey, they're probably all krewe members," Bert said, referring to the secret groups, similar to those in New Orleans, that had built floats for the old Veiled Prophet parade. Now, as individuals, they helped power the Fair Foundation that staged the VP Fair and parade that celebrated Independence Day. "After all, we're dealing with *gen-try* here." Bert exaggerated the word.

"Not in that neighborhood. At least, her address book has lots of names that I never see on the business or society pages. A lot of them are probably tenth-generation journeymen just like their ancestors. Some are even Irish upstarts."

"God forbid," Bert deadpanned. "And where are you off to?"

"I'm going to take that Family Album office apart piece by piece if Terry Girard will let me. Maybe she can tell me how these other people relate."

"I get the torch-carrying codger and you get the chick."

"Those are the breaks."

"Seriously, Dan, don't you think you ought to tell her it was murder? She'd probably want to know it wasn't suicide."

"Oh, she's convinced it wasn't that. She's busy as can be

trying to prove it was an accident or a stroke or something. I think if she knew right now that her aunt was murdered, she'd be out trying to find who did it. And we sure as hell don't need amateur help."

Bert looked hard at him, his eyebrows climbing on his forehead. "I think we could use some help, given the time frame. Thursday's not that far off and we have to assume the threats aren't a hoax."

"I *know* the schedule. I just don't want to see . . . civilians get hurt." Dan shuffled the crime scene pictures into order, bouncing them on their edges longer than needed to line them up for their envelope.

Bert said nothing. Dan thought he saw a trace of a smile but the man was halfway to the door before Dan figured out what it meant.

Go to hell, he told Bert's back. But instead of getting back to work, he sat there thinking about his attitude toward Terry Girard. Yes, she was more than just another citizen. Yes, she was a knockout, not that he'd ever put looks that far up his list, but just watching her walk across a room drove him wild. And yet it wasn't just a physical attraction. She seemed to have a basic honesty that he saw all too little of in his work, and she was smart. Independent, too, more than most. But a cop's wife had to be—God Almighty, what was he thinking? He hadn't even asked her for a date!

Business first. Where was she most likely to be? He decided to start with The Family Album.

The phone rang as Terry reached for it and she jerked her hand back before overcoming the urge to let it ring. She pulled it to her ear after the second ring.

"The Family Album." It came out as a weak sigh.

"Dan Kevlehan, Miss Girard."

His voice came booming over the phone so that she had to hold the receiver three inches from her ear.

"I hate to bother you again so soon but there are a few pieces of information I need and I thought if you were going to be there a little longer, I'd come by—you wouldn't have to stay if you just let me in."

In spite of the fear and exhaustion, something stirred in her and she blushed as she recognized it. *Like a schoolgirl,* she chastised herself. "I was just going to call you. Can it wait? You have to listen to Sister Mary Michael—she left a message on my machine at home saying she has to see me."

"If she has important information, Miss Girard, a detective from the department can interview her."

"Damn it all, Kevlehan, she won't talk to you or anybody else. She trusts me and her life may be in danger!"

"Whoa, wait a minute. How do you figure that?" His voice was guarded but he didn't sound surprised.

Terry debated whether to tell him everything but that would take time. A simple statement would have to do.

"My aunt was murdered. Will you come with me or not?"

"Be downstairs in front in five minutes." He hung up without waiting for her answer.

She stopped in the bathroom before leaving and was shocked at her strained image in the mirror. Grief seemed like a black hole, ready to consume her. Settling for a quick swipe of blush over pale cheekbones, she grabbed her briefcase, pulled the door to until she heard the lock snap, and clattered her heels down the stairs.

▽

10

TERRY HAD BARELY reached the sidewalk when a black Impala rounded the corner to double-park beyond the cars that lined the curb. She paused as she opened the car door, suddenly overwhelmed by a desire to drive herself.

"Would you want to take my car? I know the way down there by heart."

"Sorry, Miss Girard. We're not supposed to use private vehicles on official business." He waited for Terry to get in and when she hesitated he shoved the gear shift into park and turned to her. "Don't you trust the way the police drive?"

Oh, hell, Terry thought, as she slid onto the seat. It's not worth the time it would take to convince him. She slammed her door harder than even she had intended. The silence in the aftermath was palpable.

"You're pretty independent, aren't you?" He stated it as a fact, but then asked, "One of those I'd-rather-do-it-myself types?"

You bet, she thought, remembering the times she'd ridden with Sean before she knew he was into coke, and how afterward she insisted on driving the two of them. "When you live alone in a large city, you learn to fend for yourself. I think it's an asset." This wasn't the time to explore latent compulsions, though.

"Mainly, I'm in a hurry. Sister Mary Michael said it was urgent." And I don't even know when she called, but I don't want to tell him. "Do you know where we're going? It's down in South County."

"I'll find it." He had crossed under I-70 and headed up the ramp. Now he stared at the side-view mirror, gauging the steady stream of rush-hour cars he could see behind them on the interstate, slowed momentarily to feed the car into a space in the lane, and accelerated quickly.

Smooth, she thought, and relaxed her head against the diagonal shoulder belt so that she could watch his reactions.

He kept his eyes on traffic. "Can we back up a little and you tell me why you think your aunt was murdered?"

Terry thought back to the first shocking realization. "When you left this morning I took a closer look at that note. It's CeCe's formal stationery, part of a letter to someone." She swallowed, trying to moisten a suddenly dry mouth. "Probably the one who killed her and left it in her car."

"What makes you say that?" His voice was neutral.

"The sentences aren't complete, and she was a bear about grammar. If she were to write a suicide note, you can bet it would be correct. It's been trimmed—the letterhead's gone."

He signaled and maneuvered onto the span that snaked around, above, and below others and became I-55. "Is that all?"

"Far from it. Nora Carpenter told you CeCe hadn't been herself." She hesitated, felt the start of a blush, but had to be honest with him. "She *was* terribly worried about something, actually. She asked Nora if I would mind very much if the business went under. Look, we're in fine financial shape, business is good and prospects even better."

"So she worried too much about public relations."

"The business is built on goodwill and word of mouth. The wrong word from an angry client about something could hurt but this must have been more than anger—maybe fear. CeCe was as honest as they come. Maybe someone wanted her to falsify some genealogical record or change some facts and she wouldn't do it. She thought they would just ruin the business. I think they killed her."

"That's your opinion, not a fact. Have you got something solid, something I can hold in my hand?"

She debated whether to tell him or not. Would he believe her? Was she even sure?

"Our office was searched."

"What?" His head swiveled to look at her but instinctively returned to the road as he pounded the wheel with a fist. They had passed by the Busch brewery and the faint smell of beer or its makings drifted in the open driver's window. "How do you know?"

"Things were removed and put back differently in my drawers. I can't find anything missing, but that would be hard to do as far as CeCe's desk is concerned."

"When was this?"

"I noticed it today. I don't know when things were shifted—sometime over the weekend, I guess."

"And you don't know who." He exhaled noisily, and passed another truck.

Turning to look out her window she saw Carondolet Park stretching off into the distance and wished she were home in her room, safe, looking out at the park of her childhood.

"There was one couple in this afternoon wanting me to do something, maybe not illegal but certainly unethical. We agreed to drop the contract. I'm not sure their story is the whole truth—CeCe may have known more. And there may be others who couldn't get her to bend."

He surprised her by shoving an open notebook across the seat to her. "Is that couple in here?"

She looked down the list, raised her eyes, and, when he glanced back to her, nodded.

A muscle in his eye twitched, drawing the lid down almost in a wink. "Do I have to pry it out of you? We're talking about someone who may be your aunt's murderer."

She gasped, flinging the notebook back at him. So he did know it was murder. "How long have you known, you—you liar!"

Her anger had no visible effect on him. "I had a hunch this morning. You were so sure, and even if I said different, the family is often the best judge about something like that.

They see, at least in hindsight, when there's a problem—or when there's not."

"Then why did you let me beat my head on the wall? Get off at the next exit."

"You're next of kin, Miss Girard. For all I knew at the time, you could have done it." He spared another second from the road to glance at her before easing the car onto the ramp. They passed the concrete acres of shopping center on one side and a cemetery on the other.

When they exited the interstate, she thought about beaning him with her briefcase, the only hefty object she had, but traffic was intense here and reason finally ruled. By the time they reached the road leading to the convent, she had calmed and was trying to see the whole tragedy from an outsider's vantage.

"Implausible as I find your suspicion, I'll accept it. But I may as well tell you now that I'm going to find out who did it if I spend the rest of my life at it."

The alarm on his face was comical. His full, peaked eyebrows shot up, his cheeks puffed out, and the skin flushed.

"Whoa, now. Don't start with the sherlocking around. That's our job."

"So far, I think we've been neck and neck. I know the people around CeCe so much better than any detective with pad and pencil."

"For crissake, you don't seem to understand. You could get hurt. We're not talking about a tax dodger here, or a jaywalker. This is murder and the private citizen can't—"

"I'm not going to arrest anyone. Turn in just around this curve." She lifted her chin in defiance, knowing how boastful it was going to sound. "When I find out for sure, I'll get in touch."

His mouth dropped open slightly as his eyes came wide open to stare at her. Seemingly by instinct, he followed the road, bounded by blazing fall trees, around the curve to the entrance of the retirement center.

"You wouldn't mind if we do a bit of the spadework, just

to keep our hand in?" His tone, though quiet, betrayed the effort to control anger. He topped a rise in the drive and slowed as they neared the main entrance to the modern building. An eerie glow that changed his face from blue to red drew Terry's eyes to the windshield. They had parked behind an ambulance.

She bit her bottom lip, afraid to let her breath out as she watched uniformed men close the back doors of the ambulance, get in the front, and make a U-turn to head back down the drive, whirling light still flashing in place of a siren. She finally exhaled. "Oh, my God!"

"Take it easy. Don't forget this is a nursing home—old nuns get sick here."

But she was out of the car and running toward a cluster of sisters, all in bulky sweaters and longish skirts, under the porte cochere. "That isn't Sister Mary Michael is it? Please, is she here?"

They looked at her with a quizzical expression that made their faces as alike as their clothing. Finally one spoke up in a quavery voice. "Why, yes, that's Sister Mary Michael in the ambulance. She's had a stroke or something."

"What do you mean by 'or something,' sister?" Dan Kevlehan was at Terry's side, holding out a leather badge folder that the nun seemed to ignore.

"Well, they found her down by the shrine—heaven knows how long she's been there. She must have gone down to pray sometime after lunch. When she didn't show up for afternoon prayer, they went looking for her."

"Did the paramedics tell you it was a stroke?"

"No one's told us anything yet."

"What hospital?"

"What's this all—" the nun began, but when Kevlehan shook the folder in her face, she told him the name.

"Thank you, Sister. Let's go." He took Terry's arm and steered her back to the car. She allowed him to open the door and help her in.

"I wasn't there for her when she called," she said as he

helped her buckle the suddenly stubborn seat belt.

"Don't be silly," he said and slammed her door. Even this didn't bother her, though she knew she was being anything but silly. It was the truth: she hadn't been there, hadn't even played the message back for hours. She closed her eyes, heard him start the car, felt him circle around to follow the ambulance.

Terry felt numb, which was worse than feeling sick. Something she sensed tickled her awareness but she couldn't locate it. Something . . . to hell with it. She just wasn't with it.

"I never seem to be there when I'm needed."

It sounded like she was fishing for a denial but that wasn't it at all. It was the truth.

▽

11

THE DISINFECTANT ODOR DRIFTING from the emergency room cubicles into the lobby brought with it the memory of the morgue. *Please God, don't let Sister Mary Mike be dead,* Terry prayed. The molded plastic chair, hard against her back, seemed little penance to pay for not returning Sister's call.

It was after six o'clock. They had been there twenty minutes and Dan Kevlehan had not stopped, much less sat down. After exhausting the informational capacity of every clerk and nurse within earshot, he started in on her again.

"What was it she said on the phone? Her exact words?"

Terry ran the tape through her memory again. " 'Terry, this is Sister Mary Michael. Call me as soon as you can. I need to see you.' That was all, but she sounded urgent, almost . . . I don't know . . . scared. She didn't give me a clue about why. She couldn't hear well on the phone and hated talking on it."

"Well, no one will tell me anything. Until the doctor finishes examining her, we're stuck." He threw the notebook down on the seat beside her but still didn't sit down. Instead, he stood with his hands thrust into pants pockets, his raincoat flaring out behind his elbows. "So you might as well relax and explain who those people are."

"*I* should relax." He looked like a Fourth of July rocket ready to launch, steam all but coming out of his ears. She couldn't help but smile. The smile led to a giggle, and suddenly her shoulders were shaking, her breath was beating a tattoo against her chest, and the tears were tickling down her cheeks. Her mouth ached from the unaccustomed smile that had now, she was sure, turned into a grimace. She crossed her arms, cupping each shoulder with a hand until the spasms stopped, then brushed her cheeks with the back of her hands.

"We'll both relax," he said, accepting her outburst as normal. He eased down next to her with legs outstretched, ankles crossed, one foot barely jiggling. He picked up the notebook and held it open in front of them like a shared hymnal. "We need to know who among these people are clients, who would have a grudge or benefit from her death. And remember—"

She turned, only to find those eyes, like blue aggies out of her childhood marble collection, too close. They wouldn't turn her loose.

"Remember, someone in there is a murderer." He stabbed a finger at the open pages.

Terry trembled. As if she could forget. Every familiar face she saw until the murderer was caught would be colored with suspicion. And if that someone were never found . . . The thought outweighed the ethical transgression of revealing client information. Kevlehan was right: whoever had done this wasn't worried about ethics.

"All right, but you have to understand that it isn't just the paying client. We cover the whole family and anyone involved may have a secret they don't want revealed, much less immortalized."

"How about this afternoon's secret?"

Terry flipped the page and pointed to the Sullivans. "Maura Sullivan's grandfather and grandmother had fathers who were brothers. That made them first cousins and of course they shared the same last name. The Sullivans wanted me to concoct a new identity for Julia Lynch, the grandma."

"Sounds pretty thin for a motive."

"Their daughter is marrying—above her station, as they used to say—and they're afraid Jim Gaines would throw her over. It doesn't make sense, because Jim is a decent sort."

"We'll check into it later. Let's try some of the others. I understand the Barrons are clients."

"Micheline Barron is, our biggest one ever. She was a few years older but she and CeCe grew up together. She was a Dechant before her marriage. Both families were descended from the First Thirty who came up the river with Laclede, like ours, but they bought property, went into railroads and steel and grew rich, and our men went into law."

"And didn't do badly either, I'd say."

Terry kept her head lowered to the book but gave him a sidelong glance. Was he put off by all this concern about pedigrees? Did he honestly think she was from the idle rich? Maybe it would be best to keep that idea alive, though. It would maintain a necessary distance between them.

"We weren't as poor as most in Carondolet—they called the district *Vide Poches*, empty pockets, by the way. But there was a distinct economic line drawn between the Dechants and Barrons and the likes of us."

"Tell me about the family."

"Well, I know more about them than I used to. I spent a couple of hours out there this afternoon, getting pictures chosen for their album."

She interpreted his inquiring look as akin to Nora's. "I wasn't wasting time. I thought I could learn why CeCe was so worried."

"And did you?"

She stopped to think. "I really don't know. I thought it might have to do with pictures, but now . . ."

"Start anywhere and tell me everything, then. Maybe I can spot something."

She sighed deeply. "I'll start with Claude. He's the youngest, about forty-four. He plays violin in a chamber music group and runs a fine arts newspaper to which he is inordinately attached. '*Beaux Arts* is me,' he said today. He doesn't get along with Hugh. He's married to a former artist's model. They're childless and I think they live mostly off the trust fund Louis Barron set up for each of his children." She paused. Everything, Kevlehan had said. "And I've always felt he undressed women with his eyes. He's a lech."

"Next?" He was making notes.

"Frances is the younger of the two sisters, a well-preserved midforties matron. She and Evelyn married the Devereaux twins. She's married to Robert, who might run for governor next year, and—" Terry remembered her promise about not revealing plans for the presidency; she would keep it "—and she's pretty ambitious for him. Their only child drowned in a pool accident years ago."

"I've heard that about Devereaux. How does she really strike you?"

Terry looked at him. "Like Micheline with a southern drawl . . . oh, this all sounds so catty. CeCe would be appalled!"

"We call it gathering evidence," he said, slapping his knee with the notebook. "You think you have the advantage because you know these people better than we do, but it can actually work against you. It's so damned hard to see them as suspects. Tell me, did CeCe know the Devereaux family?"

"Of course. All the Devereaux clan were clients of my grandfather. She knew everyone. Wait until you see the crowd at the wake."

The picture of CeCe laid out in her favorite blue, pushed to a shadowed corner of Terry's mind since she'd left Fourcault's, was suddenly before her. She couldn't talk past the lump in her throat.

"You've had too many shocks for one day," Kevlehan said finally.

"It's just that I dread seeing her there."

He laid the notebook face down on his knee. "You'll do fine. You're a survivor."

He had hit the core of it. Terry had survived. Irrational as it was, she felt she would never shake that guilt. She suddenly found her face buried against his raincoat sleeve, the tears running down the water-repellent surface. His arm went around her and he patted her awkwardly on the back.

"It's okay, kid. It's no sin to survive."

She was about to protest that she was no kid when she saw the doctor coming toward them. She sat upright like a teenager caught necking in the parlor. Kevlehan's arm was suddenly gone and he was standing. By this time the doctor had stuffed a stethoscope into one white coat pocket and with his other hand flipped a hospital chart open.

"Are you relatives of Sister . . . Mary Michael Cassidy?" He had to check the chart for the name.

"Her family is all gone—"

"Sergeant Dan Kevlehan, Central district—" They both talked at once, but the badge Kevlehan held up drew the doctor's eye.

"What can I tell you?"

"First, how is she?"

At least he had that much feeling, Terry thought.

"She's had a stroke, and probably a concussion from the fall. They found her a few yards into the woods and it looks like she'd been there quite a while—maybe since right after lunch. She's in a coma." His voice softened as he turned to Terry. "It doesn't look like she's going to make it. You say you aren't a relative?"

"I'm Terry Girard. My aunt was her oldest friend. Sister called this morning to ask me to come see her. Do you think she knew it was coming?"

"No, it was really sudden. The paramedics said she didn't even have time to sit down on a nearby bench."

"Can we see her?"

"For a moment, if you hurry. First cubicle on the right." He motioned over his shoulder. "She'll be moved to ICU in a few minutes, as soon as the bed is ready."

"You go ahead," Kevlehan told her. "I'm going to have a word with the nurses in ICU. I'll see you in a few minutes."

Terry walked quickly, resisting the lifelong urge to tiptoe in hospital corridors, until she reached the curtained off area and slipped through the opening. Sister Mary Michael's familiar habit was gone, revealing short wavy white hair that still bore traces of blood. A breathing machine was already hooked up, the pale hose taped to her wrinkled mouth with translucent white strips. It forced air into the nun's frail chest, which rose and fell to the rhythm of the noisy apparatus. Blue-veined hands lay at her sides atop the sheet.

Gently, Terry picked up one hand and leaned a cheek down to it.

"Did you know?" she whispered, not expecting an answer. "I'm sorry. I'm so sorry."

A nurse bustled in then. "Excuse me, ma'am, we're moving her now. If you want to wait in the ICU lounge, you can see her in about twenty minutes."

Terry stared at the nun's closed eyes. There was no flicker of consciousness, no sign of life. "That's all right. It's too late now, anyway." Terry brushed past her, wanting only to find Kevlehan and get home.

Now there's a guy I wouldn't mind comforting me, Janet Gordon had thought, stealing another glance at the couple sitting thirty feet from her emergency room reception desk. He was a cop, had shown her a badge when he asked her about the nun. How she wished she'd had something to tell him, anything to help. And who was the girl? His wife? She was about to ask if she could "get your wife some coffee," just to see, when Dr. Hardesty came out to talk to them. The girl moved off and Hardesty came over, plunked the chart into the rack, and led the cop off. Had the patient died?

The phone interrupted her reverie. A relative of the nun. They all found out in a hurry, considering the cop hadn't called anyone, nor asked her to. Stretching over, she grabbed the chart, flipped over the metal cover, and gave out the designation of critical. She had to follow orders: no further details. Please contact the attending physician, Dr. Thomas Hardesty. She cradled the phone. It wasn't much, but she decided to report this small bit of information to the detective—Kevlehan, the ID had said—when he came back by.

But the swirling lights through the plate-glass doors announced another arrival. Paramedics jammed a gurney against the doors, not waiting for the automatic opener to fully function. One called out to her for a Code Blue. The handsome detective Kevlehan was forgotten.

It was too bad about Sister. Mumpet sat with phone to ear until the line went dead, the hospital receptionist's words still echoing. Critical. Not dead. Still a threat?

Her voice on the machine this morning had niggled at Mumpet until the possibility of her knowing something, of her telling Therese, couldn't be ignored. There was no plan, only a frantic attempt to stop the latest eruption of flames from spreading, destroying. A phone call had garnered the information that visiting hours for ambulatory residents were held in the morning and following afternoon prayer. That might be too late. Cecile had mentioned at one time, though, that Sister always strolled around after lunch if the weather was bearable. Standing in the shelter of trees, wondering whether to hope for that familiar stooped frame to appear or not, Mumpet watched the old nuns filter out of chapel and saw the sweater Cecile had given Sister. The figure wearing it moved down the paved walk to a grotto. Mumpet circled around through the orchard and came up on the grotto from the back, still with no plan of action, afraid to even think about it. Perhaps Sister could be reasoned with, appealed to. Perhaps . . .

Just the sight of Mumpet, appearing so suddenly and unexpectedly, sent the nun into a swoon. No time to find out what she knew; only a few fleeting seconds to catch her, to lift the slender frame into the dim bower of trees. To recognize the drooping eyelid, the slackening side of the mouth, to hold a handkerchief against that mouth and nose—long enough?—before voices sounded nearby and Mumpet slipped back through the trees to the drive, with heart beating painfully against breastbone.

The car was stuffy, the air pungent with Granny Smiths,

welcome as it flowed through lowered windows. There seemed never to be enough air lately.

A suppertime call to Gethsemane garnered the information that Sister had survived Mumpet's attempt and now the hospital strung out the suspense. Critical. A stroke? Did that mean coma? Each nerve in Mumpet's body seemed to vibrate with energy of its own, energy derived from determination. Too bad for Sister. She had no right. How dare they snoop and carry tales! But there was nothing to do for now but wait.

"A guard? You really think that's necessary?" Terry asked as she almost skipped to keep up with Kevlehan.

"Not police and not in the ICU itself. The nurses there can see everything. The hospital's security guard is going to station himself outside the unit for a few hours, at least until I check back with him. Just in case."

They had hooked up again amid the bustle of the emergency room lobby and now they walked down the drive to Kevlehan's car.

"My God in heaven . . ." Terry let her breath slowly escape with the words, then drew cold air in and trembled as it hit her lungs. The idea of someone deliberately hurting Sister Mary Mike was inconceivable, and yet there was CeCe, on a cold slab.

"Can you drop me off at my car?" she asked before he could close the door, and then watched the expression on his face turn grim as he went around the front to his door.

"Let's talk about that," he said as he got in. He eased the car out of the hospital lot.

"What's to talk about? I have to go by the funeral home before I call it a night. You don't want to haul me all over town. If it's not on your way—"

"It's not that. I just don't think you should be tooling around by yourself. Is there a friend you can stay with for tonight? How about Mrs. Carpenter?"

"I don't need a sitter, Sergeant. I'm a big girl and there are excellent locks on our doors . . . my doors."

"That's just it, you're alone in that house now."

She recognized the awful feeling that spread through her body as if carried by her blood: an emptiness generated by abandonment. It had the familiarity of an old enemy. He didn't have to remind her.

"And besides," he continued, "my back gives me trouble when the nights turn cool."

"Your back?"

"If I have to sit outside your house in this car all night, my back is sure as hell going to hurt in the morning."

"And what would my neighbors think if you did that?"

"I'm not worried about your neighbors." He pulled the notebook from his raincoat pocket and waved it between them. "Just your friends. When did you eat last?"

"You sound like Nora." Caught off guard, she had to think. "I grabbed a sandwich about eleven-thirty, just before I went to Fourcault's."

"This morning? That's not enough to keep body and soul together."

"Now you sound like Hugh Barron and his clichés."

"You must be starving. So am I. How about stopping in the Landing or somewhere for supper and we'll argue about where you go after that?"

"I don't want to argue. I'm too tired for that." Her voice sounded tired, even to her. He seemed to sense her weakening.

"My brain shuts down if I don't stoke up and I skipped lunch, too."

"Dutch treat," she said. After blubbering on his arm, she wanted to get things back on a professional level.

"Whatever. Just let me get a plate in front of me."

She had to admit that her stomach had been growling for hours.

They ended up at Carmichael's on South Grand. The neighborhood diners' conversations drifted up with the cigarette smoke toward the pressed tin ceiling, and the trio on the small corner stage played Irish ballads she had never heard before. The friendly atmosphere did more than the smell of food to raise her spirits.

"Now you can finish off the list," Kevlehan said, looking at his watch after the bar waitress had brought them beers.

"Did you want to call . . . home first?"

A wry smile made his mouth twitch. "No one there to answer. I'm the despair of my mother: an Irish son who moved out without having a wife for an excuse. But my crazy hours were keeping her up all night, wondering if *I'd* had dinner."

Terry was glad the dim lights hid what she knew was the flush on her face. "I just didn't want to . . . keep you from more important matters."

"We're cooperating, okay? So who else have we left out?" He laid the open notebook on the table between them.

"We were up to Evelyn Devereaux. She's married to the state representative and she has two kids, a girl who's twenty and Superboy, who's twenty-three and about to take over the world, in her opinion."

"Wrapped up in her kids?"

"Understatement. Especially the boy. She tries to stifle it around Frances but she can't."

"And her older brother? What's his claim to fame?"

"He's a lawyer—our lawyer, for what little we've needed. Never married, handles the trust from which all good things flow, lives with Micheline on Lindell, and may be the least dominated by her. Pretty dull." She thought of the look he'd given Claude today. "Ever hear of a man named Schindler?"

"Alvin Schindler? He died a few months ago, big wheel in commodities until he got Alzheimer's disease. Why?"

"Claude was needling Hugh about choosing a picture with Schindler. It made Hugh mad but I don't know why."

"I think I read where Barron was Schindler's conservator and executor of the estate. I'll check it out." Kevlehan made a note in his book. "That leaves Mama."

"Micheline?" Terry let out a long sigh. "She is the only daughter of rich, doting parents, and married a soon-to-be-rich man who continued the doting. She is dedicated to maintaining her life-style, getting her way, and lighting candles at the Barron–Dechant family altar. She likes to tweak her children—positively cruel at times—but today, when I thought she'd stick it to them, she went belly-up. I can't figure it unless she's going 'round the bend."

"Are there any other current clients?"

"Only two: the Davidsons and the Caldwells. They were so easy CeCe let me do all the research. Neither CeCe nor the clients have seen anything yet." Terry buttered a piece of the warm soda bread set out on a cutting board. "That sort of narrows it down, doesn't it?"

"Providing this is connected to a client. But that's not to say she hadn't come across some damning fact about a friend of hers and kept it at the office."

"CeCe's friends?"

She lifted her eyes to meet his and they conducted a staring match. When he won she blamed it on fatigue.

"Listen to me." His fists went down on either side of the service plate as he leaned across the table. "You aren't the best judge when it comes to friends. You can't see them committing the ultimate crime of murder—it isn't civilized, for crissake! But everyone is capable of murder."

"I'm not saying they're my friends; they were all CeCe's friends, but I look on most of them as an extended family—people you see on holidays, whether you particularly want to or not. For heaven's sake, Uncle Barry taught me to roller-skate."

"I know of a serial killer who taught his girlfriend victims to ski."

She shook her head in frustration. Kevlehan obviously didn't look on long-standing friendships the same way CeCe did. She trusted people, and they trusted her. Terry remembered the tortured look on Barry Malone's face this morning. CeCe may have turned down his marriage proposal years ago, but he was far from a jilted suitor. CeCe didn't jilt her friends.

"What was that you asked?"

"I said, did your aunt disapprove of any of your friends?"

Terry could feel her face warming and held the menu close. Where did he get his information? "Why do you ask?"

"Because she sounds like she wanted the best for you, and if she thought someone, say a male friend, didn't match her expectations—"

"She let me live my own life. After all, I spent nine years in D.C. without her to chaperone."

"You're not in D.C. You're here and she cared."

"She did that, all right. She fixed me up with a Mizzou professor this past weekend. He was boring."

"We know about him, but have you dated someone recently who wasn't your aunt's cup of tea?"

Damn him. "Gathering evidence, right? I suppose you have my entire circle of friends detailed to their sock size by now."

"All I'm asking is that you not rule out anyone. *Any*one, okay?"

"All right. What do you want to know?" She had dropped the menu and now ticked off her last three dates, finger by finger. "Steve Robinette, the son of my father's former law partner: eminently eligible by CeCe's standards. Jay Gelker, a stockbroker friend of a friend. We just took in a ball game and a pizza, so CeCe wasn't measuring him for a morning suit. Let's see . . . Pete Davito, intern at Barnes and my old high school beau, who has charmed CeCe since he was fifteen. They are so far from being murderers—" She shuddered at the word. "It's ridiculous."

Kevlehan's eyes told her he didn't agree, but the waiter interrupted his rebuttal. They decided on the Beef Ballynoe, a dish whose boiled potatoes resembled a stone formation of the same name, Kevlehan informed her. Then he went back to it.

"You'd be surprised how many doctors, lawyers, and, yes, stockbrokers kill their wives or mistresses or the one person who can blow the whistle on them."

"I've had maybe a couple of dates with each of these men. CeCe knows—knew—I wasn't involved with anyone."

Kevlehan was quiet. Had she convinced him?

"Why not?"

She looked straight at him, not quite believing he'd ask such a question. But then, he was a detective, and if he was digging into pasts . . .

"I lost someone close to me in D.C. I'm not ready for . . . for someone new yet."

"Right." He took a long drink from his mug of beer. "So how about girlfriends?"

"Sheesh!" This time she rolled her eyes.

Kevlehan waved his hand as if to brush an annoying fly away. "Hey, don't get defensive. Gathering evidence, remember?"

She wanted to get up and leave him to choke on his boiled potatoes, but dammit, she was paying for her share and she would eat it.

"Nora's two daughters, Kate and Bryn, are about all I have time for," she said around a bite of tender beef, "and they've been in Chicago for a week."

"Okay, I give up. Let's just eat." And he dug into his dinner with the same determination he had used to pry out information.

When they had reached the trifle, Terry felt energized enough to broach the subject of where she went from here.

"You know, there's really no need to worry about me. I took care of myself for years in D.C. and that's not a mecca of safe streets."

"But your aunt wasn't killed in D.C."

"Besides, I have to stop off at Fourcault's and see if everything is all right."

"Better call first. It's possible the M.E. ran behind."

"All right, I'll call. Then will you take me to my car, please?"

She didn't wait for an answer before heading for the phone next to the bar. She tried to muffle the mouthpiece so that the lilting Irish music wouldn't scandalize the younger Fourcault but then abandoned it when he told her that "the deceased" couldn't be picked up until tomorrow.

"We'll do it first thing in the morning, but the medical examiner's office didn't call until a few minutes ago."

Everything would be ready by two tomorrow afternoon except for the deed to the plot—that was probably with her aunt's copy of her will, wherever she kept it.

Anger made the beef feel like lead. "But your brother said it was in your files! Have you checked thoroughly?"

"Perhaps it is. I usually just remind people as a matter of course, but if George said . . ."

"Yes, George said, so please check." Terry promised to be there by one o'clock, which would give her an hour alone before anyone was admitted. If need be, she would run to the bank at lunchtime and get the deed. As she turned from the phone, Kevlehan was standing at the cashier's desk. She was just in time to see the total of the bill and divide by two. When they reached the pavement, she held out her share, plus tip, which he jammed in his coat pocket without a glance or comment. His next gambit came as they walked to the car.

"There's another facet to this that I don't think you've given any thought to. What about Nora Carpenter?"

Terry was speechless. Stored-up fury hunted for words to fight back. She stopped on the sidewalk in front of his car. "A-a-are you accusing—?"

"Chill down, Miss Girard. No, I'm saying that she saw your aunt after Sister did. Spent several hours with her, in fact. She may have been told something she doesn't even know is important."

Why did he always confound her with these sudden changes of direction? It was disconcerting to have her suspicions confirmed by his policeman's viewpoint. "I asked her what CeCe had said and how she had acted. Now that I think of it, CeCe never liked to tell Nora anything that couldn't be shared with everyone in South St. Louis. From what Nora said, CeCe didn't share this time either."

"But we can't be sure. What's more, the murderer can't be sure. Bert, my partner, says she lives alone. Probably as independent as you. She'd fight against having anyone looking out for her, but if she thought it was you who needed comforting . . ." He let the idea hang as he held the car door for her and went around to his side.

The anger roiled past Terry's satisfied hunger and a growing attraction for him. He thinks he's just too clever, she thought. He's using our mutual concern for one another to get his way. But if anything happened to Nora now . . .

"All right, dammit, I'll stay at Nora's," she told him when he was behind the wheel. "Are you happy now?"

"My back sure is. I'll take you to your car, then follow you home and see you over to Mrs. Carpenter's. And then we can both get some sleep."

He didn't even trust her to go to Nora's. What a bullhead!

The cool damp air off the river had condensed into shiny beads of moisture on her car's dark green paint. Terry ran the wipers for a few seconds to clear the windshield before pulling out ahead of Kevlehan. The traffic heading back south was blessedly light; those intent on watching their beloved Cards in the stadium or a favorite watering hole were already ensconced. Ordinarily, she would have been glued to the set, but now she clicked off the radio as soon as she heard that the Cards were winning. Listening to the game was too distracting; there was so much to mull over. She kept an eye on Kevlehan's car in her mirror and fought the feeling of security it gave her. She would be fine. She would humor him.

At home, he accepted her invitation to come inside while she called Nora and gathered her things. Terry could hear him on the phone checking with the hospital as she dumped dirty clothes from the outer pockets of her garment bag and stuffed them with clean underwear. It seemed like yesterday that she had packed for Jeff City.

"No change," he called up to her. "She isn't expected to regain consciousness at least through the night."

If only I had gone down to Gethsemane this morning, Terry caught herself thinking on the short drive over to Nora's. Maybe tomorrow Sister Mary Mike would recover enough to tell her what was so important. If not, perhaps Terry could tell, just from looking at all these lifelong acquaintances gathered to mourn CeCe, which one had ended her life.

The suspicion of murder had to be kept under wraps for now, Kevlehan had said. "Be as unspecific as you can. Suggest it was probably a stroke."

Lie, he meant, and she wasn't very good at it.

She pulled into Nora's drive and hauled her bag and briefcase from the backseat as he slowed at the curb in front. Nora, already waiting at the door for her, waved to him. Terry felt like a child embarking on her first overnight. Tomorrow the nightmare would start over.

Nora had her lower lip sucked under her Irish overbite and her ample freckled arms disappeared into the deep pockets of her flowered housecoat. Terry assumed she was worried about Sister but, instead of demanding any details, she hung Terry's bag on the oak hall tree and stared at her wide-eyed.

"The strangest thing just happened," Nora said. "I answered the phone a few minutes ago and someone was on the line but they wouldn't answer when I said hello. They wouldn't say anything. But I heard something in the background, like a church bell far off."

"Lots of bells around, Nora. Are you sure it wasn't a wrong number?"

"No, you don't understand. I heard the same tolling when I was talking to someone—yesterday or today, I can't remember because I've made dozens of calls and answered so many—but I can't pinpoint who it was."

"Probably just kids practicing up for Halloween." Terry tried for a casual tone but a shiver went through her and her hand shook on the older woman's arm as they went down the hall to the kitchen. Nora's face showed she wasn't going to swallow any false assurances.

▽

12

NORA HAD PLUGGED in a phone next to the bed so that Terry could call the hospital as soon as she woke Wednesday. The ICU nurse on duty reported that Sister was still on the respirator, still unconscious, but in no apparent pain.

Terry left the mortuary number just in case.

Her call to Fourcault's was no less disappointing. They didn't have the deed to the family plot after all. "The old man"—as this youngest Fourcault on duty referred to the founder—had insisted Miss Girard was in possession of it, and Terry would need to produce it, the archdiocese being rather sticky about such details before allowing a grave to be opened. Terry pledged to find and present it by one o'clock.

"But coffee first," she told the cradled phone and allowed herself one long stretch in the double bed she'd so often shared with Kate. The agonized soul-searching of those teenage sessions was infinitely preferable to the ordeal she faced now.

It was going to be, as Sean used to say, a bitch of a day.

The covers lay in a twisted heap after her restless night and she pulled and smoothed and tucked while trying to recall if she had ever seen the cemetery deed. But her mind would not stay on the matter at hand. Like a toddler in a mall, it wanted to dart around—back to last night and ahead to the wake, pausing only long enough to worry and not to solve.

She would call the hospital again at noon. And all the unflattering details about people she had unloaded on Kevlehan last night—what would CeCe have said? And Nora's strange phone call—Nora, who had rarely been upset by whatever practical jokes the Carpenter teenagers and their friends could devise, sensed "evil on the other end of the line," she had said last night over hot cider and banana bread.

Had it been . . . the murderer? Terry forced herself to whisper the word, but that didn't conjure up a face, only a rash of goose bumps where the Georgetown T-shirt and boxer shorts failed to meet as she stretched the faded chintz roses over the pillows.

Which face? How would she know it? Or would it mouth sympathy and comfort today, even force a tear or two, moving Terry to kiss that cheek, murmur thanks, and believe?

Yes, a bitch of a day.

"It's in her safe-deposit box, I'm sure of it," Nora said when Terry asked her about the deed.

"Oh, dammit, Nora! That means, besides everything else on this morning's agenda, I'll have to go home and hunt up the key, run down to the bank, and get to Fourcault's by one. I promised them by one."

"The key won't help if you aren't authorized. Is your signature listed for that box?"

Terry groaned as she bent over her cup, then shook her head. She had teased CeCe about not sharing her box. *Come on, there's room for my savings bonds. You don't have that many diamond tiaras*. And CeCe had closed the discussion by saying that everyone needed a hidey-hole and not everything was better off shared. Terry had rented her own box.

"I wondered why she didn't want me to have access but she was a little sensitive about it."

"CeCe liked her privacy. And they won't let you just waltz in now that she's dead, and clear it out. The IRS would be all over you."

"But they've got to!" Terry's hand slapped the tabletop enough to slop their coffee and make the salt and pepper shakers jingle in their chrome holder. Delaying the funeral yet another day because of a stupid piece of paper was unthinkable.

Nora wiped up the coffee with the absentminded efficiency born of raising teenagers and set Terry's omelet in front of her.

"Calm down. Call Hugh Barron and tell him. He has to be good for something. He can meet you at the bank with the will. That ought to do it."

"I have a copy of the will. What do I need him for?"

"They might not take just a copy unless it was notarized. He has the original. Besides, he'd have more clout if you want to be sure of getting into it, that's all."

Terry spread a piece of toast with just enough jelly to get it down and took a bite of omelet while she tried to puzzle out CeCe's actions. Her aunt had shared the house with her, never forbidding Terry to open any drawer. She had even taken Terry with her to the bank when she went to get some CDs out of the box before Terry left for Georgetown. And when Terry came back to St. Louis, CeCe had shared an office with her—but not the safe-deposit box.

CeCe had something in there that she wanted kept secret.

The note on CeCe's calendar flashed across Terry's mind: CeCe had converted some CDs Friday—had she taken out whatever it was, or added to the contents of the box? Had she decided to take action on something? Or to keep something secret? Why . . . and what?

Terry shivered. It was eerie trying to walk around in her aunt's mind.

She stood while she polished off her omelet.

"Didn't you always say anything eaten standing up didn't count as calories, Nora?"

Nora smiled weakly. "You should care."

Terry looked up the number for the bank.

"I'm going to try to bully my way into the inner sanctum. If I lose, I'll call Hugh."

Terry showered, applied a minimum of makeup, and then compromised with CeCe, wearing the teal silk paisley blouse that had been her aunt's last Christmas present to her and the charcoal flannel suit CeCe hated but which would look suitably somber for all of CeCe's contemporaries.

Finally, Terry marshaled her self-confidence, dialed the bank, and plunged in. "My name is Therese Girard, and I've been told to retrieve my aunt's deed to our cemetery plot. As her executrix, I have to gain access to her safe deposit box. Whom do I see about this?"

"Are you a signator on her box?" a polite voice asked.

"No, I'm not, but surely that isn't a problem, is it?"

"Are you an heir of the estate?"

"Yes, but—"

"You'll need to bring along a notarized copy of the will, ma'am, and have a witness as you open it."

Terry thanked her. So that's that, she grumbled.

Steeling herself to deal with Hugh Barron's clichés two mornings in a row, Terry dialed the Barron number, hoping she could still catch him.

His monotone oozed through the receiver. He could have been a psychiatrist, Terry thought, but he might also have driven patients crazy. Only too happy . . . in this time of trial . . . best-laid plans . . .

She suggested coming by his office for the notarized copy but he was bound to be helpful.

"We can kill two birds—oh, my dear, forgive me—but I can take a quick inventory of any assets while we're at it. I'm afraid, though, that I can't meet you there until noon. Will that do?"

Her heart sank. She had wanted to get it over with. "All right. I appreciate your taking the time." It took another minute to ease him off the line.

Terry rearranged the list she was making, inserting the bank after several other stops. She was checking her purse to make sure she had everything when the phone rang.

"It's your Detective Kevlehan." Nora's strong voice carried up the stairwell.

Terry resisted the urge to shout back a denial of ownership before she lifted the receiver.

"This is Terry Girard."

"You talked to the hospital?" No greeting, no preliminary small talk.

"Yes, there's no change."

"That's what they told me, too. What's your itinerary look like for the day?"

Terry could feel her temper rising. "I didn't think I had to check in during daylight hours."

"I'm just trying to make sure the case doesn't get bigger than I can handle when my back is turned. So you're headed down to the funeral home?"

"After a lot of errands. Then I have to get CeCe's deed to the cemetery plot, if you must know. I'll be at Fourcault's by one."

"Back to your house for the deed? Why didn't you—?"

"Back to the house for the safe-deposit key. The deed's in her box and I have to meet Hugh Barron there at noon. If that's all right with you." She poured as much sweetness as she could manage into the last.

"All right. Just promise me you won't leave Fourcault's this afternoon without telling me. Leave a message if I'm out—but try not to leave at all until I get there. And don't mention murder to *anyone*, including Mrs. Carpenter."

"I'm overwhelmed by all this attention, but I don't think it's necessary. I told you last night, I don't know anything dangerous."

"Excuse me, Miss Girard, but I have to go down and interview some nuns at Gethsemane who might have seen something."

The implication that Sister Mary Mike had known enough to be attacked—if she had been—left Terry with a queasy feeling as she went downstairs to coordinate schedules with Nora.

". . . and I'll be along about three so you can have a break," Nora finished her recital of the day's plans.

"You mean so I can have the lunch you're sure I'll forget to eat."

Nora gave her a don't-make-fun look. "Father Healy will

be there at seven-thirty for the rosary tonight. I hope you don't hold it against the pastor that he wouldn't move the funeral to the Old Cathedral. I still don't understand why you didn't want it at the parish."

"Nora, I've tried to explain. Daddy's funeral, his coffin there in the aisle where I had to genuflect every day before I went into the pew for Mass. I saw it for months—years—afterwards. I never forgot it."

"But you were so young." Nora's tone was doubtful. "Anyway, I've ordered a sliced turkey and ham from the deli for Friday."

And some of the fish-eating diehards won't eat either one, Terry thought. Thirty years meant nothing.

"I found a pie packed in a metal box on the back porch yesterday morning and stuck it in the freezer. We can add that. How many people are we talking about?"

"Hard to say. Father will just announce after Mass that everyone's welcome, but I'd guess fifty or sixty."

Add one more, Terry thought. Kevlehan wouldn't pass up the chance to see all those people at one time. But she couldn't worry Nora any more, not after last night's phone call.

"I want to make my lemon pound cake this morning. It was CeCe's favorite." Nora's eyes filled with tears and she rummaged in her housecoat pocket for a tissue.

"Oh, Nora." Terry hugged her. "Thanks for everything. See you at three."

She made it out the door and down the steps before she realized that this postfuneral spread they were planning could be feeding CeCe's murderer.

Ticking off each stop on her list, Terry chose the coffin flowers at the florist, ordered the small rolls CeCe preferred for tea sandwiches at their favorite bakery, and—hardest of all—picked up her birthday present from CeCe at Aubergine's, a jewelry store noted for unusual settings of offbeat, semiprecious stones. Her throat tightened when she saw the malachite earrings set in a delicate filigree of gold.

By eleven, Terry parked at Laclede's Landing to start working on her hidden agenda, stopping first at the garage attendant's booth.

"Chuck, do you remember if my aunt parked here last Sunday?"

"You bet. She gave me the name of a good podiatrist for my feet."

"Any idea how long?"

"Yep, got it here exactly on the in-and-out. Got it out for a cop, came in here, wanted to know the same thing. Two-fifty to five-oh-seven. He said Miss Girard died. That true?"

"Yes, Chuck, not long after she left Sunday. Did she say where she was going?"

"Nope. We'll sure miss her, though."

"Thanks for the information. Take care of that foot."

So Kevlehan's band had preceded her. Never mind, she knew these people better than they did. The people CeCe saw daily might remember something further and tell her out of sympathy.

But the waitress who usually served them at Braunigan's hadn't seen CeCe since the previous Friday and had nothing to tell. And the other tenants in the building weren't in on Sunday. "She worked longer hours than I care to and I'm a lot younger," the coin shop proprietor offered. None mentioned that they'd also been contacted by the SLPD, but Terry sensed they had.

There wasn't much time, once she reached the office, for more searching. She did look through all the files to see if Barry's name was there, but came up empty. She went through the Barron pictures that hadn't been chosen for the album, to see if they held any secrets, a motive for CeCe's death.

Nothing struck her as significant, and she was plagued with the feeling that whatever it was had been taken already. The office trip had been a waste.

The big hand on the clock outside had just inched past noon when Terry reached the bank. Hugh Barron was already standing inside the lobby, hands clasped behind his back like a high-class floorwalker, but with a slim leather zipper case under one arm. Angry with herself, she pulled open the heavy glass doors and hurried across the marble floor.

"My dear, no need to rush. I just now got here."

She couldn't tell him she wanted to rush through the next two days, maybe the next two years. Instead, she smiled. "Thank you for taking time to help."

"That's what I'm here for." He led the way down polished stairs to a carpeted anteroom. The twenty-inch-thick vault door stood against the wall. Gleaming brass winked at Terry from door, counter, wall plaque as she stood back and let Hugh do the talking.

"Madam, this young lady is the executrix of her aunt's estate and as such needs to retrieve documents from a safety deposit box in her aunt's name. I am her attorney, Hugh Barron."

The woman's eyes grew wider at mention of the Barron name and several seconds passed before she looked down at the card he was offering. She took it by the edges, as if reluctant to leave fingerprints on it, lowered her eyes to read it, and raised them again even wider.

"What name is on the box, sir?" She started to lay the card on the counter's blotter but seemed to change her mind and slipped it into her blazer pocket. Terry was impressed anew by the power of the Barron name.

"Cecile Girard. This is Therese Girard and she has the key with her." Hugh turned to her, his hand out.

Terry had it out and handed it to him.

"I'm afraid I'll have to see some identification and proof that you are the executrix." Apology was an inch thick on the clerk's words. She barely glanced at the will Hugh proffered and the driver's license Terry flashed. "Just sign here," she pointed to a register on a small turntable and pulled a card out of a drawer behind her. "And here," she said, laying it before them.

Terry scribbled her name and followed them into the vault with the feeling she was robbing a tomb.

The clerk inserted both keys into a waist-high unit, pulled out the box, carried it to an inner room, and left them. Overhead the fluorescent light flickered down with no particular rhythm on dark chairs and table, making Hugh's face seem to change expression even though his face was still as stone.

"Sit down, my dear, and we'll see what we can find."

Terry let him push her chair in slightly as she pulled the box toward her. He took the chair next to her, scooting it closer. She had an intense desire to protect CeCe's secrets, even from Hugh, who must be immune to seeing all sorts of embarrassing keepsakes in the leftovers of deceased clients.

"I'm an old hand at that, if you'd like me to sort through the unimportant details. I know what the cemetery deed looks like."

"I—I—I just want to see if there's anything she wouldn't want others to see. Not that she didn't trust you," she added when his eyebrows climbed and the corners of his mouth turned down. "I promise I won't take anything that's part of the estate."

Terry laid the first three packets, CDs in their plastic holders, on the table between them. Two legal-size sheets, loosely folded together, opened in her hands, bearing the letterhead of the Barron firm: CeCe's notarized copy of her will.

"We'll take that, Therese. It could come in handy." He put it in the leather file.

A yellowed and dog-eared copy of CeCe's birth certificate, the copperplate faded to a warm brown, she laid gently on the table. Next up was the cemetery deed, a pale green sheet duly embossed with its seal. Terry waved it at the lawyer with a sigh of relief, then saw what was beneath it. An envelope, its creamy linen texture bearing CeCe's strong handwriting across the front: *Property of Bartholomew Malone—To be returned to him unopened in the event of my death.* The word "unopened" was underlined twice.

Hugh leaned forward to read but Terry tilted the stiff paper toward her. Her eyes ached. Overhead, the light danced to its own erratic beat so that the handwriting seemed to writhe as she extracted the envelope. So this was what Uncle Barry was worried about. Terrified about, she thought, remembering the panic in his eyes as he stood by the office door.

"Something you don't understand, Therese? Here, let me handle it." Barron reached out to take the envelope but Terry jerked it to her chest.

"No! It's . . . it's not hers . . . or ours to see either. It belongs to a friend and I know CeCe didn't want anyone to see it." As if to prove her words, Terry turned the envelope over to show him the heavy tape reinforcing the flap, whose glue had obviously dried many years ago. Even the tape was old, cracked, peeling off.

"But if it's something of value, it may be considered part of her estate. We can't—"

"Mr. Barron, there is no tax evasion here or whatever you're thinking of. It's not worth anything. Even if it were, it is someone else's property. And I'm going to give it back to the person it belongs to." Swiftly, she lifted the flap of her shoulder bag and shoved the envelope down in it. Had he seen the name?

Even the existence of it was something CeCe didn't want Terry to know. It was the reason for her not sharing the box. And if not even Terry, then certainly not Hugh Barron. Gossip that he was, he would have the story—whatever it was—spread the length of the Missouri Athletic Club dining room within a lunch hour.

"I trust that won't be a problem." She made it a statement instead of a question, staring him down.

"As you wish, my dear. I didn't see a thing. Any other securities or stock certificates in there?" His head inched closer as she spread out the contents of a manila envelope. They were high-grade corporate bonds, left by her father; the interest from them had helped to pay the taxes on the house and Terry's tuition. She and CeCe had argued over each as they matured, Terry wanting CeCe to reap their benefit, CeCe insisting they were Terry's. CeCe had won as usual.

Terry shoved the lot six inches to the left for Hugh Barron. He had been toting up the amounts of the CDs on a pocket calculator and now added the face amounts of the bonds, punching the total button with a flourish as he looked up.

"A tidy sum, my dear. Certainly enough to keep the wolf from the door."

"Can we leave now?"

"No more papers . . . jewelry . . . coins?" He fingered through the few scraps left in the box. "Did Cecile have access to your box perhaps?"

Terry blushed, and the warm blood coursing upward made her eyes hurt worse. When she had been forced to rent her own box, a perverseness—petty anger, really—kept her from adding CeCe's name to the access card. "No, she didn't, and I really have to get to Fourcault's, Mr. Barron. Surely there'll be time to clear the rest out later. You have a total of assets there."

"A preliminary total, yes, and the rest can wait, as you say." He gathered up the bonds and put them back in their slipcases, layered everything back in the box, and closed it.

The clerk had heard them leaving and intercepted Barron as he fitted the box into its cubbyhole. She locked it and gave Terry her key.

Terry thanked her and edged toward the door, relieved to be away from the blinking light but still feeling claustrophobic in the paneled foyer. The envelope in her purse weighed a guilty ton. She carried the deed in her hand, afraid to open her purse again.

"Thank you again for coming down, Mr. Barron. I'll see you later, I know, and Aunt Micheline."

"Please call me Hugh, my dear. And Mother said she'd meet me at Fourcault's this afternoon. Run along now."

Terry fled up the stairs and out the glass doors, not slowing down until she reached her car. Leaning one hip against the trunk lid, she took in gulps of air tainted with the fumes of passing cars. When the anxiety had passed she exchanged the cemetery deed for the car keys in her purse, running a finger over the edge of the thick envelope that lay deep inside. Barry would come sometime today and Terry would return his envelope. But what secret prompted the anguish she had seen on his face? Had CeCe found a reason not to be a coconspirator? Was it important enough for murder?

Terry shook her head vigorously as she edged out into traffic. Uncle Barry was incapable of hurting anyone, but especially CeCe. Terry would have to make sure Kevlehan wasn't around when she saw Barry. With his cynical mind, he would insist on knowing everything.

▽

13

"SO GOOD OF YOU to come," Terry said, not meaning a word of it. She shook Mr. Copeland's hand, passed him on to the prie-dieu behind her, and let her eyes bore into the back of her longtime neighbor. Copeland had chased Terry off his lawn and complained to CeCe if her walk was not shoveled soon enough after a snowfall. He knelt for what he was probably counting off as a suitable interval, she thought.

"She looks almost as if she's asleep," he said as he rose.

What the hell did he care how CeCe looked? He'd never cared about CeCe alive. "Yes," she lied, and was relieved when he excused himself to join two other neighbors in a corner.

Asleep. Poor old Mr. Fourcault had said the same when she arrived: *I hope we've made her seem as if she's just fallen asleep.* And she hadn't had the heart to tell him that no, on the contrary, CeCe looked dead. She looked more like one of those Haviland figurines from her china cabinet than a person who had once been so very much alive. She had stashed Barry's envelope in the locker Mr. Fourcault maintained for family members' valuables outside his office. Now she had been standing near CeCe's casket for a half hour that seemed an eternity.

Someone coughed in the hall beyond the archway and Terry looked up to see a sturdy figure close a dripping umbrella and shrug out of a damp Burberry.

She moved down the room to identify who it was draping that raincoat on the closest settee. Someone who didn't trust people enough to use the rack by the back door. He was a Devereaux, she was sure now, but Robert or Richard?

Robert, she guessed; the legislative session would be keeping Richard busy. As a prospective candidate for governor this one might be here to work the crowd, if any. His power-red tie was slashed with enough black to be appropriate for the occasion and, though CeCe would have judged the somber Italian wool three-piece too continental, it showed off the trim waist and powerful shoulders Devereaux cultivated with racquetball and squash.

Reaching him, Terry held her hand out and repeated the phrase she knew would be worn out by Friday: "So good of you to come."

"Cecile was one of my oldest mentors." He took her hand in both of his while his head bent to within discreet consoling distance of her cheek. Practice made perfect. "Of course I wouldn't stay away. Did she tell you we talked only last Sunday?"

"You saw her on Sunday?" Terry tried to keep the excitement out of her voice. "Where was that?"

"Actually, she called me before she went to church. She didn't mention it to you?"

"I didn't talk to her Sunday. I came home Monday morning."

"That's right, she said you were out of town."

"It must have been rather important for CeCe to call before Mass. What did she want?" Terry held his eyes with hers.

Robert Devereaux hesitated. "Nothing much. She had some information I needed for my campaign. Your aunt was never one to hedge on issues."

Terry didn't care if she sounded pushy. Murder was pushy, too. "Was it something that would hurt your run for the governor's seat?"

Devereaux's hand, with a noticeable tremor, crept up to his temple to smooth already-tidy hair behind his ear. "That would be talking out of school, Therese. It was strictly between CeCe and me. I'll just pay my respects if I may, before too many others get here."

"I don't expect much of a crowd this early." Terry couldn't help throwing cold water on his vote-gathering.

Yes, it was going to be a long bitch of a day.

When a lull occurred, she retreated to the sun porch at the back that served as a coffee bar. A small radio beneath the counter was turned low, but she caught the news that the Cards had kept last night's lead, winning by a run. If they won tonight, then tomorrow night's game could be the finale and the wild crowds would make whatever Kevlehan was facing even more dangerous. She poured her fourth cup of the morning, two more than her usual limit. Today she'd worry about today.

Dan Kevlehan moved his steaming cup of coffee off a stack of notes. He had landed at his desk at seven-fifteen after a miserable night's sleep, abandoned around five o'clock. An hour in the sagging club chair making notes on a legal pad was followed by a quick shower and shave. He dressed in the navy pinstripe he'd bought for his sister's wedding and finally found a tie that was both conservative and clean. He vowed for the fifth time that month to take the whole damn rack in to the cleaners or pitch them.

The notes he'd made were spread across his blotter now. One list contained the names of all of Cecile Girard's close friends and current clientele in the left column, followed by two mostly blank columns and topped with "Alibis: Sunday night–Tuesday afternoon."

Dan tore the carbon copy from beneath it and waved it in front of Bert Lucas, who was heading for his desk.

"We have some tentative alibis on these but we really need to pin everyone down better. Four to seven Sunday and one to five yesterday. Okay?"

"Do I get to take my coat off?" Bert Lucas didn't wait for an answer but hung his raincoat on a hangar that was hooked over the top file drawer handle.

"Sure. Grab a cuppa, too," Dan said, watching him head for the pot by the window. Beyond dirty panes of glass, the day was not much lighter than it had been an hour before. Gray overcast where Dan could see any sky at all, wind that seeped in to rattle the blinds and his nerves. "You're in early," he said when Bert had settled down opposite him. "What did the old codger have to tell you?"

"Malone? I told you, you should have tackled him. A true son of the auld sod but uncharacteristically closemouthed. He seemed really broken up about the Girard woman but he didn't ask any questions about how she died or when. Just wanted to know if Therese Girard was going to be handling things. If he's on my half of that list, he was out for a drive Sunday, no destination in mind, didn't stop for gas, hit the McDonald's drive-through out on Gravois on the way home. Chances for an ID, much less a time hack, are probably zip."

"Wonderful."

"Do I get better prospects today?"

"You know I always try to give you the easy end." This drew a laugh from Bert. "You can check out old lady Barron for Sunday and yesterday. I'll take the other clients." Dan checked one of the lists. "Sullivan's their name, and I'll handle Hugh and Claude Barron if you'll take the daughters. Quid pro quo, as Hugh Barron would probably say."

Bert Lucas stood up and stretched. "One of these days I'll be happy to tell you where to put your *quid and* your *quo*, good buddy, a location not unfamiliar to the average lawyer—or cop, dealing as we must with the crap of society."

Dan gave that the smile it deserved but couldn't keep the worry out of his voice. "Dammit, Bert, we have thirty-six hours before we have to help with the Series crowds."

"Tell me about it. I heard on the way up that he called one of the TV stations to say the bomb threat is still on."

"Hell of a note. The trail's cooling down. People forget who or what they saw, and when they saw it. Somebody snuffed that old lady, and may have made a move on that nun. I want to nail the sucker."

"If it were the old Barron broad that got it, we wouldn't have to move over to crowd safety. Then again, if it were my grandma, we'd probably be over there already." Bert swatted him lightly on the head with his notebook. "Don't worry, patient plodding will turn up something."

"Impatient plodding," Dan called out to his departing back before dialing the hospital number. He identified himself, asked for Dr. Hardesty, and cursed silently as he was put on hold.

Bert was right. Priorities in St. Louis were still governed too much by a person's bank balance, his pedigree, or, yes, the color of his skin. RHIP was alive and well, PC thinking be damned. This city deserved its title of Dowager of the Mississippi.

"Hardesty here."

"Yes, Doctor, this is Detective Kevlehan. Has there been any change in Sister Mary Michael's condition overnight?"

"Not much. Her heart's strong enough but she's still unconscious and on a respirator."

"Do you anticipate any lightening of the coma, any chance she'll come out of it today?"

"We're going to do a CAT scan this morning to see how much damage the stroke caused. It's possible that if there isn't too much tissue involved, she could come around. Probably not before this evening, though. I have to tell you, it doesn't look good."

"Can I ask you to limit the information you give out on her to myself and Miss Girard?"

"Since Miss Girard isn't family, even she isn't entitled to any information, although the nurse did give her a status earlier. I communicated with the administrator down at the home about Sister. In fact, I was just about to update her now."

"Give me a few minutes with her. I want to impress on her that the information should be kept confidential. And thanks for your cooperation."

His next call was not put on hold at all. The director assured him that no reports would be passed on from her facility and agreed to ask the residents and staff if they had seen anyone unfamiliar on the grounds yesterday.

She called back half an hour later. Two nuns thought they

could help. They had seen someone who didn't seem to belong there. Mr. Kevlehan was welcome to interview them. Dan promised to be down within the hour. First, though, he'd call Terry Girard. This case had its advantages.

In the visitors' parlor overlooking the orchard two elderly nuns sat waiting. Wizened but with sharp eyes that could probably still see through an upraised geography book to the comic behind, one was bent over her walker; the other, perhaps not much past seventy, held herself straight as an arrow. Both had the stiff white at forehead and chest that broke the otherwise black habits. The smoothness of the starched cotton and draped wool was in sharp contrast to the wrinkled faces and veined hands. Not for them the anonymity of skirt and blouse that most teaching sisters now wore, Dan thought. They were strict anachronisms, and he felt a slight echo of the pounding heart that accompanied his many trips to the parochial school principal as he took the chair they offered.

"Thank you for seeing me, Sisters. The director tells me you may have some information for me."

"You first, young man. How is Sister Mary Michael?" The crippled nun gripped the walker with long misshapen fingers but her eyes dared him to try a lie.

"Holding her own, according to the doctor. But still unconscious. Did either of you see someone near her yesterday afternoon?"

"Not exactly near her," the younger, upright nun said. "I was helping Sister Margaret on the walk after lunch." She hesitated, reaching out to put a hand on the bent back. "We hadn't gone down the path to the shrine because it's too steep there for Sister's walker, but we heard the birds in the woods all screeching at once. Then they seemed to fly up in groups, first a dozen by the grotto, then in the middle, then by the gate. We were on the main driveway, looking toward where the birds had been. We couldn't see much, though, because it's so thick in there."

Dan gritted his teeth. If they couldn't see, what were they wasting his time for? "You couldn't see anything?" he asked, willing patience into his voice.

"Not at the shrine or in the woods, no. But down near the entrance, just after the last birds flew up, we both saw a person hurry out of the trees and down the drive."

"What made you think it was someone who had anything to do with Sister Mary Michael?"

"Still don't know," the older nun said. "But nobody moves that fast around here, not even the staff."

"That's true, Mr. Kevlehan, most of us can't rush. And this person was quite . . . purposeful," the younger one added.

"Male? Female?" he prompted.

"We talked it over and we can't even agree on that. It was someone about . . . oh, five-foot-eight and not all that thin, wearing a plain tan raincoat belted around the waist. He wore dark gray pants, or she may have had on slacks, and a rain hat that matched the coat pulled down over the head." The younger one pulled an imaginary brim down on either side of the veil that hid her neck.

"Was this person running out of the woods?"

"No, just walking quite fast. He was gone in less than ten seconds."

"You said 'he' just now, Sister," Dan prodded. "Does it seem to you it was a man? Your . . . first reaction." He had almost said "gut."

"Women don't wear pants around here, young man."

"Now, Sister." The younger one patted the gnarled hand. "Lots of the women who visit wear slacks, especially when it's cold. Even some of the nurses—but theirs are white, of course. It's just that—"

" 'Twasn't that cold yesterday." The older nun pounded the bar of her walker for emphasis.

"Because of the build or the face or the hair?"

"Couldn't see the face. *Or* the hair. We told you the hat was pulled down!" The hands were shaking on the bar now and the palsy seemed to spread to her head.

"How can you be sure?" Dan persisted but in a quiet voice. He didn't want to be the cause of another stroke.

The older nun was silent, evidently not used to being challenged on her opinions.

The younger one seemed less vulnerable to challenge and more interested in finding the truth. "It may be that we just can't picture a woman doing anything she would have to run away from. That's really old-fashioned thinking. On the other hand, you might say it was our gut reaction, Officer," she said with a slight smile.

Dan could feel his face warming. It didn't cool until he was out on the drive looking from their vantage point toward the gate. There hadn't been any more confirmation than what the two elderly nuns offered. No one else had seen anyone strange near the trees or the shrine, but he followed the administrator's directions down a macadam path to a graveled circle, with a small octagonal pavilion in the center sheltering a marble pieta and a prie-dieu. Two benches bolted to the ground faced the statue, inviting peaceful contemplation. Dan was tempted to sit and think awhile, but the subject of murder wasn't exactly suitable for meditation.

Instead, he examined the area, saw the parallel lines made by the gurney wheels on the gravel. The scuffed patterns of many people's shoes cutting across the near edge of the circle contrasted with the even gray of raked gravel in the rest of it.

He followed the scuff marks to the place just inside the trees where Sister had been found, but there was nothing to see.

The gates weren't visible from here but Dan struck off through the woods toward where he thought they would be. Someone leaving this place on foot would have to be fairly familiar with the territory. Or lucky. Had that person come just to talk or was there intent to silence a damning voice? Dead leaves covered the ground along with a few rotting windfall apples. Some of the leaves were crushed but the ground was hard and would leave no prints. He would have to take the word of two witnesses whose eyesight was obviously not perfect that someone had come out, as he was doing now, on the drive just inside the pillared entrance. Their word, and their gut reaction, he thought, laughing finally as he headed back to his car.

It was almost noon, lousy timing to catch Sullivan in his downtown office but worth a try; then he'd call on the Barron men before he went to Fourcault's. Dan accepted the surge of feeling that came with the idea of seeing Terry Girard again, then dismissed it; he needed all his wits today. Another few hours gone; the first drops of rain hit his windshield as he turned the ignition key. Great, he thought. My good suit on, my filthy raincoat left at home, and no umbrella.

Terry was talking with Nora, trying to stem the older woman's crying, which had begun with her first glimpse of CeCe in the casket, when Evelyn Barron approached them.

"I wanted to come early to apologize. We shouldn't have fussed at one another yesterday," she said, after she had hugged Nora.

"I didn't mind—we all get on edge sometimes." And reveal ourselves in the process, Terry thought.

"Well, I confess I *was* worried. What with Claude trying to bleed the trust for that newspaper, and Frances pumping her share and more into the campaign preliminaries, I was worried about there being anything left for Trep—and Leslie, of course."

It was obvious which child had the inside track; Leslie was expected to marry well and not make claims.

"But there must be provisions to conserve—"

"Provisions are made to get around. And with Hugh having to hire his own lawyer for that Schindler person's claim, it's just more than a body can take. Trep wants so much to set up his own practice, even if Richard says he ought to go with that Washington firm for awhile."

Terry didn't know what to say. Agree with her? "I'm sure Trep will succeed no matter what." As she reassured Evelyn, she spied Barry Malone in the doorway. He stood, damp-legged, slipping a holy card from the guest book rack through short, blunt fingers. His eyes under wild eyebrows were haunted, drawn automatically to the front of the parlor. "Excuse me, Evelyn. There's Uncle Barry. I know Nora can commiserate with you—she feels the same way about her kids," Terry lied again. Heaven help us, it was getting easier.

"I'm so glad to see you." Terry tried to keep the relief from showing as she walked over to him. Together the two of them moved up to the casket and Terry hung back while Barry knelt. He crossed himself and prayed for a time, then slipped his hand over the pale blue velveteen coverlet and patted CeCe's folded fingers. Terry could see a tear roll down his cheek before he hastily brushed it aside and turned to her.

"She was the only woman who never made me feel like a fool." His voice broke on the last word. "But I couldn't convince her to marry me."

Nora had come up beside her. "Don't leave me with that loony again, Terry," she whispered. "All right?"

Terry nodded, biting her lip to keep from grinning. She was saved when the Harmon sisters hobbled in with their chauffeuring neighbor to capture Nora's attention.

"Come over here, Uncle Barry, and let's talk a minute." She led the way to the couch nearest the door but paused in front of it instead of sitting. "I have something for you. I found it in CeCe's safe deposit box today."

The emotion transformed his face into a bittersweet jack-o'-lantern grimace. He didn't bother to wipe away the tears that coursed down his cheeks and splashed on the old serge three-piece. "God bless ya, Terry. You're so much like her, it hurts."

She took his arm and led him down the hall and through the receptionist's alcove to the lockers, praying that the old man wasn't in.

"I can page Mr. Fourcault if you'd like," the woman said from behind the morning paper.

"No, I just need to use his office a moment." Terry snatched her purse from the locker and almost pulled the old man into the office behind her. She wanted to close the door for privacy, but this might arouse the woman's curiosity.

"I think it's what you wanted," she whispered. "Whatever you trusted CeCe with, she kept it safe—wouldn't even let me share her box because of it." She pulled the long creamy envelope out and showed him the unbroken tape, its ends curled up and the side edges gray with old dust.

Her aunt's old suitor clutched it to his chest. "Thanks be to God. I've been out of my mind. Haven't even been able to grieve for her properly. I'd like to go back in and tell her thanks . . . and good-bye."

He turned and started to slip the envelope inside his suit coat. Over his shoulder, Terry saw Kevlehan, filling the doorway with more than his physical size, a look on his face made up of equal parts of anger and disbelief.

▽

14

"I CAN'T BELIEVE this," he said, confirming the obvious.

"Were you—?"

"Eavesdropping? You're damned right. That's part of my job. Jesus, I thought you had better sense!"

"You don't understand," Terry began.

"No, lady, *you* don't understand." Kevlehan closed the door behind him and strode over to the pair. "I could arrest you for concealing evidence." He held out one hand to Barry Malone as he flashed the leather badge folder in his other hand. "I'll take that, please."

Instead, the old man clutched it even tighter and slowly shook his head. His body trembled and Terry led him over to a chair and pushed him down on it before turning to face Kevlehan.

"Believe me! This has nothing to do with CeCe's death. That envelope has been in her box for ages. Barry wouldn't suddenly decide to—"

"That's enough, Miss Girard. Don't say anything more. Sir, I'll have to ask you to surrender that envelope as evidence in the investigation of Cecile Girard's death."

Barry's mouth was open as though he needed more oxygen for his gray face. "Are you trying to say that Cecile's death wasn't an accident? That she was . . . and you think that *I* would have done that to protect this?" He let the creamy white burden fall on his lap. "I loved that woman. I would never have disappointed her again, much less . . . hurt her."

Kevlehan moved in to pick up the envelope that lay between seemingly lifeless hands on Barry's knees. "Nevertheless, I'd like you to come with me."

Terry looked hard at Kevlehan, willing him to meet her eyes, pleading with him to listen. "Let him tell you about it, Sergeant. Here." Turning to Barry, she put both hands on his shoulders. "Trust him, Barry. Tell him about it and he'll understand. I'll wait outside."

She was almost to the door when the old man stopped her. "No, stay, child. I should have known that sooner or later it would all come out. And now with CeCe gone . . . *murdered*? . . . it doesn't seem as important."

"If Miss Girard is right and this has no bearing, your story won't leave this room." Kevlehan leaned against the desk, his arms folded and the envelope jutting from between two fingers of his fist. The raindrops made darker polka dots on the shoulders of his suit.

It's raining, just like at Daddy's funeral, Terry thought, knowing how irrelevant that was but wanting to think about anything but the pitiful secret this old man was now forced to tell. She sat quietly in the chair next to him as he began a tentative recital.

"Cecile almost consented to marrying me long before you were born, Terry. But I was sort of a good-time Charlie and I changed sales jobs once too often for her. She said she wanted a more stable life. I guess I got mad and I went out to California. Finally met a girl there and . . ."

He stopped to wipe his eyes, perhaps to choose the right words. "The old sordid story. Ellen got pregnant. We weren't married and when the baby was just eleven months old, Ellen died of pneumonia. Even before that, we knew there was something wrong with Maureen. She was a stiff baby, didn't like to be held. Then when she was about four years old—I'd leave her with my landlady during the day while I sold cars—she came down with chicken pox and the pediatrician told me she needed tests. They said she was autistic—lived in a world of her own. I knew that. I knew she was happier alone."

"Oh, Uncle Barry, I'm so sorry." Terry reached out and

grasped his hand, which hung limp over the arm of the chair.

He stared ahead. "It was just one of those things. No one seemed to have an answer. No medicine, nothing would help. We moved a lot. As she got older it was hard to find someone to watch her—she'd get so agitated. So I brought her back to St. Louis and started looking for a home."

"Did you ever write CeCe and tell her? She would have helped."

"Too ashamed to write her. I didn't tell anyone I was back but Cecile spied me downtown one day and followed me home. Knocked on the door and walked in ready to bite my head off for not writing or calling. Instead, she fell all over Maureen. There had to be some cure, she said. The child just needed lots of love." Here, Barry did look at Terry and then up at Kevlehan.

"Hell, I loved that child so much it hurt—still does. I told Cecile what the doctors said but she insisted we could bring Maureen out of herself. By this time your mom had died and I didn't want to saddle Cecile with my problems so I found a place for Maureen up in Lincoln County. For a few months Cecile begged me to bring her back. Said we could raise the two of you together, but I couldn't do that. She didn't speak to me for over a year. You know how Cecile thought she knew what was best for all of us."

His sad smile made Terry choke up more than his tears had. But still, she didn't understand the almost phobic secrecy.

"Why didn't you want anyone to know about Maureen, Uncle Barry? Autism isn't anything to hide."

"Not now, it isn't. Lordy, everything and everybody's come out of the closet nowadays. Back then, though, people fell all over you with pity if you had a child who wasn't right. Then they looked down on you if you had to put her away. I didn't want pity and I didn't want people telling me not to do what I thought was best for her."

"But all these years? Surely it doesn't matter now?"

Barry Malone was quiet, looking at the floor. Then he sighed audibly. "You might as well know all of it. Ellen had a small inheritance. As sick as she was the last week, she went down to the bank and converted it to cash. When she died, her mother and her brother found out from the bank and demanded that I turn over the child and the money. We didn't have that piece of paper that would make it legal. I knew they didn't want Maureen to love, only to get hold of the money. I left that night. For five years they chased me, had embezzlement charges brought against me. Then, when the statute of limitations had run out, I wrote them through a friend and told them Maureen had died, that the money had gone to take care of her. Ellen's brother Harold tracked me down finally, said he'd have me investigated anyway. That was about ten years ago. That's when I gave Cecile that." He nodded at the envelope in his lap.

"What's in it?" Kevlehan asked. He handed the envelope to the older man, much to Terry's surprise.

Barry pulled back the tape, slipped a wad of folded sheets out and pressed them flat. Like a blackjack dealer, he laid them out in a row on the desk next to him for the other two to see. "Power of attorney. A will naming Cecile as conservator for Maureen. Copies of every legal move I could take to make sure Maureen would have enough money to live out her life in comfort." His voice was almost a whisper.

"Just how much money *was* there in that 'small inheritance'?" Kevlehan was leaning forward to catch Barry's reply.

"When Ellen died in fifty-six, about thirty thousand. But I had a knack for investing. I took ten thousand of it and bought some stocks. It was the only time I touched Maureen's money. As soon as I doubled that money, I put back the loan and kept the rest of the profit invested. I knew thirty thousand would never be enough to keep her in a home for long—I had to make it grow. I just kept adding to it over the years. The interest is enough to keep her there now. I never wanted to have to put her down in Farmington. Maureen deserved better than a state hospital."

"Good Lord, man, how much have you made off that original ten grand?" Kevlehan was now bent over in front of the older man, more curious than official interest would deem necessary. Terry, too, was drawn into the man's tale.

The slight smile reappeared, this time with a hint of pride. "The trust has roughly half a million in it now."

"But Uncle Barry, you sell used cars for a living!"

"And a nice living it's been, luv. I never wanted anything for myself. With Harold dropping in every few years—he still doesn't quite believe me—I couldn't afford to look prosperous. And I'm not. The money is Maureen's, for her upkeep."

Kevlehan was striding around the room, trying, it seemed to Terry, to make sense of it all. He stopped in front of Barry Malone with his hands on his hips.

"It's a marvelous story, but half a million is enough to do almost anything to protect. Did Miss Girard threaten to divulge the trust to the IRS or what?"

"You still don't understand!" Barry leafed through the folded papers to some filled-in IRS forms and stabbed a shaking finger at them. "The taxes have always been paid. Everything was fine. One day I'm up visiting Maureen like I do most Sundays and the next day I get a call saying Cecile's dead. I wasn't sure if those papers wouldn't be turned over to the authorities and Harold would come running, put Maureen in one of those bed-and-board places. Cecile didn't want to divulge anything. All she did was . . . die on me." He dropped the papers and put his face in his hands. The sobs sounded loud in the office after the soft lilt of his recital.

Terry got up to comfort him. Patting his rounded back, she could see the worn edge of his suit coat collar below the crisply ironed shirt, the Thom McAn shoes polished to perfection. A salesman still putting his best foot forward. Kevlehan had resumed his pacing.

"For heaven's sake, can't you see he was just caught up in this whole awful business by mistake?" she asked him as he passed her on his pacing circuit.

"Just a minute, Miss Girard. Mr. Malone, you said you were visiting your daughter Sunday. What time would that be?"

It took Barry Malone a few seconds to pull himself together. When he did answer, hiccups interrupted each sentence. "From four until seven. I'm afraid I did lie about what time I stopped at McDonald's. It was really almost nine before I ate that night. I didn't think you'd believe I was just out driving all that time."

"You're probably right. And the staff at this home can verify you were there? Could I have their phone number?"

Kevlehan punched in a series of numbers on the phone, then the number the older man reeled off from memory. Terry found herself holding her breath while he identified himself and asked the director to corroborate Barry's story. A sheepish look spread over his face as he hung up.

"I'm sorry to put you through this, Mr. Malone. I hope you'll accept this with my apologies." Kevlehan nodded at the raft of papers. "It's my job to find out who killed Miss Girard and I have to suspect everyone."

"I understand. And I'm actually relieved to have had to tell you about Maureen. It's been a burden only Cecile shared with me and now that she's gone . . ."

"About Miss Girard. We'd appreciate it if you didn't mention murder in connection with her death. The coroner's verdict is still . . . under wraps."

Barry looked at Terry and back to Kevlehan. "Certainly. Whatever you say. God knows, I can keep a secret." He bestowed a weak smile on both of them before gathering up the papers and stuffing them in the envelope.

Terry knew he didn't understand the implications, but there wasn't enough time to explain. She wanted to settle things with Kevlehan. "Will you be all right, Uncle Barry? Would you like me to ask Nora to drive you home?"

"Gracious, no, I have my car. I want to visit a while with Cecile if that's all right. And Terry, thank you for all you've done." He nodded to the envelope before slipping it in his inner jacket pocket.

"Not another word about it. Please tell Nora I'll be along in a minute."

When Barry Malone had left, Terry turned to find Kevlehan already on the phone again. She made no effort to look busy and uninterested. Instead, she stood close enough to listen to his end of the conversation—which unfortunately consisted mostly of "yes," "no," and "try anyway"—and tapped her nails on the desk. Tapping her foot on the deep pile of the rug would have been wasted on him.

"Oh, and Bert, scratch Barry Malone off your list. I just confirmed his alibi. . . . Yep, doing your work for you again. I'll check back when I get there." He cradled the phone and faced her. "What do you have to say for yourself?"

"What—what do I—? Oh, that's good, that is. I'll tell you what I have to say. I think it was humiliating what you did to that poor man. I told you I was a better judge of CeCe's friends than any outsider and this just proves what a—a—"

"Insensitive clod I am?"

"I was thinking more along the lines of stubborn ass but that will do for openers. I've known Uncle Barry just about all my life. He taught me to roller skate, he—"

"He had a secret worth everything to him, more than the half million. I'm not sure he wouldn't take out greedy old Harold if it came to that. From where I stood, you were just asking to be the third one in line."

Terry sank back onto the edge of the desk, that leaden feeling spreading upward from her stomach. "What do you mean, third?"

"I just talked to my partner, Bert Lucas. He told me Dr. Hardesty called to say he'd reexamined Sister and that there was some bruising on either side of her nose and around her mouth, as though someone had tried to smother her."

Terry gripped the desk and let her chin sink almost to her chest. "Oh, dear God! How could anyone . . . ?"

"Not anyone. A murderer. Someone determined that nothing will stand in the way of . . . whatever he or she has in mind for happiness. That could have been Malone."

"No, it couldn't." She lifted her head to look at him. "I *knew* he couldn't have hurt CeCe."

"Excuse me if, with my slightly longer experience around murderers, I decline to share your trust in people." He fished out a battered notebook from his pocket, punched in a number from one of its pages, and shoved it back. While he waited for an answer he caught her eye and held it.

"I'm not taking any chances. From here on, I stick to you like fleas on a dog, Miss Girard—this close." He held his thumb and forefinger together in front of her face before turning his attention back to the mouthpiece. "Security, please."

Terry wasn't sure if he was serious. How was she going to explain his constant presence in the parlor outside? As if she didn't have enough questions to answer from all of CeCe's friends. She realized he was talking to the hospital security chief when he told them to expect a police guard for Sister Mary Michael and requested increased security until the officer arrived.

"There's just one problem, Miss Girard," he said when he hung up. "I have the rest of the afternoon and tomorrow until five before I have to switch duties for the Series crowds. I want to go through all your aunt's files to see if there's any clue to her death. And I need you to help explain things to me."

"But I have to be here. CeCe would never—"

"Your aunt would want you to prevent whoever killed her from achieving what she gave her life to stop. Will you help?"

Terry felt torn. She longed for an excuse to avoid that parlor in there, yet CeCe deserved to have her standing by, making everyone feel welcome and appreciated for coming. But she had vowed to find out who killed CeCe. On the other hand—dammit, she sounded like that Mizzou economics prof explaining voodoo economics.

A knock at the door interrupted her thoughts and old Mr. Fourcault stuck his head in. "I don't mean to intrude—feel free to use the office. But I wondered if there was anything we could do?"

"I'm sorry we've monopolized it, sir," Kevlehan said. "We're almost finished." He turned to her, hands clenching and unclenching at the sides of what must be his best suit, Terry thought.

"Well?"

"Yes, I'll help," she said. "At least for a while."

Out in the wide hall again, the smell of flowers and the hush of filtered air enveloped them like a cocoon. Everything seemed safe, normal, yet some fear nagged at Terry's consciousness. She had forgotten to tell Kevlehan something. When they reached the double doors to the parlor and she saw Nora, she remembered.

"I'm worried about leaving Nora now. Last night, just before I got there, she had a strange phone call. No one said anything but she heard a church bell in the background and she swears it was the same as one she heard when she was talking to a friend of CeCe's yesterday."

"Which friend?"

"She can't remember, but now that we know Sister was deliberately hurt, I'm afraid Nora may be in danger too."

His mouth was a grim line. "You're right, but I don't think my lieutenant will pull any more uniforms off the streets for me."

"Could we ask Mr. Fourcault to keep someone in the parlor here until we get back? If there's a staff member watching, no one's likely to try anything."

"I don't exactly like to tip our hand to the staff. No telling what they'll say to people. Let me take care of it. Tell her you'll be at the office and I'll meet you at the door."

Terry gritted her teeth. *Easier said than done*. Nora was going to make a scene, at the very least, if Terry deserted the ship.

"There you are, Terry. I wondered where you'd disappeared. Come meet Dorrit Wilson. She went to school with CeCe and she's still at the library."

Terry let herself be introduced and made small talk for a few moments, until Miss Wilson glanced at her watch.

"I'm afraid I have to be going. The doctor said he'd see me at two-thirty—you know how hard it is at the last minute—so I arranged to have a late lunch hour today."

Lunch. That was the key. Terry walked the older woman to the doorway, helped her on with her raincoat, and then pulled Nora aside.

"Speaking of lunch, you were right. I didn't stop to eat. Would you mind holding the fort for just a bit? I won't be too long."

"Lordy, child, you do look pale. There's an Italian place a couple of blocks up on Grand and you could bring me back a sandwich if you don't mind."

"Actually, Sergeant Kevlehan and I are going to order up corned beef from Braunigan's while I get him some files." She saw Nora's expression harden with the old after-all-she's-done-for-you look. "I'll order you one, too," she finished lamely.

"I don't believe it. You can't stick this out for two days? She buried your Dad and helped bury your mother and brother. The least you can do—"

"Nora, I can't explain everything now, but this is really more important." Terry saw Kevlehan talking to Uncle Barry in the hall. "If you need anything, ask Uncle Barry."

Nora looked back at the coffin as if to ask CeCe for guidance. "Go," she said, without looking at Terry again.

▽

15

THE OFFICE WAS stuffy and the first thing Terry did was to open both windows. The rain had settled down to a misty drizzle that bore an array of smells into the room: mud from the river, beer and cooking from downstairs, spices and tobacco from a shop across the street, and the hint of licorice again. Behind all of them hovered the old-mold smell of buildings that have stood by a river for over two hundred years.

Terry called downstairs and asked Danny to bring up four corned-beef specials and then spread out the Barron file on CeCe's desk, leaving the slimmer manila envelopes from her own two clients on the library table.

"Oh, for heaven's sake!"

"What is it?"

"It's just now hit me, Sergeant, that I destroyed the Sullivans' file in their presence. They were so adamant about not letting it out and . . . I confess I was pretty mad myself."

"You don't have anything? Can you reconstruct it from memory?"

"I told them no one would read it," Terry said, but her eyes were drawn to the computer in the corner behind her desk.

"Got it!" His grin was triumphant. "You forgot to destroy the disk, right?"

Dammit, was she so transparent that he could just pluck thoughts out of her head? She didn't know what to say. Yes, she had the entire file still on disk, but she had promised.

"Miss Girard, may I remind you that I can get a search warrant in an hour and print that file? And you don't have any privileged communication relationship with these people—you're not a lawyer or a doctor."

Terry felt her face warm with anger. "No, I'm not a professional. I just act like one, keeping my promises." Except she'd already told him the gist, she thought.

"I'm not questioning your ethics, but you simply don't have a legal leg to stand on. You might as well print it out now as later and save us some time."

Without a word, Terry marched to the small computer stand behind her desk and flipped the on switch on the printer and the surge protector. When the logo appeared on the screen, she punched Enter repeatedly, called up the directory, and moved the cursor to *Sullivan.* From the corner of her eye she could see him watching her—almost a leer, really—but when she turned her head to glare at him, he had resumed his pacing. She pushed Print and the laser printer began its muffled hum. While the sheets fed through, she tilted back in the chair behind her desk and tried not to imagine Frank Sullivan standing at that railing with CeCe.

Kevlehan was now wandering around the perimeter, his head cocked sideways, reading the titles of books—abstracts, histories, picture books—on the shelves that covered almost every foot of wall. "You mentioned a file of embarrassing items last night. Can I check those?"

"I've already looked through them. Nothing in there has a date within the last six months." She got up anyway, retrieved the bulging folder, and handed it to him. She was learning that he wouldn't take anyone else's word—and a small worm of fear inched around inside: he was too much like her. But she'd worry about that later. "What makes you think we'll find an awful secret here?"

He seemed not to have heard her, engrossed as he was in flipping pages of copied news items. Finally he handed back the file. "I'm not sure we will." He lifted the Sullivan pages off the printer and settled down in the barrel chair across from her. It didn't take long, and he tossed them on the desk.

"Nothing more there than what you said, not even childhood deaths, which may rule out genetic problems. How do you work this family album business? What do you collect and how?" He shoved her pen stand, letter box, and calendar toward her blotter and spread the Sullivan file out on the edge of her desk so she could use it as an example.

Now she was in her element. "Originally, CeCe ran a straightforward genealogical research service. Our basic research is kept on three kinds of sheets. The ancestral chart—we call it a pedigree chart—the family group record, and the history sheet. The pedigree takes one person—yourself, say—and lists each parent, then each of their parents, and so on." She pointed to the first page that showed Kim Sullivan on the left with her parents in the next column.

"Just like they do with dogs, right?"

"Yes, if you want to look at it that way, but don't be difficult. You have to know a little about what you're looking at."

"I'm just trying to understand the process. Are we likely to find any secrets in one of these?"

"The problem with Maura Sullivan's grandmother certainly shows up, because you can see the same names repeated on both branches. There was just no way to cover that up short of lying, and the next person to happen on it would see the fabrication."

"Then that isn't the secret your aunt was killed for. If they're the ones, there's something else involved. We'll come back to them. What's next?"

Terry picked up a blank from a stack on the corner of her desk. "The family group record features a husband and wife, and gives their parents' names plus a list of all their children and the spouses of those children. Sometimes it gives other information like subsequent or preceding spouses or details about grandchildren."

"This is more likely to have an incriminating tidbit in it?"

"I think so, because they involve a lot more relationships, but our best bet are the history sheets. They can be just about anything—burial accounts, wills published, deeds, land grants, lawsuits, whatever scrap of information we can find. Some of it is transcription of oral accounts, interviews with people who knew these people and remember what happened."

"What if those old folks have faulty memories?"

"Oh, we don't take it all as God's truth. We tape them and then go check up on as many facts as we can verify. That's part of what I was doing in Jeff City."

Kevlehan smiled and Terry, puzzled, watched the humor spread to his eyes, softening his whole face. He sat back in the barrel chair with his hands behind his head. He had taken off his jacket and loosened his tie, but the black leather harness holding his gun ran snugly across his chest. "That sounds like the same way I spend my days! Except that the people I talk to are much more likely to be lying their heads off."

Terry smiled in turn. The frustration over betraying the Sullivans' secrets was fading. Beneath her desk, she slipped both feet out of her pumps as she usually did when no one was in the office.

"Some old-timers do embroider a bit, but I didn't find any mistakes this time. I just needed some specific dates that people were vague about."

"Is that all in here, too?"

Terry had to stop and think for a moment. The trip to Jeff City seemed like a lifetime ago. "No, I haven't even had time to unpack my briefcase. It's—I think it's in the trunk of my car."

"It's not important. Whatever fact your aunt discovered, it was before you left. Let me start on a file and if I have questions, I'll ask."

Terry padded over to CeCe's desk and came back with the Barron ancestral charts and family group records and started in on the voluminous history sheets she and CeCe had compiled about the Barron–Dechant family. Something niggled at her as she turned page after page of material.

"I know you didn't take me very seriously when I said someone had gone through my desk. But what if CeCe's killer has already taken what we're looking for?"

"I was afraid you'd get to that eventually. We *can't* be sure it's still here. If it's gone, then we're back to square one, checking alibis and interrogating people. My partner's doing that now. But it's the only way I know to find a motive—and that will be the key. There was no weapon to trace and maybe dozens had the opportunity. Lots of people, innocent as lambs, can't account for their whereabouts or prove it. But someone had a reason strong enough to kill a nice old lady."

Terry was thinking about how CeCe would have laughed at being called a nice old lady when someone knocked on the door. She saw Kevlehan reach across his chest for the gun as he motioned her to stay out of his line of sight.

"Do your murderers generally knock first?" Terry whispered, but he ignored her. Instead, he took her arm and led her over to the bathroom door.

"Who is it?" There was authority in his voice.

"It's Danny, from downstairs," a man said over his rapping on the door glass.

"Jesus!" Kevlehan's breath exploded on her cheek.

"Nah, just Danny, I said." And he came in with their tray of sandwiches, almost dropping it when he spied the gun being reholstered.

"It's all right. He's a cop, Danny, a nervous cop."

She insisted on paying for hers and Nora's but let Kevlehan add the tip—after all, he'd been the one to scare Danny. They ate while they read and she explained various history sheets in the Barron–Dechant file for another hour, but nothing resembled a discrepancy or furnished a motive for CeCe's death. At four-thirty, she closed the last manila folder and stretched.

"I've worked my way down through old Maurice Barron, Micheline's father-in-law."

"What was he famous for?"

"He sat on the Board of Aldermen, helped to finance the World's Fair, ran for mayor and lost, worked his way back from the brink of bankruptcy in the panic of nineteen and built a real estate empire, then died a pillar of the community. I'm sated with benevolent paternalism and I really should get back to Nora. She'll be starved."

"Do you mind if I take the rest of these folders home and go over them?"

"If anything happened to these I'd be out of business, Sergeant. Do they have to leave the office?"

"I'm on a very tight deadline, Miss Girard. If I can finish these in the wee hours, it won't use up good investigative time."

"Go ahead and take them, then, if you think we've overlooked anything. Just bring them back intact. It's taken months to assemble this material and I'm determined to honor CeCe's commitment to the Barrons."

He gave her a strange look, shaking his head finally.

Once they were back in Kevlehan's car, the seatbelt harness dug into her chest as Terry bent over to massage her temples. It was failure, however, that weighed on her. She had hoped so much to find the key to CeCe's murder somewhere in the thousands of pieces of data.

"What happens now? Will whoever killed CeCe get away with it?"

"Not if I can help it. But my main worry is that she wasn't the last of it. There's Sister Mary Michael to consider, and Nora and you, even if you both claim not to know anything about it. Unless we find who did it, there's no telling where it will stop. It gets easier, you know, the second and third time."

Terry shivered as she watched the raindrops that now coursed almost horizontally on the window. The thought of being trapped like CeCe, forced up against that cold iron railing, made her ache with helplessness. Kevlehan wanted to stop it from happening again . . . but what if another attack was the only way to flush the murderer out? She was willing to risk almost anything to bring CeCe's killer to justice.

The question was, what to use as bait? What could Terry know that would make her dangerous? Some piece of information that CeCe had discussed with Sister Mary Mike and possibly, or so the murderer feared, with Nora. She could dangle some general-sounding threat that would cover any number of secrets, but they—he, or she?—might see that for what it was, a trap. The fact remained that she didn't know where to dangle the bait. And the more she considered various ploys, the more CeCe's drilling in thoroughness made her consider two other questions: Was she brave enough to try it? And was she smart enough to survive?

▽

16

"I WANT TO try something." Terry studied Kevlehan's profile above the steering wheel. He winced as though she had just given him a flu shot.

They were in Fourcault's parking lot, still in Kevlehan's car. Her umbrella and one of CeCe's "extras," found in the office bathroom, lay across her lap, but a sudden downpour blowing at a steep slant made both useless for the moment.

"Miss Girard, you've done enough this afternoon. I appreciate your help."

"But we didn't find anything! And I don't want to live day by day wondering if someone will decide I'm too much of a risk."

"We'll turn something up. It just takes a lot of hard, methodical legwork and paperwork."

"But you said yourself that you won't have time. Tomorrow night—"

"—is the game, I know. But we'll be back hammering on doors the day after. Don't worry."

"Just hear me out, all right?"

He eased his back closer to the door, unbent his knees a little to rest his feet on the hump of the drive shaft, and waved at the windshield. "Go ahead. We're trapped anyway."

He was humoring her, which was infuriating. But at least he would listen.

"Most everyone you seem to think is a suspect will be coming through that parlor this evening. They'll shake my hand, kiss my cheek, and tell me how sorry they are." She paused, already daunted by the thought of enduring a wake.

"And?" he prompted.

"I want to tell them that I know why she died."

His legs pushed against the hump, making his head bang on the window. Talk about knee-jerk reaction, she thought. He rubbed the spot on his head, making the hair stand up in wings on one side.

"You're crazy!"

"That's what a lot of them will think, the ones who aren't involved. Some with long memories will think I mean she committed suicide because of something I did, some argument we had. But even if I don't say it to the right person, it will get back. This is a microsociety with a wonderful telegraph system. That person will *know* what I mean."

"That's sociological crap. You can't do it. It's the silliest way to get yourself killed I ever heard of. Here I am, trying to keep you in one piece and you want to go stick your neck in any number of nooses to see if one is a perfect fit."

"If you're nearby, what can it hurt? Honestly, I'm not a martyr. Dying is not going to bring CeCe back, but even my death might not reveal who's responsible if you let the murderer choose the time and place."

"No way. It's against police policy." His arms were folded on his chest and he looked immovable.

"You send people in with wires to set up drug buys or to get judges to admit to kickbacks, don't you?"

"That's different. Those people are already involved—they're usually trying to save themselves hard time."

"Exactly. I'm involved, and I'm trying to save my own life."

"I can put you in protective custody if you keep on like this, lady."

Terry gripped the handle of one umbrella. He'd need protective custody soon if she didn't keep her cool. "Not forever, you can't," she said, more calmly than she felt inside. "What if I go ahead anyway? Will you stick around?"

"If I thought you were serious about this, I'd head this car straight down to the lockup. It would mean my badge if I went along with a cockamamie scheme like that. Besides, I can't stick around after five tomorrow."

"That leaves more than twenty-four hours."

Kevlehan straightened up behind the wheel and turned on the ignition.

"Don't." She leaned over and put her hand around his on the key, unprepared for the shock of pleasure that stirred in her.

Without a word he turned off the engine. Their faces were inches apart and suddenly he was kissing her, so quickly and gently that she could almost believe it hadn't happened. He seemed as surprised as she. She could hear him take in breath and let it out as she leaned back against her own seat and stared straight ahead.

"I'm sorry. That's against departmental policy, too," he said.

She could feel the anger warming her neck. At least she chose to call it that. How could she press him to agree now? It would look like she had thrown herself at him in order to get him to go along with her. "I don't live by departmental rules," she said evenly. Damn him, anyway. She shoved one of the umbrellas across the seat as she reached for the door.

He hurried around the front of the car but she was half-running up the walk. He caught up with her just outside the back door.

"I'm not sorry, if you want the truth. And I'll think about it, okay?"

"Don't strain yourself." She wrenched open the door, hating him for using a kiss to shut her up, hating the damn umbrella for not wanting to close, and, once inside, hating herself for leaving Nora's sandwich in the car. She turned, only to see his back.

"I'll get the sandwich," he called, heading out into the rain again.

He was reading her mind again and she hated him for that, too.

* * *

Dan Kevlehan was camped in the downstairs office of the head mortician at Fourcault's. He had extracted a promise from Nora Carpenter to send for him if anyone on a list of people he gave her showed up. He didn't trust Terry Girard not to implement her plan in his absence, and he was beginning to care more about what happened to her than duty required. He *wasn't* sorry he'd kissed her; he should have taken her in his arms and done the job right. Still, it had taken half an hour before he could breathe normally. Now, with the receiver cradled on his shoulder, he dialed headquarters and gave the numbers of Bert Lucas's extension. He stared at the strange surgical steel instruments in a glass-fronted cabinet above one counter, speculating on their possible uses, while he waited for Bert to answer.

"Lucas here."

"You're in from the field early, friend."

"Who says I'm finished? Robert Devereaux is next on my list. I thought I'd start with some of his office people and maybe some enemies."

"What have you got so far?"

"It wasn't easy, believe me, but old lady Barron said she was home all day after church with a sick headache. She says her oldest son Hugh can confirm it as well as Claude and Marie Barron, who evidently showed up sometime in the late afternoon. Emma Conway—that's the maid—spent the day in her room, though, so here we go again."

"How about phone calls?"

"She made two—doesn't remember what time—one to each daughter, but doesn't remember anyone calling in. Mind you, that doesn't prove she was home when she called them, only that they were, if she did reach them like she says. Let me emphasize, all this was given with the graciousness she reserves for gardeners who track mud into the parlor demanding high tea."

"I hear you. These people don't breathe the same air we do. Were the daughters any more approachable?"

"Let's say they didn't quite slam the door in my face. Both Devereaux women were alone in their respective homes. Robert Devereaux was on the golf course, according to his wife, Frances. The country club she named doesn't show him accorded a tee time for Sunday. Haven't been able to reach him, but he's not the first husband to get his golfing buddies to cover for a little hanky-panky."

"Or a lot more. How about Tweedledee—Richard, is it?"

"Richard D. was closeted with some politicos in Jeff City until seven-thirty that evening—the only one I can definitely draw a line through. It's been a helluva day so far."

"Not much better here." Dan detailed his visit with the Sisters first.

"Next, Frank Sullivan says they were lunching with friends over in Elsah and went on to Pere Marquette for a long walk to see the leaves."

"And the park rangers don't keep track of license plates for Sunday drivers."

"Right. Then I talked to Claude Barron, who was indeed at his mother's house with Marie but claims they were engrossed in a television special on a pay channel they don't get at home. They didn't see or hear anybody. His mother left a note in the kitchen saying she was not to be disturbed and even if he'd heard Hugh Barron, he's not speaking to his brother."

"Weird family. Did big brother agree with that?"

"Claims he was in and out, went to a movie to get away from the pollen—he has hay fever—came in at six, and fixed himself and his mother a cold dinner of leftovers around eight. No mention of seeing Claude."

"Do they treat that place like a hotel and bar?"

"Certainly saves on liquor bills. I also checked around the courthouse for scuttlebutt about Hugh Barron's relationship with a Schindler. Seems the man was an Alzheimer's victim for years before he died and Barron was the conservator. Now he's the executor and the heirs are unhappy with his stewardship."

"Unhappy enough to sue?"

"Looks like it—that, or get him audited."

"When I mentioned that Claude had been at the house, he indicated those two were *always* there, that the newspaper they run is about to fold, and that he'd refused to advance them more from the trust."

"They may breathe different air, but it stinks, brother."

"Home sweet home. I spent a couple of hours with Terry Girard and the client files—nada so far." He ignored the is-that-so humming on the other end of the phone and plowed on. "Now fill me in on yesterday's alibis."

But before they could get that far, the receptionist was at the door, telling him the hospital was on the other line.

He told Bert he'd call back and punched the red flashing button. "Kevlehan here," he said. Something heavy seemed to rise up between his ribs and push at the back of his throat.

"Yes, there's been some slight improvement in Sister's condition," the nurse told him. "She's drifting in and out of the coma but that doesn't mean she's improving. I don't know whether she's lucid yet or not."

The hospital was fifteen minutes away from here. Would Terry Girard consent to go with him? She was probably the only one the nun would talk to.

Upstairs, Terry's face lit up when she heard the news. She led the way over to Nora.

"Of course you have to go," Nora Carpenter assured her when Terry asked if she minded yet another absence from the duties of meeting and greeting people.

"We won't be long, I promise," Terry said, giving Nora a grateful hug.

It didn't take long. The ICU consisted of a nurse's station surrounded by a semicircle of patient segments, each separated from the others by chest-high banks of equipment below curtains and from the station by electronically operated glass doors. A silent nun sat next to the bed, praying the beads that hung from her waist. She nodded a silent greeting to them, then rose and walked out of the ICU.

Sister Mary Mike lay motionless on the bed. She looked so thin and insubstantial she seemed barely to make an impression on the firm hospital mattress and pillow. The respirator was still hooked up to her mouth. The tape curling up on the edges reminded Terry of the tape on Uncle Barry's envelope: both sealed-up secrets, she thought.

She took Sister's hand in hers and willed the warmth and life force from her body to the frail form.

Sister's eyes, closed before, became slits and then slowly opened but didn't focus.

"It's me, Sister. It's Terry—Therese Girard," she said in a loud voice as firm as she could make it around the lump in her throat. Bending over the nun's face so she could be seen easily, Terry noticed the faint bruises on her nose, lower than the marks made by eyeglasses, and larger.

The eyes looked down and the right hand made feeble attempts at movement. Terry could see the intense concentration to remain conscious and the strength fading. Terry lifted the hand toward her own face, as though to prove by touch that she was who she said. But the hand pulled down toward the wrinkled face instead, down to the hose that was forcing air in noisy measured blasts into her old lungs.

Terry looked up at Kevlehan and then at the nurse. Did she want the respirator off? Could they make that choice?

"She's been doing that every time she comes to. She may want to say something or she may just want to let go. We can't be sure she knows what she's doing," the nurse whispered from the far corner of the cubicle.

"Would it hurt to take that hose out for just a minute or two—put a nose gear on her?" Kevlehan asked in the same hushed tone.

The nurse's eyes grew round. "Oh, we'd have to ask the doctor about that."

"Do it, please. Stat," he added. His hands were jammed in his pants pockets as though it were the only way to keep them still, but he didn't jingle his change or keys while he and Terry waited for her to dial from her desk.

She was back within a minute, crossed to an equipment bank nearby, her skirt making more rustle than her shoes, and brought a thinner tube with forked earpieces like a stethoscope. She hooked these around the old nun's ears and inserted the ends in her nostrils.

"She may be able to tell us what she wants. If not, I'll have to hook this up again in less than a minute." Then she peeled off the tape quickly and removed the hose with gentle expertise.

Sister's eyes seemed to intensify as she focused on Terry's face. The words were there behind the face but nothing came and the face went blank again. Then, as Terry was about to shout for the nurse to help her breathe again, Sister's eyes opened wide. "You came," she managed without the timbre of vocal cords, only lips forming the words, with almost no breath behind them.

Terry nodded, making her tears roll that much faster down her face. The dry and cracking lips worked hard to contract while the eyes held Terry's. "M . . . um," Sister finally managed before her eyes seemed to glaze over. Terry felt a squeeze on her fingers and then limpness.

The nurse moved her aside to reinsert the respirator hose but a whine was already coming from one of the machines and Terry looked across the still form to the screen where a blip had been forming small, pointed mountains at slow intervals.

Now there was a straight line.

Terry stood over Nora's heavy frame, sunk in one of the couches placed around the parlor at Fourcault's. She patted the broad back encased in navy gabardine. "It was so quick, Nora. They said she wasn't in any pain."

Nora made an abbreviated sign of the cross in the air in front of her, not touching her head, chest, or shoulders. With one hand in Terry's and the other on the arm of the couch, she struggled to her feet. "Thank God you went when you did. At least she had someone there she knew."

Terry knew she should be glad of that, but she couldn't forget that they had come up empty. Terry hadn't told Nora it was she and Kevlehan who had asked to have the respirator removed. The nurse had reassured them that it wouldn't have made a bit of difference. Sister had no chance of recovery; even her seeming consciousness might have been reflex actions. Terry believed the nurse with her head—like a child, Sister had thought Terry was her mother—but Terry knew she had seen fear in those eyes. It must be hard to die, she thought, and the idea made her wonder if she would really risk dying to avenge the dead.

"I'd better make a trip before Father Healy gets here," Nora said.

It was almost seven-thirty and soon the associate pastor who was Terry's favorite would be there for the rosary and wake service. The pastor, a chum of CeCe's since grade school, had given up driving at night and would say the funeral mass Friday morning.

"Ther*ese*!"

Terry knew before she turned that it was Claude Barron. Only he could put the accent with such vibrato.

"Marie and I grieve with you for Cecile. And Mother is beside herself—aren't you, Mother?" Claude turned to his mother, who was as tall as he was and not in need of the solicitous arm he was forcing on her. Hugh came up behind the trio, his face a somber study.

"Don't fuss, Claude." Micheline Barron brushed at him as she would a pesky gnat. "Be a good boy and take this coat. Of course we're all devastated by the loss of Cecile. Hugh, a chair please." It was as though none of them had seen her since CeCe's death, as though they were on stage with certain lines to be said.

Terry moved away to help Hugh with a chair whose arms ended in carved eagle heads. "Sister Mary Michael passed away about an hour ago. You might want to tell your mother before she hears it from the others this evening."

"Goodness, this is so sad, coming on the heels of Cecile's

accident. Did the retirement center call just now?"

"Oh, you hadn't heard. She had a stroke yesterday and was in the hospital. I was there when she died. She never really came to, just . . . I think she was glad I was there."

"I'll break the news to Mother. Goodness, there's someone over there who seems to be waving. Go on, I can manage this."

The waver, a nosy woman from their block who knew when her neighbors had a cold before they sneezed, was soon dispensed with. Terry dared not try out her gambit of why CeCe died with this one.

When she returned, Claude and Hugh, with Marie between them, were lined up on the prie-dieu in front of the casket and Micheline was sitting in the eagle chair, a lacy handkerchief to her temple.

"My dear, Hugh told me about poor Sister Mary Michael. How absolutely awful for you. God certainly has made us bear our share of tragedy this week. Did she know you at the end?"

"I'm not sure. She said, 'You came!' but then she seemed to think I was her mother . . . and then she was gone. I don't think I'll ever forget it."

The old woman scrubbed the eagle's beak with her hankie, her gaze intent on the task. Finally, she looked up. "Ah, well, she had a good long life. I hope to have that many years myself, if my arthritis lets me." She slipped a swollen toe out of a custom-made pump and grimaced at what looked like a bunion before launching into a description of the doctor's explanation of it.

This was going to be harder than Terry expected. She couldn't just blurt out the words, even if Micheline paused in her litany of hardship long enough to let her say a word.

Finally, when Micheline stopped for breath, Terry started. "Micheline, I know—"

Father Healy walked up at that point, preempting Terry's chance to cast her bait. And behind him, she saw Kevlehan coming upstairs, crooking a finger to her from the hall. "Excuse me just a minute, Father."

"I've been on the phone to Hardesty," Kevlehan said when she was close enough. "They don't think there's enough evidence to do an autopsy. Her doctor says she's been threatening a stroke for a year now and that's the proximate cause of death. He's already signed the certificate. If she was deprived of oxygen, they couldn't be sure, and in any event, it didn't kill her." He looked furious.

"And you think it did—or at least helped."

"I'm dead certain. Listen, don't try any heroics with that gang in there, promise?"

"I told you before, I won't promise anything. You and a lot of other people have been telling me what to do all week. They order, they make me promise, they hint at what a grateful and dutiful niece should do. I don't think playing it safe is going to help anymore. I don't want to have CeCe in the cold ground and her killer walking around free just so I can say I was a good girl."

She turned and hurried into the room. The Barron family was almost complete, with sons, daughters, and two out of three spouses ranged around Micheline on the left side of the room. Micheline had positioned herself so that she could see everyone entering.

The Sullivans had arrived, and Terry spied Barry Malone among a large group of CeCe's friends from church, with Nora in the middle of them. She didn't know where to start first, but she had her little speech rehearsed: "I know why CeCe died." And to hell with what everyone else thought.

"In the name of the Father and of the Son and of the Holy Spirit, Amen," Father Healy began.

All those who could were suddenly down on their knees and Terry, standing in the doorway, was forced to kneel too. Behind her and to the left, she could just see Kevlehan, his hand over the lower part of his face. She didn't think it was a matter of devotion; he was laughing, dammit.

Far removed from the hail-mary-glory-be that her mouth was saying, her mind worked at a dizzying speed, totally involved with its own sorrowful mysteries.

When the rosary was over Father Healy spoke for a few minutes about his several innings with CeCe. They were mostly anecdotes about her community service and self-deprecating stories of how he came out the loser when arguing theology or parish policy with her. After the litany of the saints as a finish, he headed for Terry.

"Do you think she would have liked that?" he asked when he reached her.

"The only thing she wouldn't like is you having the last word," Terry teased. She found that, far from making her cry, Tim Healy's spiel had actually made her laugh.

When he left, his place was taken by people whom she hardly knew, old college friends of CeCe's who confessed to not having seen CeCe in years. Kevlehan appeared at one point and, having been introduced as "a friend" to knowing smiles, had hovered at her elbow. Would he clap a hand over her mouth if she started to carry out her plan?

She noticed that the Sullivans were standing nearby. They hadn't come up to her yet—probably wouldn't—but they were within earshot. When there was a lull in the reminiscing, Terry turned to the woman next to her.

"I know why my aunt died," she said, loud enough to carry.

"It was God's will, dear. That's all we need to know." The woman patted her arm and scurried off, obviously leery of any delicate theological argument with the younger generation. As if she'd somehow rubbed a magic lamp, Kevlehan appeared beside her, took her elbow, and hustled her in the opposite direction.

"Cut it the hell out, Miss Girard."

"She's harmless, Sergeant. CeCe hadn't seen her in years. I just wanted to try out the words."

"Tryouts are over. The show folds in New Haven."

Terry's throat constricted from sheer rage. He had no right to dictate to her. She was about to tell him this when one of the younger Fourcaults approached them.

"A call for you, Sergeant. You can take it in the office there."

"Fold," he repeated, with a parting squeeze on her arm and was gone.

Not on your life, she told his back silently. She scanned the crowd for likely candidates, stepping back to see around the bulk of a recent client, and bumped into Claude.

"Excuse me, my dear." He steadied her with a hand that lingered longer than necessary around her waist. "I've been wondering about that young man who seems to stick to you—is he some sort of bodyguard?"

"He's not my keeper. I don't know why he wanted to come tonight. But Claude? I . . . I know why CeCe died." There. It was out. And it was easier the second time.

His eyes had widened, smoothing the skin a bit where crow's feet etched the corners and fanned out to his temples, but at first he said nothing. His arm slowly disengaged itself.

"Why?" he asked finally.

Damn it all! How could she have been so stupid? She had not thought of an answer to give should the statement be turned back on her.

"Because I . . . because she . . . oh, I can't tell you right now." Her face burned and she stared down at the soft swirls in the carpet, out of embarrassment and not remorse.

"You're upset, Therese, but it will all be over soon. Listen, how about a glass of sherry after this ordeal tonight? You deserve to relax a little. I know a quiet little—"

"Thanks, Claude, but I wouldn't dream of keeping you and Marie out any later on a night like this."

He stood there a few seconds with his mouth slightly ajar, the lips shiny with moisture, before he squeezed her arm again. "Well, take care of yourself."

She stepped out of his way and immediately saw Robert Devereaux ease out of the Barron circle and head her way. He hovered a few feet off until Claude was out of earshot and then glided swiftly and silently across to her.

"Therese, let me say, first, that I didn't mean to seem mysterious earlier today. Cecile and I did talk in generalities about how the precampaign was going on Sunday. Secondly, I wanted to reiterate how very sorry I am about Cecile."

This sounded like the opening of a campaign speech. What was point three? "Thank you," Terry said automatically.

"Do you suppose we could talk out in the hall for a few minutes?"

"Well, I . . ." A sudden shiver of unreasonable fear coursed through her—first Claude and now Robert—and Terry looked around for Kevlehan, who was nowhere in sight. She breathed deeply. Don't be silly, she told herself sternly. You don't need him for protection—or direction. "Certainly," she said, and let Devereaux guide her firmly through the crowd.

▽

17

WHEN THEY WERE seated on a Louis XIV reproduction settee in an alcove, Robert Devereaux lost little time getting to the point.

"I realize you may not take kindly to this suggestion, Therese, but the safety and prosperity of the state are at stake. Cecile has accumulated quite a dossier on the Barrons and the Dechants. Because Richard and I are intimately connected with them, whatever turns up in your files impacts on us."

"What are you getting at, Mr. Devereaux?"

"I'll put it bluntly. Cecile suggested I hold off announcing my candidacy for next year. I don't know what she has—had—to make her say that. What I'd like—"

"But that's incredible. Maybe she thought you just didn't have enough backing or something."

"Hear me out, Therese, please. Cecile knew nothing about campaign financing. True, she didn't give me any reason, just said to trust her. As I was saying, what I'd like to do is preview the material you have so far, to make sure there is nothing that could damage my campaign for the governor's chair—or Richard's career either."

"Mr. Devereaux, we don't publish slurs in these albums. We don't even have any facts that could be remotely unfavorable to either of you."

"Perhaps not personally damaging, I realize that. But whatever reflects on the Barrons will rub off on us. And I'm afraid that, with so little experience in this business, you can't be a good judge of what is or is not detrimental. Have you, for instance, gone through the entire file yet, to be able to assess its potential for . . . mischief, shall we say?"

A small alarm went off in the back of her head. She wasn't about to tell him that not only had she gone through the file but Kevlehan had, too. Better to temporize.

"I worked on certain sections of it. CeCe did others. I brought the pictures out to the house yesterday. I've seen all of it, unless CeCe misplaced some things. You know she wasn't the most organized person."

Robert Devereaux smiled his politician's smile. "I wouldn't argue that point. And I realize this is the worst possible time to pressure you. But Therese, you *were* out in the capital over the weekend. Richard saw you with the son of an old fraternity brother we've done business with. We simply want some advance warning if you're investigating, and a chance to see any material with our names on it. How about it?" The smile grew wider, if that was possible. His hand reached out to take hers and was withdrawn when she kept her tightly laced fingers in her lap.

A tingly feeling inched up the back of her neck and iced the nerves in her scalp. She stared at those teeth wondering what it was he was afraid she had stumbled on in Jeff City. And wondered what his reaction would be if she dragged the fly on her line across his nasty little backwater. *I know why CeCe died.*

The tingle became a shudder. He might not have to ask why. She had to force her voice down to a normal register in order to snow him with detail.

"Mr. Devereaux, I was in Jeff City to find census data, to check military records for the Barron and Dechant men who fought in the Civil War, and to talk to a researcher about helping us. I don't mean to denigrate your importance to the state, but you and your brother don't figure in the album at all, except as spouses of Frances and Evelyn. There is a photo of the four of you when Richard was elected, and wedding pictures, but that's it as far as I know."

The smile faded only slightly while he digested her explanation. He realigned the crease on his trouser leg and shot his shirt cuffs out a fraction more from his sleeves as if to gain time for phrasing his next attack.

"Still and all, our reputations are so closely linked to the Barron and Dechant names that any . . . unguarded revelation, shall we say, could do irreparable harm between now and November of next year. I think the state needs me and I intend to win. May I have your word?"

Another promise. Damn these people and their promises! "My word? On what?"

"To let us preview any questionable material, my dear," he said, as though to a slow-witted child.

She was seething now. "If I have questions about any material, I'll ask whoever is involved, Mr. Devereaux. But Micheline Barron is my client and she has final say. Thank you for coming." She stood up and moved quickly down the hall to the ladies' room. She had to get away from people bent on telling her what to do.

Once inside, she wet a paper towel, sank down in the wicker armchair, and pressed the cool dampness against her eyes. Another hour tonight, ten hours tomorrow, and then the funeral on Friday. Could she hold out that long? Could she keep from telling some of them to go to hell? Did she really want to live here—work with these people—without CeCe? Terry was the researcher, more comfortable burrowing through libraries and archives for data; CeCe had been the meeter and greeter, the one who could stroke egos and mollify customers, the one who was at home with everyone. Maybe it would be simpler to shut up shop and go back to Washington.

And let whoever silenced CeCe go free? Not a chance. Terry stood and examined the damaged mascara in the mirror. She used the towel to flick dark specks from her cheeks. *I'll be damned if I give up now,* she told the swollen eyes reflected there. She slapped at her cheeks, bringing back color to dispel the shadows that threatened to swallow up her face.

Over her shoulder she saw Frances coming through the swinging door. God, not another one.

"Don't worry, darlin', Robert didn't send me in as reinforcements." Frances breezed past her to one of the stalls in the corner. From behind the metal door she continued. "I did see him buttonholing you. I'd apologize for him but I let him mend his own fences. That's his strong point as a politician."

It certainly wasn't timing, Terry thought. "He seems to think there's some detrimental information I'm going to spring on your family to kill his chances for nomination. I confess I don't know what he meant. Do you know anything about it?"

"Something unsavory? How ridiculous!" Frances said over the noise of the flushing toilet. She opened the door and looked straight at Terry. "But if I did think that you even contemplated messing with our good name, there's just no telling what I'd do."

Terry watched the older woman wash her hands and help herself to a liberal dose of hand cream from the counter. No amount of lanolin would help those age spots, she thought. And no amount of southern charm would make this woman likeable. But Frances wasn't stupid. Would she say such a thing if she had already—

Frances interrupted her train of thought. "It's not that I pine to be the governor's lady. Spending four years stuck in Jefferson City is a wifely duty. It's the White House I have my sights on, and no piddly little book better get in the way."

"Then you *are* Robert's reinforcements."

"No, darlin'." Frances propped the door open with a stiff arm. "I'm Robert's main army and his GQ. This li'l ol' southern act is gonna charm the socks off the power brokers but it doesn't mean squat next to strategy. And my strategy is to keep the slate clean."

The door swung closed with a whoosh of air that made Terry shiver. So much for retreating from the battlefield, she thought, giving Frances a fifteen-second head start before she moved into the hall.

Before she could reach the parlor, Kevlehan appeared in the doorway, crooking a finger toward her. What was she, a servant to do his bidding? Didn't he trust her an inch? When she didn't move toward him immediately, he navigated around several groups in the hall until he reached her.

"Have you been at it again?"

"No, I didn't have to. People have been at me." She told him the highlights of her conversation with Robert Devereaux and Frances, repeating verbatim the veiled threat Frances had made.

"Do you think she's capable of murdering your aunt?"

Terry remembered the steel in Frances's voice: Scarlett declaring her intentions to save Tara. "You're damn right I do."

"Then why advertise the fact by threatening you?"

"I don't know. You're the expert on the criminal mind. You tell me."

"Ah, Miss Girard. You claim to know these people so much better than we do. Now you can see just how dangerous baiting them can be for you," he whispered as they reached the parlor door. "I'll hang around, if you don't mind, and follow you back to Mrs. Carpenter's whenever you're ready to leave."

Kevlehan was as good as his word, never more than a few feet from her until the crowd thinned. When everyone had left and they had all said good night to CeCe, he walked them out to the parking lot. He escorted Nora to her battered station wagon and then stopped at Terry's Mustang as she fitted her key in the lock. The storm was long over, leaving only a few puddles on the concrete, a few large drops on her hood, and the sharp odor of wet leaves in the air.

"I was just thinking. You didn't really dig up anything on Devereaux in the capital, did you?"

"Of course not. Besides, I thought we had agreed that if there is something to worry somebody, it turned up before my trip."

"Right. Just wondering. Drive carefully." He held the now open door for her, pushed down on the lock, and slammed it once she was inside. Only when he peered through to check the backseat and make sure the other door was also locked did he step away.

Maddening, Terry thought, as she shoved the stick into gear. He is impossible. As if she hadn't been driving around Washington for years. But then she remembered when she *had* been scared; when she'd gotten lost that night and ended up on a sparsely traveled street. When someone had tried her passenger door handle at a red light. Her heart raced now just as it had then, and her foot jabbed the accelerator to send the engine racing, too.

This is South St. Louis, Terry told herself. To forestall panicky feelings she began listing what she'd done in Jeff City, but could think of no incriminating information turning up. When she pulled her car up behind Nora's in the Carpenter driveway, she could see Kevlehan's car as he pulled in behind her. She locked the doors and went around in the glare of his headlights to open the trunk and retrieve her briefcase. She would check through it just to be on the safe side.

Kevlehan was behind her when she pulled it out with one hand and tried to slam the lid before he could do it for her. Somehow, the lid caught his thumb in the maneuver.

"Son of a—" He grabbed the base of his bleeding thumb with his other hand and moved it up and down in front of him, grunts stifled behind lips pressed firmly together.

"Oh, I'm so sorry! I didn't realize you had your hand—"

"Forget it, dammit. It's okay. Just get inside and lock the doors, will you?" He moved down the drive to his car, his broad shoulders drawn forward, left hand still clutching his right, both of them held in front of his crotch.

"Damn it all," she whispered. It had been an accident, not intentional. She started down the drive but he waved her away. That was one way to avoid an awkward moment on the doorstep, she thought. Oh, well, she just couldn't win.

Inside, over a cup of chamomile tea, she told Nora about her session in the office and her conversations with Robert and

Frances Devereaux. She omitted the bit about hurting Kevlehan's hand out of self-preservation; Nora might launch a lecture neither of them had the energy for. They turned on the late news to find that the Cards had won again, 5–3. That made it three to one. Of course there was no mention of Sister Mary Michael's death—she was just another stroke statistic. Terry didn't tell Nora about Kevlehan's suspicions regarding Sister's death. If Sister had been one of the last to talk with CeCe, then Nora, being later, could be in even greater danger. Grudgingly, Terry acknowledged the wisdom of bunking in with Nora. Kevlehan was probably right again, blast him.

She hugged Nora good night and climbed the stairs to her guest room haven, still thinking about Kevlehan. Had she hurt him badly? Her stomach had that funny, knotted-up feeling she got whenever anyone hurt himself, even if she hadn't been the cause. Her mind lingered on the pained look in his eyes. Those expressive blue eyes unlike any she'd seen. The knot moved lower and changed to something else.

Oh, no, not now, she thought. It had been, as predicted, a bitch of a day.

Hearing an engine start up outside, she reached the window in time to see a tall black man stooping over to talk to Kevlehan through the driver's window. This must be Bert Lucas, the partner Kevlehan had mentioned. Kevlehan's car pulled out of the driveway and the other man pulled an identical car into its place. The changing of the guard. And Kevlehan had come up with a sore thumb instead of a sore back. She pulled the old-fashioned chintz shade down with a snap to shut out the reality: they would not be providing protection unless they thought there was danger.

Terry shed the suit gratefully and settled into her shorts and T-shirt. She found an old chenille robe in the closet and wrapped it around herself, more for emotional comfort than for warmth, sat Indian-fashion on the bed, and opened the briefcase.

On the bottom were photocopied sheets of census rolls and regimental lists. Ticked off in light pencil were the names of Barrons and Dechants, innocent citizens and honorable soldiers. She could find nothing remotely incriminating as she leafed through these. Clipped to the pockets above were several business cards she'd collected, including one each from the boring professor and his researcher mother. She hadn't even met his father, the old frat brother Robert Devereaux mentioned.

Inside the first pocket on the lid were all the last-minute papers CeCe had grabbed up from the lower tier of her vertical file—the "to-do" stack. Unfinished business to stir up more guilt; she should just leave it be until after the funeral. But her sense of thoroughness overcame exhaustion. She would have it done with.

The first sheet contained dates to be confirmed when a Sullivan had served in the legislature—trash those, she thought, tossing them aside. Ditto for the next four sheets dealing with military service for other Sullivans, Murrays, and Lynches. A memo in CeCe's handwriting to check when the Dechant Foundation was established—that could be done from here in the city.

When Terry leaned over to deposit the Sullivan papers in the wastebasket, a narrow sheet in the stack slipped away and fell to the floor. It was yellowed with age and folded in thirds; a faint odor of mustiness rose from it. Bending over from her perch, she retrieved it and gently opened up the layers. She almost tumbled off the edge of the bed.

"My God in heaven!" she whispered.

Scrambling the rest of the way to the floor, she carried the brittle document close to the nightstand's lamp. She looked at the other sheets, then at the one she was holding. Minus the robe, which had fallen off, her bare arms had hairs standing straight up, and a shiver started between her shoulder blades. She sank down hard on the edge of the bed and let the wave of shock pass. Outrage was building somewhere deep inside but she wouldn't acknowledge it yet.

Calm down, she told herself finally. How had she gotten this? Where?

With another chill of realization, she saw the scene again: CeCe staring at a yellowed document—this document—when Terry came sailing into the office Thursday afternoon. CeCe jumping in her chair, refolding and shoving the paper into the pile, making inane small talk that Terry wondered at briefly and dismissed as CeCe being CeCe. Then, Friday morning, CeCe scooping up these pages and stuffing them in Terry's briefcase at the last minute—"Verify these if you have time, but don't worry about them. Have some fun." Forgetting in her inimitable fashion that they held what she had hidden.

In her mind's eye, as though she were rerunning a film, Terry saw herself squaring up the pile, not wanting them dog-eared before she even got to them. She had filed them in the pocket unlooked at as she mulled over the suggestion to have fun, suspicious even then about the setup with the professor. CeCe had handed Terry the very secret she had tried to keep.

That's what this is, she thought. A secret anyone would want to keep. Terry examined every inch of it. The intricate indentations of the notary seal, though softened by age, still soaked up shadows from the lamp, still set the nerve endings of her fingertips afire. The calligraphy was faded but the names stood out clearly under the Old English heading: City of Saint Louis . . . Transfer of Property Deed . . .

She took a deep breath. It was what they had searched for this afternoon, she was sure of it: a deed transfer for land. She read the specific boundary designations, mentally transcribing old street names for new, recognizing what had been several square blocks of a solid residential area and was now prime commercial property worth millions of dollars. It was being sold for $400,000, still a small fortune in those days, to Frederic Lavelle.

In ten days, a small corner of it would be dedicated as a public park. Barron Park. The seller was Maurice Barron, Micheline's father-in-law, and the date was 1919.

When she'd first come back to The Family Album, Terry

had seen a newspaper clipping about a Lavelle dying suddenly and the mysterious disappearance of most of his fortune. Terry thought she could now point to the circumstances behind Barron's recovery from near-bankruptcy. He had received the money and, when Lavelle had died hours or days later, had somehow gotten back the deed. She looked at the signature of the recorder of deeds: René Dechant. Micheline's uncle. Of course. Friends make fraud a lot easier.

Unless there was some explanation. The shiver retreated up her neck into her scalp. Maurice Barron could have bought it back when he'd regained financial stability. Somewhere there would be a piece of paper on file showing this. And CeCe would have demanded and gotten that proof.

But CeCe was dead. People killed for money and this represented a fortune. It was also a felony, a shame brought on both the Barrons and Dechants. She held in her hands the reason for CeCe's murder.

But who? Who would snuff out such a life, silence her aunt for this? And how would Terry find out who it was?

Her hands began trembling and she let the deed fall onto the spread to keep from tearing it at the vulnerable folds. Nothing must happen to destroy this: it was her evidence. And evidence meant police. Should she call down to whoever had taken over for Kevlehan?

She went to the window and pulled the shade out slightly from the window. The car was there, its roof reflecting the shine of a nearby streetlight. A stream of smoke curled up from the driver's window. She looked down at her T-shirt, at her nipples hardened by the shock, at the rumpled boxer shorts and the fuzzy ridges of the pink chenille robe left in a heap on the bed. She couldn't, not like this, and she couldn't bring herself to get dressed again. Besides, that was a perfect stranger down there.

She moved to the phone and dialed the number she'd memorized. A bored voice told her it was police headquarters.

"This is Terry Girard. Would Sergeant Kevlehan still be around?"

"No, ma'am. He's off duty. But Sergeant—" he hesitated as if checking a roster, "—Lucas is outside if you're still at the Carpenter residence."

"Yes, I saw the car."

"Do you need anything?"

"We're all right. But would it be possible to reach Kevlehan at home?"

"I can't give out that number, and besides, he called in that he was on his way to the emergency room for treatment half an hour ago. Seems he smashed—"

"Yes, I know. His thumb. Thanks, anyway."

Terry cradled the phone. Something else to feel guilty about. She turned on herself the rage that had been building inside, but instead of prompting her to action, it brought on a light-headed exhaustion. It wasn't just from the stresses of the day—and God knows, she couldn't remember a worse one—but from the horrendous realization of evil. Much as she wanted to puzzle out the answer tonight, her body would not cooperate. Her eyelids drooped heavily, her arms were deadwood, her mind was a swamp refusing to yield up a living thought.

She sat back down on the bed, folded the deed carefully, and put it back in her briefcase. Like an automaton she snapped the latches shut, fished out the keys from her coat to lock both sides, and slid the case under her pillow. It would keep until morning; no one was going to try anything while Cerberus was outside. She snapped off the light, climbed into bed, and, despite the firmness under her head and the awful questions still unanswered, was asleep in seconds.

The first inkling of fear began to nibble a hole in Mumpet's confidence and questions poured through. Why were the police dancing attendance on Therese? What did they suspect? Why had they asked where everyone had been? Did they know it was murder? Had Therese found the incriminating document? If so, then why hadn't the questioning been more thorough?

But now something was wrong—there was too much activity. Tomorrow was none too soon for Therese to be dealt with, before she had the entire police force in Fourcault's parlor.

▽

18

THE MUFFLED PATTER of rain became a soft tattoo of drums, a ceremonial farewell at CeCe's grave in the dream Terry had been having. When the alarm sounded, she pushed the last shreds of that scene from her mind and stretched.

She raised up slightly to pull the briefcase from beneath her pillow and laid it on her stomach. Nestled inside the brown leather was one answer, but it led only to more questions. Who had, or thought they had, the most to lose by allowing the deed to become public?

She ranked them easily: Micheline, of course; her status as grand dame was endangered and the rest of her life would be clouded by this scandal. But did Micheline have the strength—and the nerve—to hurt her old friend? Is the pope Catholic? Terry asked. Just because they all waited on her made people think of Micheline as weak, but Terry had seen her pull open that heavy French door hard enough to unhinge it. And last night she had hitched that chair around easily so that she could watch the doorway for socially prominent arrivals. Nothing, not even friendship or decency, was as important to Micheline as living out the privileged life she was used to.

Robert Devereaux had even more reason, because this would certainly be judged in those smoke-filled rooms as cause for abandoning next year's governor's race. CeCe had seen that at once, and he'd made it clear last night—was that whole conversation a smoke screen to make him look innocent?

The retreat from the campaign would bother Frances—maybe even more than Robert. Robbed—relieved?—of her child, Frances had thrown herself into mothering a candidate. She was the brains and will behind the handsome product. Either of them could have done it, Terry thought, and not blinked an eye.

How about the others? Would staid Hugh stoop to such a thing? Kevlehan had passed on the information about the threatened lawsuit and Claude's newspaper troubles. If Hugh was in a financial bind, the money lost in returning the land might worsen it. He seemed fixated on money. She remembered the way he handled the bonds in CeCe's box, much the way Evelyn fondled her kids' pictures.

Claude fondled too—ugh, how she hated him touching her. But he liked that paper even more than he did young women, it seemed. If the trust were depleted, his last source of funds was gone. And by rescuing family honor, he'd be respected by his older siblings at last—if he had the stomach for it.

Marie had the stomach for it—both literally and figuratively, Terry thought—but Marie wouldn't lift a finger to save the Barron name. On the contrary, she'd laugh up her Mexican serape if it were tarnished. But if money was involved . . . how closely attached was she to *Beaux Arts*?

Evelyn was sturdy enough to have pushed CeCe, and there seemed to be something . . . unbalanced about her. She was obsessed—was that too strong? No, that's how she sounded when it came to Leslie and Trep. Nothing should hurt them or stand in their way.

Except for Marie possibly, CeCe would have agreed to meet any of them at the lookout, and Terry was convinced that someone had set up a meeting there.

Enough. She was ready for action. Hyped. She lifted her hands off the briefcase and watched them tremble. She realized she didn't know how to force someone out of hiding. But there was hope; should she choose to cast her rod and line across the Barron waters, she knew what fly to use this time.

She swung the briefcase to the foot of the bed and her feet

to the floor in one motion. Maybe later she would run some of these possibilities by Kevlehan, if he was back on the job.

She raised the shade and checked the driveway: beyond the windshield of the cruiser, a uniform badge caught the early morning sun—not Kevlehan or even his partner.

In the shower she thought again about the accident and his pained departure last night. It must have been worse than she thought to send him to the hospital. He was partly to blame, of course. He shouldn't have sneaked up on her like that. She could close a trunk lid, for heaven's sake! Nevertheless, she tried out different speeches of apology as she toweled off. None seemed quite right.

She was brushing her teeth when she heard the phone. The last two mornings had started with conversations with Kevlehan. Considering last night, the third time was not likely to be a charm.

"Telephone for you, Terry. Can you take it?" Nora called from the other side of the door.

"Who?" Terry managed around a mouth full of pasty foam.

"Who do you think?"

She rinsed her mouth. "Kevlehan." She didn't even bother to make it a question. Her watch on the bathroom shelf read seven-thirty.

"Shall I tell him to call back? I have breakfast ready."

"No, I'll come on down and take it." And apologize in front of Nora to do extra penance. She shrugged into the chenille robe and knotted the belt so tightly it hurt. *Masochist,* she thought, and loosened it.

"I need caffeine," she called ahead to Nora as she padded downstairs.

"I thought you were dressed already. I'll pour. You talk."

Terry would tell him about the deed first; that should cheer him up. Then an apology. As Terry picked up the phone, Nora put a steaming cup on the kitchen counter.

Terry smiled her thanks. "Hello," she said into the receiver.

"You sound extremely cheerful—does slamming car doors do that for you? Get the aggression out of your system?"

"Are you trying to make me feel bad? Because you were partly to blame. I'm not used to people creeping up behind me to stick their hands in my trunk."

She thought he mumbled "or anywhere else" but she wasn't sure. "What was that, Sergeant?"

"Nothing. I called to tell you that Officer Hartwig will be on duty this morning. Lucas had the night shift."

"I know. I watched you trade—"

"Please don't interrupt. I've only got about two minutes before they do a little minor surgery on my thumb."

"Oh, God!—"

"Shut *up*, Miss Girard. Please. I'll be out in a few hours. After all, I've been waiting around the whole goddamn night!" He stopped and she could almost see him counting to ten. "I just wanted to let you know there is someone in charge. Don't do anything dramatic. If you need anything, ask Hartwig. *Yes, I'm coming*. Listen, I have to go. I'll come right to Fourcault's. Remember, no opening night performance down there!"

"Good luck," she managed before he hung up. She wouldn't promise anybody anything today. And her heart sank when she realized she hadn't had a chance to tell him about the deed.

Nora's eyebrows were about as high as they could go on her forehead. "What was that all about?"

"Last night I slammed my trunk lid down on his thumb and evidently broke it. They're just about to operate on it."

"You didn't apologize."

"He didn't give me much chance." Terry tried to keep it from sounding like a defensive whine.

"He just sounds like he really cares what happens to us. He asked me if we'd gotten any more strange calls."

Terry had almost forgotten about that. She looked closer at Nora and saw the dark circles under her eyes and the slight quiver in her chin. Telling her about the deed would be too much for her to handle right now.

"Did you lie awake all night waiting for one?"

"No, but I didn't sleep much either."

"You sit down and let me at least serve you this morning."

Nora was having none of it. "Don't be silly. I feel better if I'm doing for someone. Go get some clothes on in case someone comes to the door. There's a car in the driveway, you know."

"That's Officer Hartwig, I was informed. Do me a favor and don't invite him in for coffee." Terry took her cup, and her secret, upstairs.

She slipped on clean underwear and stepped into the only other outfit she'd brought from home: the navy tissue wool with the Irish crochet collar that she'd worn to dinner Sunday night. It looked severe in the watery light from the window—perfect. CeCe would hate it.

She was just buttering a piece of toast at the kitchen table when the phone rang again.

Nora let out an exasperated sigh that carried over into her "Hello." The brusqueness was instantly smothered in a respectful, "Oh, Father!" She held out the phone to Terry, her eyes round. "Father Morgan," she whispered, even though her hand covered the receiver.

The conversation was brisk and brief. Terry would have to come by this morning and decide which hymns for the funeral plus a myriad of other details. It was unusual—the old pastor stressed the word—that the family would let it go until the last minute. After all, a funeral mass wasn't something you threw together on the spot.

"Yes, Father. I'll be down as soon as possible."

When the phone was safely cradled, Terry allowed herself a short expletive that drew a wince from Nora. She was doing the best she could.

Her spirits lifted an inch when she read the headlines over breakfast: the Cards' best hurler, who had been a questionable starter, would pitch tonight. Those Series rings were almost on their fingers.

"Be sure you tell him 'Amazing Grace,' " Nora warned as she cleared the plates. "I know you aren't fond of it but CeCe loved it."

"Right." Terry sighed. By now, she didn't much care if they played "Twelfth Street Rag," another of CeCe's favorites, but Terry bowed to CeCe's taste, to tradition and syrupy glissandos. "Amazing Grace" it would be.

"Are you going straight to Fourcault's when you get dressed, Nora?"

"No, I'll stop by the bakery and pick up the order. We can take things over to your house and set up tonight. You sure you don't want to have them back here?"

Terry could almost hear CeCe snort at the idea. "No, she'd want me to have it. It's the last thing I can do."

Not the last thing, really. She had transferred the deed from briefcase to shoulder bag to make carrying it less conspicuous; now she gripped the bag firmly.

"I'll tell Officer Hartwig I'm off to the rectory so he can stay here. Surely I can't get in trouble as long as I'm with Father Morgan. See you as soon as I can."

Outside, Terry hurried down the drive. Nothing had dried yet, and the sun looked only momentarily in charge of the day. Hartwig's police radio was turned low so that the dispatcher's urgency was muted. She saw a thermos on the seat and watched as Hartwig spied her. He put the steaming cup in a dashboard holder so fast he almost scalded himself.

"Officer, I'm going to the rectory for a while if you'll let my car out. A few blocks down. I'd appreciate it if you'd stay here with Mrs. Carpenter if you have to stick around at all."

"I'll have to check on that, Miss." He rolled up the window, spoke into a hand-held mike, waited for what seemed like ages, and then spoke again. One more short wait and he nodded as though the listener could see him. Down came the window. "We'll be on our way as soon as possible, miss. Someone will be here to cover for me in less than five minutes."

"But I'm in no—"

"They said Sergeant Kevlehan was firm on that, ma'am. I'm to stick to you like glue."

How original of him. Terry thought up other adjectives as she sat in her own car waiting. She was even leery of showing the deed to Kevlehan for fear he would take over and make her stop. No opening night, he'd said.

Father Morgan accompanied each choice he offered her with a sermon on which answer would have pleased CeCe most. To save time, Terry agreed with most of his selections. Still, she didn't emerge until Father Morgan's hunger pangs got the best of him. The morning sun now hid behind a solid ceiling of clouds and Terry shrugged her raincoat closer to her body to keep out a sharp wind.

Hartwig gave her a stoic nod when she leaned down to the window to apologize for taking so long. She had wondered how the police officers managed to spend hours just sitting but she saw that the thermos on the seat had been exchanged for a perfectly constructed box score for tonight's game. "For your sake, I hope they don't change the batting order," she said with a smile.

It was after one when Terry finally crossed the patterned carpeting to the couch at Fourcault's, but Nora's manner showed more commiseration than disapproval. Funeral planning was more legitimate than yesterday's foray to the office, it said. She still had that edginess Terry had noticed ever since the phone call, and Terry was glad she hadn't mentioned anything about the deed.

"Was it hard going with Father Morgan?"

"About what I expected. I gave in to his opinions on most everything—including 'Amazing Grace.' "

Nora relaxed visibly. "I guess you think we're stiff-necked. But CeCe was old school, too. Tell yourself it's for her."

"Right."

"Did you stop to eat? CeCe wouldn't want you to get sick over this, you know."

"We had a big breakfast, Nora." To keep from arguing the

finer points of her digestive system or what she should be doing for what reasons, Terry went up to the casket. CeCe looked exactly as she had yesterday and the absurdity struck Terry: now that the greatest change a human could undergo had taken place, the morticians struggled mightily with cosmetics and curling irons and whatever to stave off any further change. And none of it mattered; CeCe, the real CeCe of the sharp wit, the keen mind, and the soft, all-encompassing love for Terry, was gone forever.

The tears that filled her eyes as she turned her back on the casket kept Terry from seeing who was striding toward her until he was just feet away. But Hugh Barron's hushed tones were depressingly familiar.

"My dear, I hardly had any chance to comfort you last night. Such a crowd of people!"

"CeCe had a lot of friends."

"Well, to make up for it, I canceled my caseload for today because I thought you might need me. If there's anything I can do, anything, I'll be here."

"Oh, you shouldn't have done that. There's really nothing I can think—"

"Moral support, if nothing else. A strong right arm."

Terry's heart sank. Could she stand a whole day of his clichés? But he was a Barron, and clichés might be the least of his crimes. Better to have *all* the Barrons here where she could watch them, perhaps maneuver them into giving something away. She forced a smile.

"What would we do without friends like you at a time like this?" That had a nice trite ring to it. "Why don't you see if you can give Nora a few words of encouragement? She hardly slept at all last night."

"Poor Nora. It won't be the same for her without Cecile. I'll see what I can do."

Clutching the shoulder strap of her black leather bag, Terry escaped through the doorway intent on getting another cup of coffee in the sun porch. Instead, she bumped hard against a navy blue-suited Kevlehan.

He threw his arms wide, the left hand holding a wet raincoat at its collar, the right hand swathed in white gauze bandage, concentrated on the thumb.

"Gee-zus, lady! Stay clear for a while, will you?"

"I'm sorry. I didn't see you coming—and I didn't see you sneaking up behind me last night either, but I'll apologize for that, too." Terry looked closer at his injured hand. The bandaged thumb resembled one of those rubber "number one" fingers sports fans waved at the television camera. She softened. "How much of that is you?"

"Less than you'd like, I guess. Most of it is to protect against flying females. They set it, put on a splint, a few stitches. I hardly even noticed the nine hours I spent waiting to get them."

Terry rolled her eyes to show that she would not grovel, but she did feel contrite. More than contrite. Protective. Wanting to care for him. Her chest felt tight.

"Let me get you some coffee. I want to show you something." She took the dripping raincoat, a newer and cleaner one than he'd worn before, and walked with it back to the sun porch, leaving him to follow. A rainy-day rack had been set up next to the back door, with a tray beneath to catch the water from coats and umbrellas hanging there. As she added his she looked out the back windows to the rainy parking lot for his car. "You didn't drive?"

"Can't for the next twenty-four hours. One of the uniforms dropped me off. Now what's new with you?"

Terry bent her head but watched him from the corner of her eye as she busied herself with the flap of her handbag and put her hand on the folded document. His eyes traveled down the blue wool and a quirky smile pulled at one corner of his mouth. The fist in her chest opened and a floaty feeling took its place.

"I found it," she said, gently lifting out the paper, not even trying to keep the excitement out of her voice.

"Found what?" He started to reach for it, seemed to realize that he couldn't manage the task of unfolding something that delicate, and waved the white digit impatiently at her. "Come on, you moved fast enough last night."

She took time to glare at him before she peered past his shoulder. She didn't want Hugh Barron or anyone else eavesdropping. Then she opened out the deed so that he could read it.

He glanced down the wording, looked at her fiercely, then reread it carefully, just as she had done.

"Well, I'll be a son of a—"

"I know. It's what we were looking for, isn't it?"

He kept staring at it until he, too, looked behind him as though the whole of South St. Louis were peering through the windows. "I'd say it's about as sure as the Cards taking the Series. Where in hell did you find this?"

When the deed was safely in his coat's inner breast pocket, she explained how CeCe had hidden and then inadvertently given her the document. "I never even looked at that batch of papers until last night."

"You found this last night? Why didn't you give it to Lucas?"

She blushed. "I was in my pajamas. I was tired. I knew it would be safe under my pillow with him outside."

His elbows went out and he tried to put his hands on his hips but the bandage wouldn't let him. Instead, he reached both hands in the air as if to implore God to infuse her with a brain.

"I tried to call *you*," she offered, "but they said—"

"I was mauled by a nervous citizen. Oh, well. This does narrow it down. Now we just have to figure out which of the Barron clan had the opportunity and the . . . the . . ."

"Coldheartedness? Any one of them. It doesn't narrow it as much as I'd like."

"I think we can cut the picture down a little. Pour me a cup of that, will you? Then I'm going to do some phoning from downstairs. That office where we talked to Malone isn't private enough—anyone can walk in."

"And does," she couldn't help adding, but he just smiled broadly this time.

"Can you see the stairs from the parlor?" When she nodded, he said, "I want you to make sure nobody comes down there until I'm finished."

Terry watched him walk out into the wide hall, moving carefully, as though he wasn't used to carrying hot coffee in his left hand. The lightness in her chest continued, as though the paper she'd given over had had a real weight. Hope was part of it, and she wouldn't let herself think about what else it could be. She didn't want to be disappointed again. She waited until he disappeared down the stairs and then gulped down a couple of scalding swallows of coffee and went back to the parlor, unable to squelch the feeling that it would all be over soon.

▽

19

THE WATERY LIGHT outside, visible only from small windows near the ceiling, didn't add much to the cold blue light of the fluorescent tubes in the embalmer's workroom. But Dan Kevlehan didn't care. Despite the lack of sleep—they'd finally given him a gurney to doze on when he refused to be admitted to the hospital—he was charged with energy. With the phone in his left hand, he stared at the rain beyond the panes and saw instead a blue dress that curved in all the right places, a head of dark chestnut hair that wanted to curl around the edges, eyes filled with sympathy. Why was he thinking of Terry Girard, for crissake? Anything to avoid guessing at the uses for those damned instruments in the glass-fronted cupboard, he told himself. The last three fingers on his right hand had already worked their way free of constricting gauze and drummed the desk until Bert Lucas's sleepy voice came on the line.

"Yeah, Lucas here."

"I know you've just had three or four hours in the sack but I need some help here."

"How's the hand, Romeo?"

"Very funny. I told you she was closing her trunk. I'll feel a lot better if we can wind this up this afternoon." He itemized what had to be done. "I'll leave the how up to you. Better have a good story if you're spotted. I'll hit neighbors, employees, see if someone can shed a little light. When you turn up something, call back here and run it by."

"*When*, not *if*?"

"We need a break. We have four hours left."

* * *

In spite of the weather, close to a dozen people were in the parlor when Terry came through the wide double doors. Micheline, flanked by Claude and Frances, was ensconced again in the eagle-armed chair. Terry had told herself she wanted them all there, but she really hadn't expected another Barron invasion today. She tried to hide the revulsion that forced her jaws shut and stiffened her lips in a thin line. Had it been a family affair? And if so, who had been elected . . . ?

She forced her mouth to smile at them as she crossed to where Nora sat on the couch nearest the casket. Luckily, Hugh had been diverted to Malcolm Hennessey, an ancient, retired judge who had been her grandfather's crony. Four Barrons she had to keep an eye on. Evelyn Devereaux walked in, brushing a speck of something off a short mink jacket. Five. It was a harder task than it seemed. When Nora introduced a genealogical colleague of CeCe's from downstate, Terry had to crane her neck to keep everyone in view. Before long, she noticed that the genealogist was weaving from side to side with a puzzled look, trying to keep herself in Terry's line of vision. Finally the older woman glanced behind her. "Am I in your way, dear?" she asked.

"I'm sorry, I thought someone over there needed me. You were saying?" But Terry couldn't concentrate on what was being said. Suddenly, she clasped the woman's arm in a polite embrace. "Thank you so much for coming."

Claude was almost to the doorway.

Terry moved after him, the effort to keep from running almost unbearable. When he turned right toward the restrooms instead of crossing to the stairs, she was stranded in the middle of the room.

"My, you are skittish this afternoon, Therese," Micheline said from her makeshift throne.

Terry felt the blood creep up her neck. "I just can't seem to sit still. I hardly slept at all last night," she lied.

"Well, come sit in Claude's chair for a few minutes. Take

some deep breaths; that's what my doctor recommended to me when I'm upset, and I can guarantee it works." She patted the chair on her left.

Terry gauged the angle between chair and door, saw that it would afford a view of the stairs, and sat down on it with her heart racing. She had worried about Nora giving away the show instead of her own inability to play the naive niece. She rubbed her temples with both index fingers and glanced furtively at the door while pretending to close her eyes.

"Was that the same handsome fellow going downstairs who was here last night? Someone said he was a policeman," Frances asked.

Terry's heart, racing until now, seemed to skip a beat or two. She looked up at Frances. The carefully filled-in eyebrows arched above wide-open eyes.

"Oh, the man with his hand bandaged? Yes, he's the one who made me sign for CeCe's autopsy." This last was no secret. She knew that Hugh would have passed on the information. "I wonder what he's doing here again today? Probably more papers."

"I had a black detective come ask me where I was Sunday and so on. I didn't appreciate it one bit. If they think CeCe's fall wasn't an accident, they ought to look at some of those neighborhood gangs."

"Hugh and I were bothered, too. It's . . . embarrassing, Therese. Can you tell them to stop it?" Micheline finished arranging the Hermès scarf at the neck of her navy suit.

"I couldn't even stop CeCe's autopsy. I'm afraid I'm helpless."

"Odd," was all the older woman said, but the one syllable hung on the air.

So relieved was Terry when Claude came back from the direction of the men's room that she let out a breath she wasn't aware of holding. "I'll let Claude have his chair back. I want to see if Nora . . . picked up the rolls for tomorrow," she finished lamely.

"Calm down, child. You'll be a wreck by tomorrow."

Micheline seemed to be peering directly into Terry's thoughts.

Terry escaped to the front of the room, circled around so that she faced the door, and bent over to Nora, who was blessedly sitting alone.

"Would you like to go down the street and grab some lunch? I'll hold the fort."

"I promised the girls I'd be here. They said they'd leave Chicago before noon, so if they haven't eaten, maybe we'll sneak out for a bit."

Terry relaxed her clenched teeth and eased the muscles in her shoulders. Just the thought of seeing those two friendly faces made things seem almost normal until she spied a younger Fourcault threading his way past Hugh and the judge and heading toward them. He bent a conspiratorial head that she could have clobbered.

"Miss Girard? The gentleman downstairs asked if Mrs. Carpenter could join him for a few minutes. Right away."

Nora looked up at Terry. Her face was paler and her eyes held a puzzled look. "What do you suppose it's about?"

"I don't know, but we'll find out soon enough." Terry helped Nora to her feet.

There was no sidling out of the room unnoticed. With the young Fourcault leading the way, Terry tried to make small talk with Nora as they passed Hugh and then the quartet of Barrons. She mentioned limousines for the morning and times for assembling, but to her ears it sounded like so much babbling.

Downstairs, Kevlehan ushered Nora to the desk chair he'd obviously been sitting in. He still held the phone's receiver in his left hand. "Mrs. Carpenter, I want you to listen to this sound and tell me if you recognize it."

He held out the phone to Nora, who at first recoiled. Then she seemed to gather her courage and almost grabbed it from him. She put it to her ear as though it would contaminate. For several seconds her face was a mask. Then she nodded to him and Terry could see the blood drain out of her face.

"It's the same chime, I'd swear to that. Where is it? Whose phone?"

Kevlehan took the phone from her gently, but ignored her questions. "It's confirmed. Thanks, Bert," he said into the mouthpiece. He hung up and finally looked at Nora. "I don't think I'm ready to say just yet. But thank you for your help."

Terry met his eyes above Nora's head and mouthed a silent but insistent *"Who?"*

He barely shook his head. "If you'd like, you can go back upstairs, Mrs. Carpenter. Miss Girard will be along in a minute."

"Miss Girard will be *back* in a minute. I'm going to get Nora upstairs to the office where she can lie down. She's had a shock, in case you hadn't noticed." Terry helped Nora up and started for the stairs. "Are you sure you can make it?"

"I'll be all right. I just feel a little weak in the knees." Nora stopped for a deep breath that she let out through an open mouth.

"Here, use the elevator." Kevlehan led the way across to the far wall where he pushed a button. The door slid open on an unusually deep compartment. "Thanks again, Mrs. Carpenter."

It was like riding in a hearse, and neither woman spoke until the doors slid back to reveal the main office. "Good," Terry said. "No one will know you're in here."

Nora sank down on the leather couch. Terry helped her lift her swollen feet up and stretched them out on the tufted surface before asking the receptionist to bring Nora some water. She took the elevator downstairs again, wondering for the first time why Kevlehan had asked her to watch the stairs. He knew this was just as likely a way to reach the lower level. Was it busy work? Was he humoring her? She charged out of the elevator as soon as the doors opened.

"Are you trying to keep us all in the dark with this 'watch the stairs' and 'don't ask' routine?"

"I figured she'd want to know we'd traced it, even if I couldn't tell her where."

"I thought she was going to faint. Didn't you realize how upset that call had made her?"

"I don't want to tip off anyone and I don't think she could play a part very well in her present state."

The fact that Terry had to agree with him made her mad. "It's the Barron house, isn't it? But which Barron, for God's sake?" His silence made her madder. "I can't play a part either, is that it?"

He slumped down in the desk chair and shrugged his shoulders up to his ears before relaxing them. "You could be the Sarah Bernhardt of South St. Louis, Miss Girard. But it's police business and I don't see your badge."

Her throat tightened. "You're right, I don't have a badge. Just a dead aunt upstairs. And a deed that I trusted you with."

He sighed heavily, and the foot that was stretched out began to jiggle. "Okay. It *was* the Barron house. I'm still not sure enough to say which one of them—could be any of them because they're in and out all the time. I'm on my way to check out a couple of leads now."

"What sort of leads?"

"Just—leads, dammit. Before I go, tell me who's upstairs."

"Hugh Barron was still there when we came down, and so was Micheline, with Frances, Evelyn, and Claude in tow. Is it one of them? Or one of the spouses?"

"For God's sake, woman, keep your shirt on. What I'd like to do is drop you and Mrs. Carpenter off at headquarters on my way and—"

"Don't be silly. I'm not leaving again. People will be swarming in here after work or on their way to the game. And Nora's had enough upset for one day. She probably needs to go home with Kate and Bryn."

"Who the hell are they?"

"Her daughters. My female friends, remember? I have to hold the fort, can't you understand that?"

"Can't *you* understand? I can't protect you if you're spread around the city."

"I'll be fine."

"The hell you'll be fine!" But before he could finish, the phone on the desk rang hollowly in the tile-walled room. He clutched the receiver as if to strangle the person calling, then snatched it up to his ear. "Kevlehan here," then silence.

"What the hell?" He listened again, checked his watch against the one on the wall: 4:05. "All right, fifteen minutes. Twenty if the game traffic's started." He replaced the receiver with exaggerated care. Terry thought he would have preferred ripping it out by the cord.

"I have to be at the stadium. Now. Hartwig will have to take me."

"I'll be okay, really. I'll be with dozens of people for the next five hours."

"Then promise me. No, no, don't get your back up," he said as she started to protest. He put a finger to her lips and she felt a tingle that shot through her body, making her happy and angry at the same time. "Promise me you won't leave until I come back to pick you up."

"What about Nora? I don't think she can last the whole evening."

"Are those daughters of hers married?"

She nodded. "They're all driving back from Chicago and coming straight here this afternoon."

"Tell them to all go home to Mrs. Carpenter's if she has to leave. That will make five of them, safe as we can get. One way or another, I should be finished with this detail in a couple of hours. Any questions?"

"Are you going to put that in a safe place?" She flicked her finger toward the lapel of his jacket under which lay the deed.

"As soon as I can get in to the evidence room, I'll lock it up. Listen, I have to go."

Terry went upstairs with him to the sun porch. She was surprised to see that it was almost dark outside, a premature nightfall composed of dark gray flannel clouds, with the misty rain barely visible against their faint reflections in the windows.

"Geezus! What a night to play ball!" He struggled with

his raincoat and muttered something when she held it so that he could put his left arm through the sleeve. As she draped the rest over his right shoulder she could see the squad car pull up even with the steps outside, its headlights making two white cones filled with tiny liquid diamonds.

He opened the back door of the sun porch and turned around. "You'll stay?"

"I'll *be* here."

Terry watched him run down the two steps and across to the dark blue car, not bothering to use his umbrella. When he fumbled for the passenger door with his left hand, the wind billowed out his raincoat, almost forcing it off his shoulder, and even through the door she could hear him swearing. Patience was not Dan Kevlehan's strong suit. What was, she wondered? With great reluctance Terry dragged herself back to the main parlor, already missing him.

▽

20

DAN KEVLEHAN LEANED AGAINST the seat belt and drummed the fingers of his left hand on the smooth vinyl seat. He hoped the nut who had threatened to bomb Busch Stadium would not get the chance. The Cards deserved to win.

His mind wandered to that last game of the previous Series between the two, when noise and a dome of ball-hiding grids made fielding sheer hell. What a way to have to play a ball game! What a stupid way to build a stadium, where the home team's cheering could completely shut out communication between fielders, and a fielder, even when he successfully waved off a team member with sign language, could lose the ball against that confusing background. Why couldn't the Cards have won in a year when the National League had the four-game advantage as home team?

All this to keep from thinking about the case he'd just left. And the girl. He couldn't trust her not to do something foolhardy. He would have to settle for safety in numbers and hope that if she tried a stupid trick, it would be around lots of mourners. But he had to admit she'd helped. She was feisty, he didn't understand her, and he knew she was more than just a name in the file.

Hartwig had cut over to take I-55 as a quicker and safer route than crosstown, with its numerous stoplights. Even a siren was not enough to make a diehard Cards fan slow down when he had a green light and the opening pitch awaited. Now Dan's foot pressed the rubber mat in an empathetic braking as Hartwig swung the Ford off the highway, down the off ramp, and onto the congested street by the stadium.

Here, mounted policemen tried to maintain order, one giving them a wave-by that made room for them to cross the stream of cars and shoot through Stadium Plaza. A uniformed patrolman rushed to move a further sawhorse barrier and Hartwig pulled up finally near a gate that was strangely vacant of fans.

Inside, the leader of a SWAT team was quietly issuing last-minute instructions to half a dozen men dressed in flak jackets and protective helmets. Dan recognized a crime reporter from the *Post* trying to wheedle some facts out of Simms, the public information officer. Above, somewhere in the vast expanse of ramps and hallways that surrounded the field, a bullhorn squawked unintelligibly.

"Sergeant Kevlehan?"

Dan nodded. The corridor seemed even darker than outside with only the fluorescent tubes above, making the name tag pale and unreadable. The patrolman's face was even paler.

Dan's eyes adjusted and he made out the letters on the man's tag. "What've you got, Lueckmueller?"

"In the men's john over here, sir." He pivoted stiffly, led the way to a door with no knob, and took up his post next to it, looking relieved that he didn't have to go farther.

Dan pushed it open with his left elbow, glad that he'd left his raincoat in Hartwig's cruiser. At first the room appeared empty except for the familiar beefy presence of Harold Jordan, evidence technician and expert wielder of all the tools contained in the black box at his feet. Sweat darkened the light blue shirt and beaded a forehead the color of dark chocolate, but his smile said everything was under control.

" 'Bout time."

Dan had learned how to work a crime scene from the grizzled veteran, who stood with thumbs hooked in his belt loops—the better to keep from messing up evidence—and one foot propped on his black case.

"Had to come from South Grand. Been waiting long?"

Jordan shook his head. "He's still warm, I'd guess." He

motioned to a stall whose door stood ajar. "Door was latched when a ticket taker came in. Not many people here yet, so he looked under to see if it was occupied and saw the stocking feet. Called out, then stood on the stool next door for a peek and screamed his head off. Dispatch got the call at four-oh-three."

Dan edged the now-unlatched door open wider with the flat of his fingernail. Propped on the commode was a middle-aged man in dingy white boxer shorts and an undershirt yellowed at the armpits. His eyes and tongue bulged out in a faintly blue face from the pressure of the wire that cut into his neck so far that only one stiff end was visible sticking out behind his left ear. Even with the distortion, Dan could make out that "Why me?" expression he'd come to recognize and dread.

"Anybody know who he is?"

"The ticket taker knew him. Bob Hawkins. Security guard. Our bomber did him for the uniform he was wearing. SWAT's trying to trace his path from here but someone said there was a hostage."

"Any word on how it's going up there?"

Jordan shrugged. "I've been in here minding the store."

Dan felt the anger pounding at his heart. Anger at whoever regarded human life as being so cheap that he would trade it for a suit of clothes. But underneath, the beginnings of relief eased the tension in his shoulder muscles. This homicide was going to be clear-cut; no prolonged investigation that would tie him up for days and keep him from the Girard case. They had the murder weapon, the motive, the most likely suspect tabbed, and all the evidence a reasonable jury could ask for. He backed out of the stall and took a deep breath. He still had to go through the motions.

"Let's get started."

As if on cue, Lueckmueller held open the door for the medical examiner on call. Behind him, Jordan's partner, a trim blonde in her late twenties, trundled in with a camcorder in one hand and a still camera in the other. Around her neck hung a satchel stuffed to bulging with other apparatus.

With almost nothing said, they began the standard operating procedure for homicide scenes, staying out of each other's way, moving around in a strange ballet to examine the body, take photos, dust for prints, and all the other grisly but necessary chores. When things were well in hand, Dan headed out.

"I'll interrogate the ticket taker and anyone else who was around to hear or see anything. I won't be far if you need me." He heard Jordan chuckle as he left. Jordan didn't need any help.

Lueckmueller was no longer guarding the door. In fact the hall seemed deserted, not a soul in sight. Strange.

"Drop!" The one word echoed down the hall.

Dan dropped to the floor in the prescribed procedure. "It's Sergeant Kevlehan." He knew better than to reach for ID. "Who the hell are you?"

"SWAT, sir. Please return to the room you exited. We have this hall secured until further notice."

Dan got up and retreated to the men's room, brushing his suit only when the door was closed. "Dammit all, we're stuck here. Not a word of communication. Who's running this show, anyway?"

"Relax," Jordan soothed. "Wash up and let's see if you still remember all I taught you. It could be hours."

Dan swore.

Terry stopped to pour and drink a glass of iced tea before she headed down the wide hall again. Though the gloom matched her mood, she wished the drizzle would stop. CeCe had loved the brilliance of autumn leaves and hated when they were prematurely destroyed by wind and rain. Terry wanted every tree in Mount Olive Cemetery dressed in its finery tomorrow. CeCe deserved it.

She deserved more: her killer caught. Terry hadn't reached the wide doorway when she saw familiar faces coming through the front door.

Kate Carpenter Flynn hurried down the hall to throw her arms around Terry. Her black curly hair had fought the humidity and lost, frizzing up around her face and tickling Terry's nose as they hugged. "God, Terry, I'm sorry I couldn't be here sooner."

Bryn followed her sister quickly with a hug of her own, and then the husbands, less demonstrative, came forward to offer their condolences.

"Where's Mom? She said she'd meet us here."

"She's lying down in the office. She had a bit of a shock. Do you think you can take her home and stay with her for a while?"

The sisters gave each other a worried look but it was Kate, the leader, who spoke.

"What sort of shock? Did she faint?"

Terry glanced through to the parlor to see if Kate's lecture-hall voice had turned any heads, but couldn't be sure. "Come on down here."

When they reached the side hall she told them quickly about the phone call and that Nora had identified the source of the bell sound. "I think she'd feel better tucked up on her own couch. I can manage fine here and Sergeant Kevlehan will follow me back to your mom's house as soon as we close up."

From beyond the office door, Nora started to protest. "I heard that and I'm not leaving you here by yourself."

Terry moved across the office's thick carpet and helped Nora sit up. "I'll feel a lot happier if I know you're home. Tomorrow's going to be a b—, a beastly day and you need to get a good night's sleep."

"Then let Bryn and Larry stay and bring you home."

"I have a key and Kevlehan will not only see me to the door, he'll probably come look under Kate's old bed to make sure it's safe."

Nora's eyebrows shot up and her mouth opened.

"She's just kidding, Mom, but she's right," Bryn chimed in, taking Nora's pulse with professional efficiency. "Give us five minutes to pay our respects to CeCe. We'll bring your coat out with us."

But Nora insisted on one last visit to CeCe's casket. Walking behind the five of them, Terry could see how shaky Nora's legs were and how the two girls supported her weight between them. Nora began to sob as she bent over CeCe, her shoulders heaving so that Kate and Bryn had to lift her from the prie-dieu. With Larry and Jack's help, they hurried her out to Kate's car.

It was best for Nora to go home, she knew, but when they had left, Terry felt alone and vulnerable. As mad as he made her at times, she wished Kevlehan were here to . . . to what? To tell her she'd survive, she thought, and walked back into the parlor.

The after-work crowd had arrived and people approached her immediately. Trying not to be obvious, she looked around to see how many Barrons were still in sight but could see only Micheline talking with an old Family Album client. But if she was still here, the rest were nearby, and one of them guilty of a murder, possibly two murders.

"That handsome police officer get tired of us, Therese?"

Terry spun around. Claude had come up silently behind her and, being just shorter than she was, spoke at her shoulder. The cherub gone sour had his wife at his side. Marie's desert sunset shawl had been traded in for a gray-and-black poncho with stylized figures, making her look like an oversized Acoma pot.

"He must have finished whatever paperwork needed doing here."

"I didn't mean to startle you. Mother said you were rather jumpy." His own nervous giggle made Marie's lips compress to a thin line.

"I'm fine."

"Well, we're all here for such moral support as you should need." His esses came out with just the hint of a lisp.

Terry was speechless. She could only nod and accept Marie's pat on the arm, which preempted Claude's soft, plump hand reaching for her.

Without Nora, Terry was even busier acknowledging her friends and CeCe's. People she didn't know or could only vaguely remember and people she'd seen last week, all wanted to express their sympathy and tell her their favorite story about CeCe. Time seemed to rush by instead of crawling as she'd feared.

"See you in the morning, darlin'," Frances called to her with a cheery display of teeth, when Terry caught her eye. After Claude, none of the Barrons had been able to get her ear, for which Terry felt grateful. She didn't know what she could say to them anymore. Looking around to check for the others, she realized that not only were they gone but so were most of the other people.

Alarmed, she looked at her watch. Eight-thirty! And no sign of Kevlehan.

Before another person could approach, Terry slipped out to the phone, identified herself to the same policeman she'd talked to last night, and asked if Sergeant Kevlehan had left any messages.

"No, ma'am. They had to secure the stadium. The game was postponed and there's a hostage situation. Turn on your television and you'll probably get more than I can tell you."

She knew better than to ask for an escort. Every available man would be dealing with the crisis—as well as the disappointed crowds and the ghouls who came down just to watch.

"Thank you. If you see him, tell him . . ." That I'm reneging? That I'm going home even if it scares him? "Tell him I'll be at the Carpenter home by nine-thirty and I'll be fine. Thanks."

A small television had been brought in for the game and she found a group of mourners and one or two Fourcaults watching it.

"Any word on the hostage?" she asked the nearest man.

"No change. They're talking to the bomber by bullhorn but he won't come out."

Terry's heart sank. She couldn't ask the Fourcaults to stay until he came; it might be all night.

"Terry?"

Terry turned to see Marilyn Deickmann, the widowed neighbor two houses down, who had offered ice, chairs, and help with cleanup for tomorrow. She was shaking her umbrella in frustration.

"What's wrong, Marilyn?"

"My car has a flat tire, and you know how the cabs are as soon as it rains. Do you think I could catch a ride home with you?"

Terry hesitated. She had told the police she'd leave but hadn't really committed herself, hoping for a miracle, that Kevlehan would appear so she could keep her promise. But Marilyn had been so helpful, and it would mean she'd be alone just for the ride through the park to Nora's.

"Of course. That is, if you don't mind waiting until we close up."

"You're sure you're going home after this? I don't want to take you out of your way."

"I'm staying at Nora Carpenter's tonight—just through the park. It's not a bit out of my way."

"Thanks. I'll get someone to fix it first thing in the morning and ride up with the Haydons."

"Sit down and watch the excitement and I'll be back in a few minutes."

Terry went back to the parlor and made a circuit of all the people she hadn't spoken with already. Then she took a few minutes to say her own special goodnight to CeCe and offer a few prayers. When she turned, everyone was gone and young George Fourcault was hovering. She could hear a vacuum already running in one of the other parlors.

"I didn't mean to keep you. Are there any last-minute directions?"

"Just that the limo will pick you up at eight-thirty in the morning."

"Fine." Not fine, she thought. It was too soon. She didn't want to bury CeCe tomorrow. Or at all.

Marilyn was waiting for her by the backdoor. Had the

game been on, the workers would probably be clustered around the television. Instead, its screen was dark and a lone teenager was wiping off the coffee counter.

The rain was so light they didn't bother with an umbrella, but they could hear thunder rumbling to the south. The hearses were lined up in a row, their shiny black surfaces dulled with hazy patches of mist. The air smelled of wet cement and moldy leaves. Automatically, Terry checked the area surrounding her car: no one lurking, no suspicious shadows. She had her keys out long before they reached the Mustang.

Inside, she turned the defroster on as soon as the engine caught, and even before the windows were clear she pulled out of the parking lot. Marilyn, who had buried her husband just a year ago, filled the trip south with hints about the postfuneral reception.

At eight-forty-nine, Dan heard the soft explosions, followed a few minutes later by the rumble of booted feet down the hall. The SWAT had finally acted, after what seemed an eternity of squawking bullhorn negotiations. Tear gas, it sounded like. No bomb going off.

They had been trapped in the men's room with the corpse for three and a half hours. Jordan, his blond assistant, and the M.E. had badgered him to join a poker game on the cleanest patch of floor, but his complete inattention to the game convinced them to let him drop out. He had paced—miles—ever since.

At eight fifty-seven the all-clear was passed down the hall. Dan was first out the door.

"Quick, where's the nearest phone?" He asked the uniformed figures rushing by. They ignored him.

"The hell with it." He crossed the hall and shoved his good hand against the safety bar of the door. The cool air hit his face like ice water. Only yards away stood a jumble of cruisers, their light bars flashing. He could still reach her at Fourcault's and tell her to wait.

"Let me at that radio." He flashed his badge at the uniformed driver, who unlocked his door and unwound his huge frame from behind the wheel, not quick enough for Dan.

"Come on, dammit." He sank onto the seat and grabbed the mike. "Patch me into Fourcault's Funeral Home, quick."

"Identify, please."

Furious, Dan got the ID from the uniform standing outside and repeated it.

"What was the patch again?"

"Fourcault's." He shouted. "South Grand area."

He could hear the ringing. Finally, what sounded like a teenager answered and Dan didn't wait for him to finish saying the name.

"Hello, this is Police Sergeant Kevlehan. Get Miss Therese Girard to the phone, please. Now. Hurry."

"I don't think anyone else is here but the manager. I'll go look."

The seconds crept slower than the last few hours had.

"Nope. Everyone's gone but us. Who was it you wanted?"

"Girard. Therese Girard."

"Yeah, she left a few minutes ago with somebody."

"With someone? Who?"

"I don't know any more names. Hey, man, I got, like, work to do. No one's here, okay?"

Dan switched off without another word and got back to headquarters. He identified himself this time.

"Oh, Sergeant, was that you before? Miss Girard left a message that she'd be at . . . the Carpenter house by nine-thirty, and she'd be okay."

"Did she say who she was going with?"

"No, that was all the message. You need a ride?"

"I need this unit and another one for backup. Everything's cool here—plenty to spare. Anyone south by Carondolet Park?"

"Nearest one's on a call just now. Where do you need 'em?"

With panic pounding at him, Dan tried to sort facts from surmise. She had left with someone unknown. If not the murderer—who could be taking her God knew where—she was on her way to Nora Carpenter's like she said. It was the only plausible place and he gave the dispatcher the name and address, then yelled at the uniform to get in and drive.

The patrolman turned on the ignition and, like a chain reaction, the sky lit up with jagged lightning and thunder rattled the car windows. Just what we need, he thought, hoping he wasn't sending everyone on a wild-goose chase.

▽

21

THEY WERE ALMOST HOME when the next wave of clouds rolled in and lightning flashed in her rear view mirror. The car behind her turned off, gunning its motor just before the thunder sounded. Together, the noises drowned out the latest hint Marilyn offered.

"You're going to need that umbrella to get in," Terry said as she pulled in to Marilyn's driveway. The rain beat against the windshield so that the wipers were almost useless. "Do you want to wait until it lets up a bit?"

"No, dear. You've had a long day and I know you have scads to do in the morning. Call me early if you need any help setting up." The older woman opened the door, slid out and opened her umbrella, almost in one motion. She ran through the glare of Terry's headlights and up to the porch. Terry waited until she saw the door opened and the hall light go on before she backed out of the drive. Now just another half mile until loving arms would welcome her.

With the heater turned up a notch and wipers on high, Terry eased down the street, past her house, and turned left into the park. As she made the second left, a car pulled out and across the roadway ahead of her. She stomped on the brake pedal so hard the engine died and it took all her pumping to stop the Mustang before it hit the other car. With chilling recognition, she saw that it was the same car that she'd watched race up the side street behind her.

Now the fear rose in her as she saw the driver climb out of the car and head toward her car. A rain hat was pulled down to reach the raincoat's upturned collar.

She fumbled for the door lock—Marilyn's door was still unlocked. When she looked up through her window, still beaded with raindrops, Hugh Barron's face looked as though it was stricken with smallpox.

"Unlock the doors, Therese, or I'll be forced to shoot you where you are." The always somber face was now a grimace, the sides of the mouth pulled down, his brows almost meeting in the middle. "I would prefer this to be painless but I swear I will shoot if you don't do as I say. One more will make no difference in the end."

Her stomach cramped in pain. The gun in his hand looked huge and she realized it was because of a silencer on the barrel. She couldn't back up; it took a while to tease the Mustang back to life after flooding. Terry unlocked the door.

Without moving his aim away from her head, he climbed in to the backseat and sat on the passenger side, where he could see her between the head rests.

"Start up the car. We're going to go back to your house now."

He would kill her in the house, maybe even make it look like another suicide. She forced breath in. "The police have the deed, Hugh. They know all about it."

He was quiet for a moment. "The deed isn't enough. Everyone has a motive to keep that deed from being published. Mine is just the greatest need. I can't afford an audit. Start your engine."

She turned the key, praying it would not start. It didn't. "It takes a minute when it's flooded. The Schindler estate—?"

"The Barron trust, too, my dear. I'm afraid the market has almost ruined me. I can't let the family know—things will turn around. Depress the accelerator to the floor, let up and try again. I'm surprised you don't know that, Therese, or are you stalling?"

She knew that the Mustang didn't work like that. She tried it. Nothing. Keep him talking. Think.

"Why, Hugh? CeCe and Sister—they were harmless!"

"Harmless! Your aunt was ready to ruin me, and that old

nun called you to tell you all about it. They brought it all on themselves." He sneezed as though to emphasize his point. "I thought you'd guessed when I met you on our patio— Mother suspected. But then she's not about to acknowledge it. The Barron name is sacred to her. Once more, Therese, and if not, we'll take my car. It makes no difference."

Sacred and powerful, Terry thought, remembering the bank clerk, the mourners in awe of that clan, her own reluctance to cross him. She turned the key and the engine hummed. Like hell was she going home to certain death. She put the car in reverse, backed up a few feet, slipped it quickly into drive and slammed into the Mercury in front of her.

Terry felt the seat belt cut into her chest and her head barely grazed the steering wheel. Hugh, with no belt to restrain him, was thrown against the front seat. Terry heard a muffled explosion. She reached for the belt's release with one hand and the door handle with the other, rolling out onto the ground and coming up in a crouch.

Behind her, he was scrambling around in there, cursing, trying to find the gun that she was sure he'd dropped. Terry ran headlong into the rain.

Where? For God's sake, where to run? Her breath was already ragged, from shock if not from exertion. The leaves were slippery and twice she skidded on them, almost falling. Where?

The police station nearby had been closed a couple of years ago; there were no lights on in any of the houses along the boulevard, not even at Marilyn's. Could she make it to Grand? To the traffic there? She had no choice. The rain pelted her shoulders, plastered her hair against her face.

She was almost to the deep railway cut that ran through this corner of the park when she heard him far behind her. Glancing over her shoulder, she saw the beam of a flashlight, probing an arc ahead of him. If she could cross over the bridge, she would not be slowed going down, over the tracks and up again—he would surely catch her then.

But he would expect her to go that way, and besides, the

streetlights on the bridge road would show her plainly. With no more self-doubt, she veered away from the road and bridge, sprinted to the edge of the cut, and tried to let herself slide down on the slick grass. Her foot caught in her raincoat, twisting her ankle hard. Pain shot up her leg like a hot flame. She tried to free it and lost her balance, rolling the rest of the way, a rag doll tossed aside. It was like a coal mine at the bottom.

Terry sat, panting, her legs out in front of her. When she bent her right leg and tried to put weight on that foot, the pain was intense. She caught her breath, looked to the top, along the edge of the slope, to the bridge. In seconds, she could see him running to the middle of the bridge, shining the light over the rail on her side—far short of her, thank God, and growing dim—then disappearing to the other side. He came back, followed the rail to the far side, his fading light swinging wildly. He was beyond reason now, she judged, obsessed with silencing her. When he came back to the middle, he switched the flash off and raised the gun like a warning flag. Her body began to shiver uncontrollably.

Terry watched as, like a slow-motion film, Hugh marched to the end of the bridge, went around the railing, and disappeared in the shadows. Like her, he must have fallen; she heard cursing above the far-off rumble of thunder. She cleared the rain from her eyelashes and strained to see which way he'd gone: under the bridge or toward the boulevard and her?

One last sputtering arc of light told her he was coming toward her. He cursed and she heard the flashlight clang against the now overgrown rails. He was about seventy yards from her and despite the almost total darkness here, he couldn't help but find her.

She had one advantage over Hugh Barron: she knew every inch of this park, particularly the railroad cut that had been her favorite hangout. But it would be, as Hugh would say, like shooting fish in a barrel.

At the thought, something between a sob and a laugh threatened to escape and Terry froze for a moment, willing her ragged breath to stay in bursting lungs. Damn Kevlehan! Where was he when she needed him?

Upright now, Terry hopped forward on her good left leg. The wind was not as strong down here but the rain continued to pelt her head and shoulders, trickling down her back inside her clothes. Raindrops stung the back of the leg she held bent up behind her, the useless foot dangling painfully.

She couldn't go much farther. Already her good leg wobbled from the strain of double duty. And then she stopped—

Barrel!

She must be within yards of the dugout she'd watched the teenagers digging on Monday. Praying that she hadn't already passed it, she leaned against the hill with both hands and felt beneath the dying grass. A yard at a time, two painful hops, another yard.

She was about to give up, to scramble up as best she could to hide behind the nearest tree, when she felt it. A reassuringly hard surface that curved beneath her scrabbling fingers. The faint smell of whiskey and wood.

With nails that snapped under the strain, Terry tugged at the staves of the barrel until they eased outward. She reached a palm in and shoved the makeshift door open a little. Hunkered down, her feet stuck through the gap, she wormed the rest of her body past and down the slope of floor. It oozed with mud.

Scrambling around so that she knelt facing the opening, Terry pulled at the staves, not knowing whether the hatch was closed or not.

I'm trapped now, she thought with a sense of rising panic. Is it really hard to breathe or am I losing it?

Terry forced herself to take in a lungful of earthy smelling air through her nose and let it escape slowly through her mouth. A rock under her knee dug into flesh that already ached from the fall. She shifted her weight and felt the sides of the cave with both hands. The hole stretched into the hillside for four or five feet, its walls not much more than a yard apart. The ceiling brushed her matted hair if she tried to kneel erect. Room for two boys in close formation—or for one absolutely stupid woman, she judged, the tears starting to pour down her cheeks.

Maybe if she scrunched at the back of the cave, he wouldn't see her even if he found the door. Terry propped herself up on both hands and scooted backwards.

Her hand touched something cold and damp.

The small scream came unbidden and unstoppable. Her hand had jerked away and she fell backward until her head hit the back wall. Again her hand stretched across the dirt floor behind her and touched what felt like a trench shovel. Of course! They were still digging and would leave their muddy tool at hand rather than explain to a nosy mother what they were up to, and where.

"All right, Therese, I heard you. We'll stop this nonsense once and for all. Come out of your hidey-hole. *Now!*"

Did he think she was an idiot? He would have to shoot her—she wasn't moving. Even through the barrel staves Terry could hear him pacing in the dead brush outside. So close, so damn close.

A sudden flash of lightning lit up a narrow vertical of bright blue in front of her. Under the cover of thunder, she thrust her head close to the crack and prayed for another flash of lightning. If she could spot him through the crack—

"Aha! So that's where you've gone to ground."

Terry cringed. Instinctively, she drew toward the back wall but just as quickly realized the futility of that. Snatching up the shovel, she crouched with her weight on her right knee and good left foot even as he tugged at the door. If he stuck his gun hand in . . .

"Come out or I will shoot you and seal you up in there!"

He had the hatch almost open. He had the gun. She had no choice.

She lunged with her whole weight against the shovel, driving it into whatever part of him she could find. Then everything seemed to happen at once. Another soft explosion like the one in the car and in the glimmer of lightning she saw Hugh Barron bent over. He screamed in pain with his hands clutched at his middle. She yanked the shovel back, brought it up once more and made her own thunder on his head with it.

He sank to his knees. The gun dropped from his hand and he sprawled facedown in the wet weeds. Tossing the shovel aside, she crawled over to where the gun glinted in another flicker from above. It was cold and wet and she aimed it at him while she unscrewed the silencer, throwing it in the long grass. Jerking the gun up, she fired off another shot, this one so loud it hurt her ears, and aimed it down at Hugh again.

Only then did the hot pain on her ear and the smell of singed hair tell her how close she had come. He didn't move and she leaned back against the door to the cave to rest her foot.

In the distance sirens wailed and the sky glowed blue and white, blue and white, above the bridge on her right.

Beautiful timing, Kevlehan. You missed the whole damn show.

▽

22

HER HEAD THROBBED. That was the first thing she noticed when she woke up, even before she opened her eyes. The second was a feeling of being muffled up, as though she had headphones on. She hazarded lifting her lids and a white cap swam into view, first with two stripes and now, as Terry opened her eyes further, with the one black band. The cap faded off to her right and she felt pressure on her arm. *No, I won't come out. Let go!*

"Easy does it. I'm just taking your blood pressure."

She was in a hospital. Not dead, obviously, but injured? In some sort of accident? She took inventory: concentrating on any pain other than the throb in her head, she moved shoulders, elbows, and knees, fingers and toes. There! The right foot was stiff and a sharp ache ran up her lower leg.

"Do you know your name?"

Silly. Of course she knew it. But the blank in her mind filled her with panic until she blurted it out.

"Terry Girard!"

"Fine, just relax. And the day?"

This time the blank wasn't filled with anything. Tears blurred the stripe on the cap again.

"That's okay. Do you know where you are?"

"Hospital."

"Right on. The doctor will be along in a few minutes. You just rest."

Terry needed no urging. She drifted back where her foot and even her head didn't hurt.

When she woke again the pain in her head had lessened but her throat was dry and scratchy. She ran a barely wet tongue over rough lips and cranked one eye open slightly to a room with drawn blinds.

"Hey, you're awake." Deep, ragged voice. Large form reaching over her toward something on the other side of her. A click. "Nurse, she's awake."

Kevlehan. She had awakened once before with him hovering. Yes, at the morgue. She opened both eyes and saw the edge of something white at the corner of her right eye. She reached up to explore.

"Just a flesh wound, as we say in the business." His hand engulfed hers and moved it gently away from her head.

So that's where her headache came from. Terry tried to recall how she could have injured herself. Bits of it—pictures—flashed like still shots run through at high speed. Hugh and the cave and that gun exploding. "It was Hugh. He tried to shoot me. I can still see him."

"It's a damn good thing his aim was rotten."

She turned her head left to face him and was shocked at the dark circles under his eyes and the pale, exhausted look. Had he been here all night? She tried to sort out times and gave up as the enormity of Hugh's actions hit her.

"He killed CeCe . . . his own godmother!" She could feel the warmth of a tear run across her temple and tickle into her left ear.

"You won't hear it from his lips. At least we haven't—he's clammed up on the advice of his lawyer."

"Well, he admitted it to me. Isn't that good enough?" Terry tried to sit up but the dizziness spawned a wave of nausea that made movement a decidedly bad choice. Even to wipe the sweat that beaded her upper lip seemed like too much effort.

Kevlehan was there, reading her mind again, swiping gently with another hanky. "Take it easy and don't try to move your head yet."

He looked up as a striking, white-coated woman, blonde

hair pulled back in a ponytail, appeared at the bottom of Terry's bed. "This is Dr. Sommers. She checked you over when you came in last night, remember?"

Did he think she was dotty? Terry wondered. "Of course. Dr. Sommers." Actually, she had no recollection of being treated last night, but wasn't about to admit it. "So, how am I?"

The young woman had a smile that reached her friendly eyes. She snapped a penlight on and checked Terry's pupils, making Terry's head throb anew.

"You had a rough time last night but luckily you have a hard head." She lifted the cover, manipulated an ice pack more snugly around Terry's ankle. "Feel that?"

Terry sucked air through her teeth. "Yes. It hurts like hell."

"It's just a bad sprain. We x-rayed it last night, if you remember, and there are no broken bones. Welcome back to the land of the living and overworked. I'll see you this afternoon." She made a few marks on the metal-covered chart and swept out.

"Thanks," Terry managed to say as the door whooshed closed. All she remembered about last night were those awful flashes of Hugh's face. "What time is it?"

"A little after eight. You didn't fall asleep until around one and they kept waking you up for six hours."

A sudden and urgent sense of needing to be somewhere overtook her.

"I have to . . . don't I have to do something?" How stupid that sounded. Where was she supposed to be?

"Nora put off the funeral, if that's what you're worried about. The doctors think Monday is the earliest you could attend. Just take it easy."

The funeral, of course. How could she forget?

"The bullet just winged your ear. Bled like a pig, and you were mud from head to foot. You must have sprained the ankle in a fall."

Terry shivered. CeCe fell. No, she was pushed. Sleep flooded in again.

* * *

When Terry woke up again, her head felt better but the rest of her body ached as though she'd been thoroughly beaten. She felt rested, though, and—she only now realized, as she smelled food—famished. She opened her eyes to watch Kevlehan cranking up the narrow table to where it fit close to her chest. A tray on the table wafted meat-loaf smells. She almost drooled.

"Hungry?" he asked, and tucked the napkin under her chin.

"Starved."

"Your friend Kate will take the next shift, but I'm glad you woke up on mine."

"Me, too," she said softly. "And I *do* remember now. Hugh was going to take me home and make it look like I committed suicide. He's . . . he's . . ."

"Evil? Crazy? Bet he goes for an insanity plea." Dan spooned some mashed potatoes into her.

"He's no crazier than I am," she said after she managed to swallow. "He admitted he raided that estate and his own family trust—they're broke and they don't know it. He even admitted trying to kill Sister—I think. He said . . ." She tried to remember what his exact words were but couldn't. Instead, a vision of Sister in the hospital bed swam up from her unconscious.

"You know, Sister told me but I didn't understand." She remembered now. "She said 'You came,' but she was saying 'Hugh came.' And when I thought she was calling me Mama, she was trying to tell me it was Mumpet."

Dan Kevlehan's eyebrows were thick when he bunched them in a frown. Sort of cute. His hand held the spoon poised in the air.

"Mumpet?"

"It was a nickname. Here, let me feed myself. CeCe called him her little one—*mon petit* in French. The other children made it into Mumpetty, shortened to Mumpet, and CeCe would call him that now and then. He didn't like it from her and he absolutely wouldn't tolerate it from the others. I saw him push Claude in the pool one Fourth of July when I was little, just because Claude called him Mumpet in front of some clients."

She watched him smile as she stopped to shovel in a few bites of pudding. She didn't care how it looked; she was famished.

"I doubt if Sister's words are admissible, but they won't be necessary. Your testimony will be plenty, and even without it, we'd have enough evidence to present to the D.A."

"You knew it was him?"

"Not until yesterday. But his secretary furnished Bert Lucas with some apple pulp she said came from Barron's shoes. It got on the office rug and she had to clean it up."

"That's what he meant!"

"You aren't coming through."

"He said he thought I'd guessed. Micheline did. She bent to pick up his file and saw, or smelled, the apple on his shoe—he couldn't smell a thing with that hay fever—and she rushed through the rest and got rid of me. I smelled it too, but I thought it was cider."

"Well, it's the same kind of apple they grow in the orchard down there at the retirement center. Then, in the same sample of pulp, the lab found traces of a new and unique chemical they sprayed around that shrine. It's only been sold to three professional gardening concerns, and the retirement center's gardener is the only one to use it so far. That locks Hugh to Sister.

"As for your aunt, his only alibi is his mother. But it's possible Marie Barron may break it down. Hugh had turned down their loan request—he didn't have it to give—and so Marie went snooping while Claude watched TV. She says Hugh wasn't in his room between five and seven. And there's you, of course." Kevlehan stared at her over a cloverleaf roll he'd appropriated from the tray.

"Help yourself," she said, belatedly. Had he been here all along? She'd think about that later. Now she wanted to know all about why her aunt had to die. "How much is that block of land worth that CeCe died for?"

"Thirty or forty million. But it's mortgaged to the hilt. We have a man going over his books now. He'll be lucky to raise attorneys' fees. I'll bet he diverted the Schindler money, too."

"Yes, he admitted that. What does Micheline say?"

"Madame Barron is not speaking to the police as yet, her lawyer says. She's under sedation; doctor's orders. My guess is she won't admit it."

Terry let this sink in. Friends from childhood. And Micheline could turn her head and let Hugh kill one of the few people who ever cared enough to excuse Micheline's faults. Inconceivable. And yet Terry could hear CeCe telling her to forgive.

Always forgive; it confounds people, CeCe used to say.

"How about the others? Frances would have helped him. And what about Evelyn and Claude?"

"They claim not to have known a thing. It doesn't matter. And Dr. Sommers says for you not to worry about it. The calmer you stay the quicker you'll recover and get out of here."

"He searched our office—I'm sure of it. It makes my scalp crawl."

"Since he had your aunt's keys—oh, by the way, we found them in his glove compartment—he probably went through the house, too. If he had found the deed, we might never have been able to pin it on him."

Terry gasped, which hurt her head but she refused to acknowledge it.

"*That's* why he was so interested in the safe deposit box. He kept wanting to help me sort everything out. He figured CeCe had put it in there!"

"She should have made a dozen copies and told him they were spread all over town."

The tears sprang up in her eyes unbidden. "No, she respected other people's privacy. She wanted to give him a chance to make it good. She didn't realize what a deep hole he was in, how desperate . . . and evil."

"Everyone knows now. The whole thing was on the news last night—played a very poor second fiddle to the bomber, but still got a mention."

"The bomber! I didn't ask you—?"

"They gassed him and rescued a hostage, but before that he killed a guard for his uniform. That's what I had to handle, and I spent hours cooped up in a men's room with the corpse while they dickered with the bomber."

"And I know how you love waiting around!" She smiled at him and he reached for her hand.

"I didn't know you'd left the funeral home until I got out. Lady, you gave me one hell of a scare."

"I don't really remember much about last night," Terry confessed. "You came down to Nora's?"

"Doing about ninety. I drove through six red lights on Grand with two patrol cars behind me. What the hell were you doing in the park?"

"I brought Marilyn Deickmann home. She had a flat—"

"A flat? *That's* how he managed it. He knew she'd ask you for a ride, you'd feel safe, and he'd get you as you left her house."

She felt her mouth drop, then blushed. "A chump, wasn't I?"

"You didn't look like a chump when I found you. There you sat, pointing that damn gun, and Barron was out cold." He acted it out, holding an imaginary gun in his still-bandaged hand.

"I'm sorry for playing into Hugh's hands, and for probably keeping you up all night. Your back—"

"My back has been through worse nights, which is probably more than you can say." He hesitated. His brows knit again and he looked like a kid owning up to breaking a neighbor's window. "And now that we're on an apology spree, I'll add mine for not getting to you in time. I don't think much of citizens taking the law into their own hands but, Miss Girard, that was one beautiful citizen's arrest."

Terry felt the warmth spreading out from her middle all the way to her throbbing ear and foot. He might be gruff and more than a little set in his policeman ways, but—in spite of last night—she knew this was one person she could trust to be there for her.

"Thank you, sir. Coming from you, I'll cherish that compliment. But do you think you could possibly switch this citizen's 'Miss Girard' for 'Terry'?"

"I'd like that. And the name is Dan."

"Unless, of course, it's official business, Sergeant."

"Which reminds me, I have to be there for Hugh Barron's arraignment." Dan checked his watch and made a face that turned into a stifled yawn. "Even though I'm supposed to be off duty."

"Well, if you're off duty . . ."

His face was blank at first. Then a slow smile crooked his mouth as he lowered it to hers. Talk about therapeutic! Every inch of her felt marvelous.

"If we're going to pursue this relationship," he murmured in her ear, "we've got to quit meeting like this."

She held his face away to look at him. "What do you mean?"

"I hate hospitals," he said.